TEN
GUILTY MEN

DANIEL CAMPBELL
SEAN CAMPBELL

Ten Guilty Men

First published in Great Britain by De Minimis, September 2015
© Sean Campbell 2015

Cover Art designed by Nadica Boskovska
© Sean Campbell 2015

Typeset by Kunj Shrivastava

First Edition

Prologue

FIVE YEARS AGO

Reporters, photographers and a television crew camped out opposite the home of Ellis DeLange. Rafe Soros had been outside since daybreak, his camera remaining focused on the DeLange residence for nearly six straight hours. It was fast approaching midday and Ellis DeLange had yet to show her face.

Rafe didn't blame her. In her place, he'd be hiding behind an eight-foot wall too. If he had one anyway. Such things were the preserve of the successful. While Rafe rarely grumbled about his lot in life, he had managed to sleepwalk into his forties with sod all to show for it. Twenty-five year old Ellis however had never had to struggle. She was the daughter of steel magnate Gregory DeLange and had been born with platinum spoon planted firmly where it still remained.

A bout of schadenfreude had struck Rafe when he got the call that morning. His wife didn't understand why he was grinning as he leapt out of bed at four a.m. Little Miss Perfect, the darling of the fashion world, had been caught smuggling coke into the country hidden inside Daddy's private jet.

Ever since, she had holed herself up in her Richmond home. The only sign of life was the occasional curtain twitch, but Ellis was too smart to give the mob a chance to catch her looking out.

It was at precisely half past twelve, after half of the reporters had adjourned to a nearby pub for a working lunch, that the front door swung open with a creak. A young man stepped out and strutted towards the gate. The front gate slid open as he approached it, as if by magic, and then closed the second he was beyond the boundaries of the DeLange residence.

A dozen cameras leapt into action, though quite what his colleagues thought they were photographing, Rafe had no idea. Likewise, microphones were thrust towards the man and questions shouted at him. The man waved an arm for silence as if to make a statement.

'She's not here,' he announced flatly.

'Hokum!' one journalist, a noxious old scab by the name of Gifford Byrnes, spat. 'We've been camped out all morning. We know she hasn't had a chance to leave.'

'Look, she's not here. Why don't you lot clear off?'

'And who might you be?'

'Never you mind. I'm only here to tell you to clear off and leave her alone. This is harassment.'

'Can't be harassment if she isn't here to be harassed,' Gifford said with a look of smug satisfaction. 'And hang on, I know who you are! You're Kallum Fielder, the Fulham striker!' The same dozen cameras immediately began snapping away in his direction. Rafe reluctantly joined in and snapped a quick shot of the young footballer. He glanced down at his camera screen and smiled. The picture was perfect. Kallum stood shoulders back with his arms folded tightly across his chest. At six-foot-six, Kallum stood nearly as tall as the gate but the house loomed larger still, three storeys of stonework which framed the photograph. It would be an easy sale to one of the weekly gossip magazines.

'So I am.'

'Are you dating Ellis?'

'None of your business.'

'If you're not, why were you in her house?'

'That's totally irrelevant. I told you she isn't home. Now you can either believe me, which will save you from blocking up the pavement all day, or you can sit here and waste your time.'

'And why would we believe you?'

'Because in the' – Kal glanced at his watch – 'four and a half minutes we've been chatting, she's gone out the back door and down the private alleyway at the back of the property. Thanks for the chit-chat.'

With that, Kal strode back towards the security gate, which opened again just for a moment, and then he was gone. The press would still get a story, but it wouldn't make the front page. Job done.

Chapter 1: Edgecombe Lodge

SUNDAY APRIL 6TH – 06:59

The call came in at precisely six fifty-nine in the morning, right at the very end of the graveyard shift.

'Dead body. Edgecombe Lodge. Richmond. Door's open.' The caller's voice was male, but it sounded distorted, almost robotic.

In the seven seconds that the call lasted, Detective Sergeant Roger Mayberry went from dozing gently in his chair to wired with adrenaline. Before he could reply, the line went dead.

'Damn!' Mayberry cursed. Things like this weren't supposed to happen. Not on a Sunday morning before breakfast, and certainly not on his watch. He'd only agreed to take the shift to keep the Superintendent happy.

Now he had to go all the way out to Richmond to prove the caller was a troublemaker.

But it was no hoax.

Edgecombe Lodge appeared to be just like its neighbours: a detached family home in the leafy London Borough of Richmond. The house was double fronted, with windows guarded by heavy drape curtains which were drawn tightly shut, and the small garden out front had been immaculately tended in an identical manner to the rest of the street.

But Edgecombe Lodge's apparent respectability was only a facade. On closer inspection, the wrought-iron security gates that separated it from the road were entwined with blue-and-white police tape, and the pearly-white paint on the window frames had begun to crack.

Detective Chief Inspector David Morton leant casually against the gate as he waited to be let inside. Morton had left Richmond Station only five minutes ago, but the moment he had turned onto Gallow Crescent the flurry of rush hour gave way to a serene quiet. Out of the corner of his eye, Morton watched the house opposite Edgecombe Lodge as an elderly lady pulled back the living room curtains only to slam them shut again the moment Morton waved at her.

Edgecombe Lodge itself was eerily still. Morton's team were already on-site but from Morton's vantage point on the pavement, there were no signs of the activity within. Edgecombe Lodge was a solid thirty feet away from its nearest neighbours and had an ugly electrified security fence running around the perimeter. Bloody eyesore but a great place to commit murder, Morton thought.

Morton glanced impatiently at his watch: oh-nine-hundred hours.

A few minutes later, a familiar figure emerged from the house and walked briskly towards him. The gate unlocked with a click, pulling crime scene tape taut across the gap between the gate and the wall. Morton ducked under the tape and extended a weathered hand in greeting.

'It's about bloody time, Ayala,' Morton said as the pair shook hands. As usual, Bertram Ayala was impeccably dressed. He had on a slim-fit suit, with the jacket slung over one shoulder. A smattering of designer stubble made him look more like a model than a detective.

'How the other half live, eh, boss?'

When Morton didn't reply, Ayala prompted him again, 'It's mighty impressive, isn't it? It's got to be worth a few million. Ten minutes from Richmond Station, but quiet enough to hear a pin drop. That's luxury for you.'

Morton cocked his head to one side. 'I wonder how our victim managed to afford it. She's in her early thirties, I believe?'

Ayala scrunched his nose up in disbelief. 'You can't be serious, boss? Ellis DeLange is... was,' he corrected himself, 'loaded.'

'You knew her?' Morton walked slowly towards the door, and Ayala trailed in his wake.

'She's like the most famous fashion photographer of the noughties... or she was. The press are going to be all over this.'

Morton shrugged indifferently, pulled a pair of slip-on evidence booties from his pocket and then leant against the wall so that he could pull them over his shoes.

'Who called it in?'

'An anonymous tip called it in this morning. DS Mayberry has gone to try and chase down who the caller is,' Ayala said.

Morton sighed. 'That berk? He couldn't find a virgin in a nunnery. But you get to stick around when you're engaged to the Superintendent's daughter.'

Mayberry had long become a running joke in the office. He was regularly sent to find tartan paint, left-handed screwdrivers and long weights. Every time someone sent him down to procurement, he came back with a puppy dog expression. 'They h-haven't got it,' he'd say apologetically. It didn't help that he had a mild speech impediment and regularly mixed up his words.

But just like a puppy seeking approval, he kept coming back for more. He'd never make it beyond Detective Sergeant, so Morton couldn't even promote him out of the unit.

'He's the one that took the call. You know how short staffed we are right now.'

The pair exchanged glances. Few officers seemed to last too long under Morton's command.

'Can't we get the Irishman back?' Ayala said.

'No chance. No officer of mine will ever beat a suspect, no matter how much they might deserve it. Anyhow, I heard he's off running some private eye outfit out of Balham. I'll be looking for another DI soon. But until then, I expect you to help make up the shortfall. Speaking of which, you get to do all the paperwork for the crime scene. Oh, and you get to double-check everything Mayberry does, just to be on the safe side.'

'No way! I'm not taking responsibility for him.'

'Oh yes, you are. At least he's finally learnt how to answer a telephone and write down the right information.'

Ayala grimaced. 'He didn't. Mayberry didn't even manage to write down the whole address. I had to check the recording to get that. Our caller didn't say much and Mayberry didn't prompt him for any details... Not even a name. The man just said there was a body at this address, and that the front door was unlocked. Then he rang off. Sure enough, when we got here the gate was ajar, and the door was unlocked.'

'What sort of accent did the tipster have?' Morton asked.

'It was a bit distorted. I'd say pretty neutral, possibly south London. Not cockney, not too street. Male, obviously. Probably middle-aged, white, definitely a smoker – I'd know that wheeze anywhere.'

'How are you doing without cigarettes? I remember quitting. I was an irritable bastard for months.'

Ayala rolled up a sleeve to show off his nicotine patch. He grinned lopsidedly as if about to quip that Morton was still an irritable bastard but thankfully, for his sake, he thought better of it. He pushed the front door open, then stood aside to let Morton pass.

'Bloody hell!' Morton exclaimed. The entrance hallway should have been the height of luxury and yet it looked like squatters had taken up residence.

Oak flooring extended towards a pair of twin staircases where a plush red carpet began, but Morton could barely see it for the mess. Several bin bags, flies buzzing around them, lay on the floor against the near wall. The stench was overpowering.

Morton darted through the open doorway to his left in search of fresher air, and found himself in an open plan living area. The lounge was just as messy but the smell seemed less pungent. Two scene of crime officers were already at work at the back of the room.

'Hard to believe this place was nominated for *The Impartial's* "Best in Design Award",' Ayala said as he ran his finger along the mantelpiece where dust had gathered nearly a centimetre thick. 'Looks like she hasn't cleaned in months.'

'Quite.'

The living area wasn't quite as messy as the hallway, but it came close. It was split in two with a lounge at the front, and a kitchen at the rear. The lounge was comprised of four dark leather sofas arranged around a coffee table atop which Morton could see needles, white powder that looked like sherbet but Morton knew it wouldn't be, and a number of empty beer cans together with a solitary wine bottle.

'Chateau Neuf De Pape,' Morton said. 'Someone has good taste.'

'Or had good taste, if it was the victim,' Ayala said. 'There's a lipstick stain on the glass next to it.'

'Well spotted,' Morton said. He called over to one of the crime scene techs 'Can you bag this please?'

The tech nodded. Behind the sofa, there were a series of artsy canvas prints on the wall. Morton gestured at them, and asked: 'Did she take those?'

Ayala nodded. 'Same over-saturated style she was famous for. I've got one you know. An early print that is.'

'Better you than me.'

'Peasant,' Ayala said quietly. 'It'll be worth a fortune now she's gone.'

Morton pretended not to hear him.

The scene of crime officers swarmed around Morton and Ayala in a flurry of activity as the two spoke. Morton watched as they worked in threes to photograph the evidence, bag it and then replace it with tiny plastic markers.

'Mind if I grab that?' one asked. He pointed at a used condom on the sofa next to Ayala.

Ayala turned to look, then jumped backwards almost into Morton. 'Eww!'

'Grow up, Bertram. There's another one over there,' Morton said. He pointed towards the kitchenette, where a second condom lay atop the counter.

Ayala shuddered, and turned away to watch one of the techs swabbing away at the stovetop.

'I wouldn't look too closely at that stove either.'

'Why?'

'Let's just say those aren't chocolate drops.'

Morton chuckled at Ayala's reaction, and walked into the kitchen. The brown pellets sat atop a film of grease that shimmered lightly. Every surface was covered with some sort of detritus.

Still more techs were dusting the walls for fingerprints, of which there appeared to be many. Morton used his foot to clear a small area on the floor. Underneath was the same hardwood as in the hallway, but Morton was willing to bet that it had been many months since it had seen the light of day.

'That doesn't look like it belonged to a woman.' Morton pointed to a large suit jacket folded on the breakfast bar which separated the lounge area from the kitchen. He picked up the jacket, and turned it over in his hands.

He turned to Ayala. 'It's nowhere near as dirty as the rest of this place. It's got to be recent.' A partially torn label was sewn into the hem. 'Ike Feltham. Could that be the owner's name?'

Ayala laughed, as if the question was so elementary that the truth should have been obvious. 'No! He's a tailor and my god, is he amazing! Well, I say he but his name isn't Ike–'

'Why the bleeding hell is Ike's name in the jacket then?' Morton asked.

'It was his old partner, an old timer who ran the tailor's before him. He's based over on Savile Row.'

'Pricey then?'

'A few thousand I'd say. For a whole suit with the trousers of course.'

'Reckon we can get DNA off that?' Ayala asked.

'Doubt it,' a voice said from behind Morton. He turned to the Chief Scene of Crime Officer, a chubby man called Stuart Purcell. 'I've got ten men collecting samples for trace, but it's going to take a week just to bag, tag and log it all.'

'Fine, but make sure that sample is near the top of the pile. I want to know who is rich enough to leave that lying around.'

'Is it really a big deal? It's a nice jacket, but compared to this house it's small change,' Purcell said. 'People leave coats behind all the time.'

'They do, but you'd come back for something hand tailored, wouldn't you?'

'Fine. But you owe me, David. And not for the first time.'

'Add a beer to my tab,' Morton said. 'Which way is the body?'

'Out back with the coroner. Through that door at the back on the right.' Purcell waved an arm to indicate a white uPVC door at the rear that hadn't been visible from the main hallway. It seemed incongruous with the rest of the house. All the others doors were wooden, complementing the period features of the house, but the uPVC door had been put in much more recently.

Morton grabbed Ayala's arm, and steered him towards the door. 'Come on then. You get to meet a real life celebrity. I doubt she'll be too talkative, but I'm sure you'll jabber on enough for the pair of you.'

The door that Stuart indicated led through to a narrow hallway. A wooden bench ran down the middle of the room while a series of cubicle doors lined either side. Morton nudged the nearest door open with his foot to reveal a bench with private shower and a small shelf full of toiletries. Morton could hear Ayala exploring the next cubicle along.

'Nice changing rooms,' Ayala called out. 'Ellis DeLange must be a fan of entertaining. You reckon anyone would miss a few of these?' Ayala held up a few miniature bottles of toiletries.

'Detective Ayala, I'll pretend I didn't hear that. This isn't a hotel.'

At the far end of the hallway a door was propped open with a kitbag that Morton recognised as belonging to the coroner. Through the doorway, Morton could see a swimming pool with sunshine bouncing almost mockingly off the water's surface as light shone through a windowed roof and danced off an array of tiny gemstones embedded in the pool floor.

As Morton entered, the heat and humidity of the room hit him, together with the sharp smell of chlorine mixed with a lingering fetid sweetness.

Doctor Larry Chiswick hunched low over the edge of the swimming pool. His shaggy grey mane, tied up by an elastic band, had been gathered into a shaggy ponytail that ran down his back.

At the pool's edge nearest the coroner, the body of Ellis DeLange floated face down, gently bobbing under the current from the pool's filtration system.

Morton crouched next to the coroner, and looked at the body. Ellis DeLange was a petite woman, with a frame to match. Morton guessed that she couldn't have weighed more than eight stone. Long blonde hair covered most of her upper back, with a tiny pink string bikini, which left little to the imagination, visible underneath.

'The curtains don't match the drapes. She's a brunette really,' Ayala said from behind Morton.

'Read that in one of your gossip mags?'

Ayala pouted. 'No – look at her roots.'

Morton followed his gaze. Ellis' roots were dark brown. The coroner used a gloved hand to sweep aside the sodden locks, which had splayed out to cover most of Ellis' back, to give Morton an unobstructed view of a striking tattoo which covered her back and sides with a floral motif. In life she had once been a beautiful woman, but her skin was inelastic and had begun to slip underneath the tattoo, giving it a somewhat distorted appearance.

Morton glanced sideways at the coroner. 'Can we get her out of the pool?'

Doctor Chiswick nodded, and few minutes later Ellis' corpse was staring up at the ceiling from a plastic sheet, giving Morton the chance to look at her face.

She had the beginnings of crow's feet, and there were dark circles beneath her eyes. Her skin was pulled taut across high cheekbones, contrasting sharply with the sagging skin of her back. A waxy film had begun to form on the skin, which turned her a pale shade of green.

'Adipocere,' Chiswick said.

Thick purple veins criss-crossed her arms and legs like train tracks.

'Drugs related?' Morton asked.

'Probably, but toxicology will confirm.' The doctor referred to the standard array of toxicological tests performed in suspicious death cases.

'How'd she die, Doc? Did she drown?'

'I don't think so. I wish things were that straightforward. I can't see any petechia in her eyes or any foam in her airways. But she appears to have suffered blunt force trauma to the back of her head. Feel under her hair at the back of her skull,' Chiswick said. He held out a box of gloves to Morton. 'That could well be our cause of death.'

Morton grimaced and waved away the proffered gloves. 'I'll take your word for it, thanks.'

He stood, and stretched his arms.

'Suit yourself. She's got some sort of abrasion there,' Chiswick said. 'There are some post-mortem scrapes where she's bashed against the tiled sides of the pool while floating, but that's it.'

'Definitely foul play then. What was she hit with?' Morton stood, then twirled slowly on the spot, looking for anything that could have been used to bludgeon someone to death.

The doctor stood up, and looked Morton in the eye. 'I can't definitively rule out accidental death at this stage. She hasn't bled out much so she can't have been struck with anything particularly sharp. We're looking for something large and heavy with a smooth edge. It's got to be heavy enough to cause internal bleeding, but not so heavy that it would have broken the skull. That means something with a large surface area.'

'How do you know that?'

'Something smaller would have concentrated the force of the swing into a small area of contact between the weapon and Ellis' skull, causing it to break. Her skull isn't that badly damaged. We're looking for something large enough to have diffused the force across the skull. Her brain got the brunt of it, but the blow didn't crack her skull open.'

'Could she have slipped and hit her head on the edge of the pool?'

'I doubt it. The impact would have been much more concentrated by the hard angle on the edge of the tiles, and that isn't the case here.'

Morton nodded. He'd worked with Chiswick long enough to trust the coroner. 'How long has she been dead then?'

'Ballpark, a week or so but I can't be sure. The water temp is twenty-three Celsius—'

'Room temperature,' Morton said sharply.

'Yep. Body's the same. Body temp while alive is about thirty-eight give or take, and the old rule of thumb is about one degree an hour, so it would have taken fifteen hours for her to hit room temperature. That's our bare minimum estimate.'

'Putting time of death yesterday at the latest?'

Chiswick crouched back down and pointed at a greenish patch of skin tinged with what looked to Morton's untrained eye like bruising.

'Normally adipocerous tissue would mean she's been dead for a fortnight or more, but the atmosphere in here has messed up the forensic window. It's so hot and humid that the skin became adipocerous faster than a buried body would have. I can't accurately say how much quicker, though.'

'Humidity in here is insane. Who in their right mind has an indoor pool?' Ayala interrupted.

'Someone with more money than sense," Morton replied.

'That's all I've got for you right now. With your leave, I'll get her back to the morgue, and let you and the forensics boys do your jobs.'

'That'd be great. Thanks, Larry. Where is she in the queue?' Morton referred to the autopsy priority queue.

'You're in luck. I've got no other suspicious deaths on my list. I'll bump her up to the top, and get to work this afternoon. Come by around five?'

'See you then.'

Chapter 2: The Old Coach House

Edgecombe Lodge had two unique buildings as its neighbours. To the east sat The Stables, while The Old Coach House could be found to the west. The three had once been one property when Richmond had been less crowded, with only a field where Edgecombe Lodge now stood. Back then The Stables had been an outbuilding for The Old Coach House, one of many of London's lost coach houses.

Once they became detached homes in their own right, they shared little in common beyond a security fence which ring-fenced the three from each other and from the rest of the block.

The Stables had begun life as the most humble building, but little remained of the original structure as glass-clad extensions had been added on all sides to maximise space. A thick row of overgrown leylandii, nearly twenty feet tall and almost as dense, separated The Stables from Edgecombe Lodge, so Morton turned his attention to The Old Coach House, which had no such encumbrance.

When Morton pressed the security buzzer at the gate outside The Old Coach House, a camera perched on top of the gate swivelled towards him and a tiny red light blinked rapidly as the camera turned on.

'Yes?' A woman's voice emanated from a speaker.

'Good morning. Detective Chief Inspector Morton. Could I speak to the homeowner please?'

'Wait.'

It was clear that the voice's owner wasn't English. A second voice, a man's this time, came over the speaker, but it was muffled. Morton thought he heard the pair arguing. Then a few choice words, definitely not English, became audible as the man grew angrier.

'Nyet, ni nada.'

'Sir? Sir! We can hear you. Can we have a few moments of your time please?'

The intercom crackled, and the man spoke directly to Morton in a gruff tone: 'What do you want?'

'We'd like to talk to you about your neighbour, Miss Ellis DeLange.'

'What she now do?'

'She's dead. May we come in?'

'Do you have warrant?'

Morton tilted his head slightly, considered appealing to the man's better nature, then decided to try bluffing. 'We can come back with one.'

The intercom clicked off, and Ayala turned away thinking Morton's bluff had backfired, and then the gate began to retract with a loud clank. The motor whirred to a stop, then started up again moments after Morton and Ayala darted inside. They were met at the door by an elderly Hispanic woman who looked furtively up and down the street as if worried she might be seen talking to the police before beckoning them to come inside. The woman led them through to a grandiose sitting room with high ceilings and thick oak beams laid bare. She pointed to an L-shaped sofa, then disappeared back through the doorway.

The Old Coach House's sitting room contrasted sharply with Edgecombe Lodge. There were few personal possessions, and those that could be seen were displayed neatly on shelves either side of the chimney. Even the logs in the fireplace were meticulously stacked. The home had an old-world feeling. It was cosy and warm, like a well-worn jacket.

Morton ignored the sofa, and moved towards the shelves. In between knickknacks there were a number of photographs. Each one showed the same man, who Morton presumed was the homeowner: a tall, Caucasian man around Morton's age but still in good shape. All of the photos showed him in action poses. One had him knee deep in a river fly fishing. In another, he posed in a military uniform with blue piping which Morton didn't immediately recognise. The shoulder boards were marked with the letters 'GB' but it wasn't a British uniform.

As Morton tried to work out which army the uniform represented, the voice from the intercom boomed out behind him.

'Ah. You like the photo of my uniform, yes?'

Morton turned to see the man from the photograph with a twinkle in his eye, dressed in a wide-pin suit, and wearing much too much cologne. 'It's very... imperial. Is it–?'

'–Russian? Yes. Now, you talk. I have' – the man glanced at a clock on the mantelpiece – 'ten minutes, so hurry.'

'I'll cut right to it then, Mr...?'

'Vladivoben.'

'Mr Vladivoben, how well do you know Miss DeLange?'

'I see her in the street sometimes but our conversation has never been more than that.'

'So you know nothing of her lifestyle?'

At that moment, Vladivoben was saved from having to answer by his maid's reappearance. She carried a tray laid with an old-fashioned bone china teapot and a plate laden down with biscuits, which she unwisely set down upon the coffee table right in front of Ayala. She poured three cups of tea, then shuffled towards the hallway. Out of the corner of his eye, Morton saw her loitering to listen to the conversation, though she busied herself dusting a bookcase.

While Ayala helped himself to the biscuits, Morton pressed on with the interview. 'Where were we? Miss DeLange. I assume you know of her fame.'

'Her infamy, yes. My daughter has a number of her prints. But her lifestyle is her own. Around here, we live and let live. People here value privacy.'

'Have you ever had cause to argue with Miss DeLange?'

Vladivoben's nostrils flared. He drew himself up to his full height and puffed out his chest. 'You dare to come into my home and imply I had something to do with her death? I find your insinuations insulting, Mr Morton. I bid you good day. Maria will show you out.' And with that, he swept from the room without another word.

'Well, that was sudden,' Ayala said. 'What spooked him?'

Morton was saved from answering by the maid shuffling in. She stared at the floor as she entered, being careful to avoid eye contact. She was about to lead them back out when Morton tapped her lightly on the shoulder.

'It's Maria, isn't it?' Morton asked in his gentlest tone.

'*Sí*. I mean, yes, sir.'

'Maria, did you know Miss DeLange?'

She shook her head slowly, a quizzical expression appearing briefly on her weathered face.

Acting on a hunch, Morton tried again. 'But there is something you know, isn't there? Did you hear or see something?'

'I am... not sure. The lighting. It was not so good.'

'When was this?'

'El Sábado,' Maria said.

'Saturday,' Ayala translated, though he needn't have bothered.

'And what did you see?' Morton asked.

'Out of my window, up in the attic. I hear noises. Someone is knocking dustbins. I look out. And I see a naked man climbing over the fence at the bottom of Miss Ellis' garden.'

'A naked man! Did you see who it was?'

'No sir. All I know. Is a man, sir.'

'Was he tall, short, black, white?'

Maria blushed furiously, but shook her head. 'I no know, sir. It too dark and I only see from behind.'

'Did he have any memorable features?'

The maid bit her lip, cast her gaze downwards at the floor and mumbled something.

'I'm sorry. I didn't quite catch that, Maria.'

'He was... a small man.'

'How short?'

'No. Not short. *Small.*'

Morton furrowed his brows. Maria saw his confusion and pointed between her legs.

Ayala smirked. *'¿Lo pequeño?'* he asked.

Maria held her thumb and forefinger aloft approximately half an inch apart.

This time, it was Morton's turn to bite his lip to stop himself laughing. He just about kept a straight face as he said: 'And how did you see this?'

'Que?'

'If he had his back to you, how did you see his... size?'

'He like this at top of fence,' Maria replied. She mimed putting one leg over a fence. 'I see everything.' Maria shuddered, as if she'd rather forget.

'Very well. Thank you, Maria. You'd best see us out.'

Ayala leapt from his seat on the sofa, snatched up a handful of the biscuits for the road, and followed Morton out.

Safely back outside, Ayala burst out laughing. 'What in God's name was that all about?'

'I don't know, but I'm going to find out.'

Chapter 3: Too Much Information

With several hours to go before the autopsy would be complete, and uniformed officers dispatched to carry out a general canvass, Morton decided to explore the rest of Edgecombe Lodge while Ayala dealt with the chain-of-custody paperwork.

There was one bedroom on the ground floor, a double right off the main hallway. From the lack of personal items, Morton assumed it was reserved for guests. A bay window opened out onto the front driveway, but the curtains were still drawn when Morton entered.

The bed was unmade and a half empty bottle of triple distilled vodka lay on its side atop the bedside cabinet. Plastic markers had been placed by forensics techs to mark where evidence had been collected, making it look like a confetti of rainbow-coloured plastic had been thrown in the air. Each disc was numbered with a colour corresponding to the type of evidence collected. So far, Morton had spotted discs up to the high three figures but it wouldn't surprise him if Purcell's team passed the one thousand mark by the time they were through processing the house.

With four more bedrooms, five bathrooms and a converted attic yet to be searched, the Forensics Department would be busy for weeks.

Most of the house was so messy that it was impossible to tell if anything was missing or out of place. A few shelves looked oddly empty, but whether that was from items gone missing or a lack of possessions, Morton couldn't tell. Pizza boxes, which Morton recognised as belonging to a local Italian restaurant, Trattoria Da Mondo, seemed to be everywhere. It must have been Ellis' favourite takeaway.

Despite the mess, the extravagant decor shone through. The entrance-way was the most decadent example of Ellis DeLange's lifestyle. Twin staircases rose to either side of the hall, a sweeping cascade of marble and oak.

The swimming pool came a close second, but although many of the house's original features were impressive, a closer inspection revealed that all the other rooms were perfectly ordinary. Morton thought they could have been picked up and dropped into almost any two-up two-down in the country without appearing out of place.

Imitation furniture, costume jewellery and high street clothing suggested that Ellis wasn't living quite the life she wanted her home to portray.

The mess continued upstairs except in the master bedroom, which was an oasis of cleanliness. A sleigh bed dominated the room, with an oak armoire next to it atop which sat a number of birthday cards which were displayed facing towards the bed. A few bore the message 'Happy 30th Birthday!' but it was the largest card that caught Morton's eye; it read *'Happy Birthday, Big Sis!'*

Morton opened the card, scanned the handwritten message. A name, scrawled in tiny lettering in such a way that made it look as if the author's hand had never left the page, was at the bottom: *Brianna*. Morton nodded appreciatively. That took care of identifying next of kin.

Morton surveyed a series of photographs in a collage covering the longest wall. Three women recurred throughout. In the centre was Ellis, petite and curvaceous. The woman on the right was Ellis' likeness, but taller and thinner. The third, on the left-hand side, was about Ellis' height, but much less careworn.

Morton peeled one of the photographs off the collage; it came away easily. He flipped it over. A blob of dried-out Blu-tack had been used to stick the photograph to the wall. Below the Blu-tack someone had scrawled in pencil, *'L → R: Brianna; Ellis; Gabriella, NYE 2012'*.

The three women had been photographed in various combinations throughout: Brianna and Ellis, Ellis and Gabriella, all three together. Oddly, there were none of Gabriella and Brianna alone. Perhaps, Morton mused, Ellis was so narcissistic that she preferred to display only photos that included her. It certainly appeared that way. None of the photos failed to feature Ellis.

One other figure seemed to be included in many of the photos, a man that Morton thought looked vaguely familiar. He was tall and rugged, and he appeared in the largest photograph with his arm draped casually around a much younger Ellis DeLange. She was smiling broadly and looked much more fresh-faced than in her more recent photos. Again, Morton took the photo down from the wall and flipped it over. The same swirly handwriting had pencilled '*Me + Kal, my 25th birthday*' in looping cursive. The 'i' in birthday was dotted with a tiny heart, as if written by a schoolgirl.

The photograph was only five years old, but the difference between the happy girl in the photo and the thirty-year-old now in the morgue couldn't be more chalk and cheese. Morton snapped a quick photo on his phone of the three girls and the man called Kal, then felt his stomach rumble. No wonder. It was getting on for three o'clock already. There was just about time to grab a quick sandwich before going to meet the coroner – if the autopsy began at the time promised, which was never guaranteed with Dr Larry Chiswick.

Chapter 4: Date with Death

Ellis DeLange's body was tiny in death, lying atop a full-size gurney which could have accommodated her body twice over. Her eyes had been closed out of respect and a paper covering guarded her modesty. Dr Larry Chiswick leant over the body to take a final sample, his bear-like shoulders almost obscuring Morton and Ayala's view.

Next, Doctor Chiswick picked up a hypodermic needle with his left hand, and spoke gruffly as he held it aloft: 'I'll be with you in a moment. Got most of your samples bagged and tagged. There was something organic under her nails. That's already gone off to DNA. On the shelf there, you've got liver, brain, bile and blood samples. Just got to get this last one.'

Chiswick swept a hand towards a metal tray behind him which held the evidence, ready to be sent over to the Met's forensics department by the diener. Morton glanced at the blood samples. The nearest one was labelled *'Femoral Artery'* followed by Ellis' name, and various numbers. The other was marked *'Heart'*.

Ayala followed Morton's gaze and frowned.

'Doc, why do we need multiple blood samples?' Ayala asked as he focused hard on the row of vials. It was his first time attending an autopsy. Morton wondered how long it would be before Ayala recused himself from the smell.

The coroner swung round, pointing the high-gauge needle in Ayala's direction. 'You said there were drugs found in the house. If we're testing the full range, we need two samples because the concentration can vary in different parts of the body. Basic science, you know.'

Chiswick turned back to the body, and used the thumb of his right hand to push open Ellis' left eyelid. Moments too late, Ayala drew back as he realised what was about to happen. The coroner deftly plunged the needle into the eye, then pulled back on the syringe end to withdraw a sample from the vitreous humour. He injected the fluid into a glass phial, then set the needle down.

Ayala retched, then bolted from the room.

'Eight minutes. That's a new record, even for you. You should get a new second-in-command. That lad doesn't seem to have the stomach for this sort of work,' Chiswick said.

'If only. I think I'm stuck with him. Besides, if I ditch him I'll only have Mayberry left and nobody wants that.'

Chiswick's expression darkened. 'I wondered who'd get stuck with him. Sorry it had to be you.'

'Office politics. With Vaughn gone, I had to promote Ayala from within and Mayberry is Ayala's replacement. How's life down here treating you, Larry?'

'Can't complain. Compared to my patients, I'm doing dandy,' the coroner joked.

Morton scowled at the coroner's dark sense of humour, and then glanced out into the corridor.

'Ayala's long gone. Let's get on with it. I'll catch him up later.'

'Right you are. Ellis DeLange, age thirty. Death was caused by blunt force trauma to the back of the head resulting in a subdural haematoma. Her brain bled out from the inside. It would have been pretty quick.'

'Definitely murder then?'

'Unless she ran backwards at about fifteen miles an hour into a solid object, then threw her own body in the pool to cover it up, I think we can rule out accidental death or suicide.'

'What was she hit with?'

'Damned if I know,' Chiswick said. 'Something oblong, reasonably heavy. The force was dispersed over a large contact area, so it wasn't as narrow as a pipe. I'd be tempted to say a brick, but there doesn't appear to be any transfer evidence to support that. You find anything like that?'

'Nope. All we found were drugs, condoms, pizza boxes and a towel in the garden.'

Chiswick leant against his workbench, and smiled. 'Sounds like my student days.'

'She was a bit old for that, and not looking too good for her age either.'

'That's nothing more than a poor diet, her make-up being washed off in the water and a touch of adipocere.'

Morton examined the tray of samples ready to go off to the lab. 'You don't think she was on drugs then?'

'Oh, she was taking something but she hid it well. No track marks, so she wasn't shooting up.'

'Oral administration?'

The coroner grinned. 'Guess again.'

'Injections between her toes? Some sort of cream?'

Chiswick shook his head. 'Sorry. Your victim liked her barbiturates taken rectally. See that baggie over there?'

Morton glanced over at what appeared to be a woollen rag soaked in a yellow goo. 'No. You're kidding!'

'That was inside her. It's definitely been soaked in some kind of nembies, and if I had to guess from the bitter smell and yellowing, I'd say its pentobarbital, most commonly used by vets to euthanize animals. We'll need to wait a few weeks for forensics to confirm that though.'

'A euthanasia drug? Are you suggesting she was suicidal?'

'Oh no. It acts like an opiate in low doses. There's a fine line between getting high and overdosing, but she didn't cross it. She'd have been high, and lost all her inhibitions.'

'That'd explain the evidence of drunken sex.'

The coroner grinned, and let out a hearty, booming laugh. 'See. Just like university.'

Chapter 5: Next of Kin

By the time Morton and Ayala arrived at home of Brianna Jackson, Ellis DeLange's next of kin, the sun was had set. They parked underneath a nearby railway bridge in a bay marked "Permit holders only", and set off on foot towards Amelia Street. It was a residential area, with a steady flow of foot traffic, but it wasn't well lit. There were few lampposts, and even where there were lights it seemed that bulbs had been allowed to burn out without being replaced. The faces of those they passed swam into view and then disappeared into the darkness just as quickly.

'Damn!' Ayala cried out.

Morton turned to see Ayala on the ground, clutching at his ankle.

'This is no time to take a break,' Morton joked, and held out a hand.

'Bloody bin bags. Didn't see 'em in the darkness.'

Brianna lived in a fourth-floor walk-up in a listed building. While exceptionally pretty, it lacked the charm of her sister's home, and there were no outer security doors let alone a perimeter fence. A terracotta archway led through to a narrow hallway with a steep spiral staircase on the right. At the very top of the stairs, Morton and Ayala paused to catch their breath.

Morton spotted Ayala wincing. 'Your ankle all right?'

'No. I'll be suing for worker's comp next week," Ayala quipped.

'That's the spirit. Mind knocking the door? I can't reach from here.'

The landing was barely big enough for the two of them. The stairwell had a solitary window through which a street lamp could be seen a few feet below casting a pale glow over the street. Three doorways at the top were marked '1A', '1B', and '1C'.

Ayala rapped his knuckles on the middle door.

The sound of shuffling preceded a woman's voice.

'Who's there?' she asked shrilly.

Morton imagined someone pressing their eye to the peephole, and trying to make out the two shadowy figures in the stairwell.

'Metropolitan police, ma'am,' Ayala said.

'What do you want?'

'Do you know Ellis DeLange?'

'She's my sister. Why?'

'May we come in?' Ayala asked. The Met had strict rules against giving death notices on the doorstep.

A chain rattled on the other side of the door, a lock clicked and the door swung open inwards. Ayala shuffled in then stopped suddenly, causing Morton to bump into him.

Morton nudged him in the back to keep moving, and then stood on tiptoe to glance over Ayala's shoulder. The flat, if it could be called that, was little more than a bed, a microwave and a curtained area at one end that Morton presumed concealed a bathroom.

Morton nudged Ayala again, and he shuffled forward just far enough to let Morton squeeze in. Morton pushed the door shut then breathed a sigh of relief. Just by closing the door, Morton had doubled the available space to stand in.

Brianna Jackson, born Brianna DeLange, sat on the end of the single bed with knees tucked up beneath her chin. She looked up expectantly, quickly glancing between the two detectives.

'Miss Jackson, I'm DCI David Morton. I have some bad news to tell you. I sorry to inform you that your sister has been found dead at her home,' Morton said.

Brianna inhaled deeply, then nodded. 'It was it an overdose, wasn't it?'

'We believe your sister was murdered.'

She clapped her hands to her mouth, her eyes flaring wide in apparent surprise. 'How? When?'

'We're not sure yet. When did you last see your sister?'

'Her... her birthday party, the weekend before last.'

'What night was this?'

'Saturday. She was stressing about turning the big three-oh.... It just seems so silly now. She'll be young forever now.' Brianna began to sob loudly. Ayala reached into his pocket, and pulled out a silk handkerchief monogrammed with a golden 'B'.

'Was the party in the evening?' Morton asked.

Brianna nodded. 'It was supposed to start at seven... but she only picked seven to get everyone there by nine. Everyone turns up late, don't they?'

'Do you remember who was there?'

'I... I've got a list. She invited everyone on social media. Pass me that laptop.' Brianna pointed at a small notebook sat on top of the microwave. She flipped up the lid, and the trio waited for the notebook to boot up in silence. Once it was on, Brianna tapped away at the keys to log in and brought up the details of the party.

She pointed at the screen. 'See, eighty-two attendees. She even invited my ex-husband, the useless git. He didn't turn up, thank God.'

'Eighty-two!' Ayala cried out.

'Miss Jackson—'

'Please, call me Brianna.'

"Miss Jackson,' Morton repeated firmly. 'Tell us about the people your sister had in her life.'

'Me. I'm pretty much almost all she had. We lost our parents a few years back, though Ellis never really got on with them. She was only two years older than me, but she looked out for me.'

Brianna might have been twenty-eight, but she looked a decade younger than her sister. In the most recent photos Morton had seen at the house, Ellis had a sunken, weather-worn appearance with waxy skin and eyes that seemed lifeless and dull; Brianna was still chubby-cheeked and cherub-like.

'Why didn't Ellis get on with your parents?' Morton asked.

'They disapproved of her lifestyle. Don't get me wrong, they were proud of everything she achieved... but Ellis got mixed up in the wrong crowd. It was that Paddy Malone that did it. He got her hooked, and she's been his meal ticket ever since.'

Ayala pulled out a notebook and pencil from his inside jacket pocket. 'Do you have an address for Paddy?'

'How should I know where he lives? He comes and goes. Most of the time he's in her kitchen with a needle jammed in his arm.'

'Could he have killed her?' Morton said.

'I doubt it. He's a loser, but he's pretty laid back. And like I said, he needed my sister.'

'Is there anyone that would have wanted her dead?'

'No... Yes. Her boyfriend, Kallum. Kallum Fielder. I saw them arguing at the party. It was embarrassing really. We all tried to ignore it.'

Morton's forehead creased as he strained to remember where he had heard the name Kallum Fielder. He hated it when things slipped out of recall.

'When was this?' Morton asked.

'Ten o'clock, maybe. Maybe a little after. I was gone by eleven so it had to be before then.'

'And was there anyone else?'

'Not that I can think of. Look, I don't mean to be rude but I've got to make some phone calls. I'm sure you've work to do anyway.'

'Of course. Do you have a phone number we can reach you at?'

Brianna scribbled on the back of a leaflet for a local takeaway, and handed it to Ayala. It had two phone numbers on it.

'The top one is my mobile number. The bottom one is the landline for my work – the Walworth Veterinary Clinic and Pet Hospital.'

'Thank you for your time, Miss Jackson.'

Chapter 6: The Boyfriend

For Morton, a quarter to nine o'clock in the morning felt like an early start for a Monday. But the man he and Ayala were at Broadcasting House to see had been up for several hours already.

Kallum Fielder, known to the nation simply as Kal, was the face of hit morning television *Wake Up Britain*! Over a bleary-eyed cup of tea or bowl of cereal, Kal would read out the morning's headlines in his deep, soothing baritone. He was also considered something of an in-joke and as celebrity-chaser Gifford Byrnes put it: "Kal speaks smart but acts dumb."

From the back of Studio One, the detectives watched Kal finish up his six 'til nine stint in front of the camera.

'And that's all from *Wake Up Britain*! I've been Kal Fielder and I'll see you tomorrow morning,' Kal signed off with a wink.

CRT monitors, which were affixed to the ceiling to show what was being broadcast in real time, cut to a preview of the next show.

'That's a wrap! Take five, everybody,' the director called out.

Morton pushed his way past the sound techs stampeding towards the snack tray out in the hall, flashed his ID at the single cameraman giving him a quizzical glance, then stepped onto the stage.

A pair of plum-coloured sofas, one used by the show's hosts and the other by the guests, were arranged at right angles in the centre of the stage. Almost immediately after Morton stepped onto the stage the heat from the lighting hit him. His suit suddenly felt clingy. But Kal was apparently immune. The television presenter sat right on the edge of the sofa with a mug of coffee in hand. His attention was focussed on holding his head deathly still so that his make-up could be reapplied.

'Mr Kallum Fielder?'

Kal waved a hand in reply, but didn't turn away from the beautician desperately trying to paint over his panda eyes.

'Who are you?' he asked.

'I'm DCI Morton. This is Detective Ayala. We need to talk to you about Ellis DeLange.'

Kal tensed visibly, and Morton saw his left biceps twitch. He pushed the hand of his make-up artist away. 'Leave.'

When the make-up artist was out of earshot, Kal continued: 'Eli's been arrested?'

'No, Mr Fielder. I'm afraid I have some bad news. Ellis was found dead at her home.'

Kal's biceps twitched again. 'No. That can't be.'

'I'm afraid it is. Her sister identified the body late last night.'

'But you've got to be mistaken. Eli is in New York! She can't be dead. She just can't be.'

Morton glanced at Ayala. 'Why would you think that?'

'She's doing a shoot there. She left over a week ago.'

'When was this?'

Kal paused to think, raising his hand to his lips to bite his nails as he did so. Morton made a mental note: two nervous tics. Finally, Kal replied: 'Sunday morning. The 30th. She had a midday flight from Heathrow to La Guardia. She's due back in a few days.'

'And when did you last see her?'

'The night before she left. Her birthday.'

'Mr Fielder, your girlfriend never made it onto her flight. We believe she was killed on the night of the party.'

'Killed? You think Eli was murdered?'

'Yes. And we know you two argued that night.'

'You think *I* did it?'

'Did you or did you not have an argument in front of witnesses that night?' Morton said.

'Yeah, but it was no big deal. Couples argue.'

'What did you argue about?'

'You'll think I'm crazy. I accidentally left my wallet on her nightstand when I got changed before the party. When I remembered and went back for it, the wallet was empty. Her room is upstairs, and our guests were in the main living room, so only Ellis could have touched it.'

'How much was in there?'

'Two hundred pounds. I had to walk home that night.'

'When the argument happened, did you leave straight after?'

'Not right away. She yelled, I yelled. She's been stressed about turning thirty for weeks. I thought I'd let her cool off. She stayed in her room, and I went back to the party. She was still asleep when I left.'

'It was all verbal then? You didn't hit her at all?'

Kal shook his head.

'So we won't find your DNA underneath her fingernails?' Morton asked on a hunch.

Kal folded his arms, hiding his hands from the detectives. Morton looked at him carefully. Up close, Kal looked a lot less youthful than on the television. His eyes were bloodshot, and his shirt looked unironed.

'Alright. So she scratched me. Doesn't that make me the victim?'

'You're still breathing. You don't look like a victim to me,' Morton said.

Kal stared in apparent disbelief at Morton.

Ayala took the opportunity to jump in. 'Kal, you know you're not at all like I expected.'

'Yeah, and what did you expect? You think I ought to be more street, just 'cause I'm black? Boy, I went to Harrow. I'm from Twickenham. Not all homies are from the 'hood.'

Ayala cocked his head to one side. He knew how prejudiced people could be. That still didn't stop him blurting out: 'But you used to be a footballer! And you spell Callum with a 'K'! What's with that?'

Kal glared, and turned to Morton. 'You going to let him talk to me like that?'

Morton shrugged. 'I'm curious as to the spelling too.'

'It's simple. Actor's Guild rules say my name has got to be unique and it was a pain having two different spellings, so I changed my name by deed poll. I am officially Kallum now. Callum Fielder ain't exactly as unusual as Detective Ayala, you see. What's his first name anyway?' Kal jabbed a finger towards Ayala.

Ayala's face scrunched up. He hated his name.

'It's Bertram,' Morton volunteered helpfully with only a hint of amusement.

Kal laughed mirthlessly. 'Your name is Bertram Ayala and you're giving me stick for an alternate spelling? That's some nerve.'

Ayala clenched his jaw. Morton saw that he was about to lash out, and quickly changed the topic: 'When did you leave the party?'

'Maybe an hour or two after we argued. The party was dying not long after midnight. I know that 'cause people left to get the last tube out of Richmond. Eli was still sleeping, so I joined Paddy in the kitchen–'

'Paddy Malone?'

'Yeah, that's him. We were playing Texas hold 'em when Gabby came running into the kitchen. She had tears running down her face, mascara going everywhere. I figured that was my cue to split. I don't need none of her drama. Besides, it was a Saturday night. We start filming the Sunday morning show at half past five.'

'Who was there when you left?'

'Eli obviously. Paddy was there trying to comfort Gabriella. On the way out I saw that prick, sorry, *Lord* Culloden, running after Gabriella. Figures that he'd be the one to upset her. I've never liked that guy.'

'So just the five of you?'

'Far as I know, yeah.'

'And where did you go?'

'I told you, home. My place in Twickenham. It's only half an hour or so away on foot.'

'Can anyone verify your whereabouts?'

'I live alone, if that's what you're asking. I went to bed. Got up the next morning, went to work.'

'You could have gone back, couldn't you?'

'Well, I didn't. So screw you and your accusations.' Kal rose, shot a nasty glance at Morton and huffed off towards his dressing room.

Morton turned to Ayala. 'He's quite the charmer, isn't he?'

'Yes, he is. Boss, is that his producer over there, the guy who called out cut earlier? We should verify he made it to work... and if he did, whether he was acting normally. I doubt anyone could murder their girl-friend then head in to work on TV a few hours later.'

'Let's find out. Hey! Wait up,' Morton shouted.

The producer spun around, and looked at the detectives curiously.

Morton walked towards him. 'You're the producer for *Wake Up Britain!*, right? Did you work last week on Monday?'

'I work every bleeding day, five in the morning 'til five at night. I'm not the talent.' The producer made air-quotes with his fingers as he said the word talent.

'Kal Fielder. What do you think of him?'

'He's photogenic, but he's arrogant and lazy. It isn't a good combination. But somehow he gets the ratings so I'm stuck with him.'

'Was he working last Sunday?'

'If you can call it that. He swanned in late, obviously drunk or high, bloodshot eyes and wearing a creased shirt. We only just made it on-air for the live morning segment thanks to the time it took make-up to make him look presentable... and even then, we had to avoid close-ups.'

'How late?'

'Half hour. It doesn't sound much, but when everything is planned down to the minute, any delay is intolerable.'

'Is he usually late?'

The producer glanced at an LED clock on the wall that Morton hadn't noticed. 'Only recently. He's been looking dishevelled all week, like he's not sleeping well. Do you need anything else? I've got to be in Studio Two in three minutes.'

'No, that's all. Thanks for your time.'

Chapter 7: Parole

The roads were gridlocked as Morton and Ayala headed back from Portland Place. Morton strummed his fingers impatiently against the steering wheel as he waited for the traffic lights to change in his favour.

Ayala sat in the passenger seat with an iPad in one hand, and a can of diet cola in the other. 'Francis Patrick Malone. Goes by the name of Paddy but that's no surprise. I bet every Irish guy has been called Paddy at least once.'

'His mother called him Francis. That's his name. I wonder how annoyed he gets when we use it. If only I knew someone who hated his first name,' Morton said, then shot a sly glance at the passenger seat.

'Whatever his name is, this guy's got a rap sheet as long as my arm. Possession, dealing, burglary, fencing and petty theft. He's not even a good criminal. He's currently out on licence for his last conviction. He got busted dealing liquid ecstasy. How'd he get to know someone as famous as Ellis?' Ayala asked. He splayed back in his seat, holding up the iPad up at an odd angle to try and maintain his 3G connection so he could peruse the Police National Computer Database that housed the details of Malone's convictions.

'School,' Morton replied without taking his eyes off the road.

'What?'

'They went to school together. 1995 to 2000, they went to Lower Holloway Community School.' The light changed and Morton accelerated sharply before turning right towards the Barbican Estate.

'How'd you know that?'

'Says so in his rap sheet. He was convicted for dealing there after he turned eighteen. She's got her school listed on her Wikipedia profile. Doesn't take a genius to use a search engine,' Morton said. He patted his left trouser pocket, where he'd stashed his mobile.

'No, but it does take a decent Internet connection,' Ayala grumbled.

'Or you could call his probation officer. I assume your phone still works.'

'Just about. Only two bars, boss.'

'Ring him. Then tell us to meet us there.'

'Meet us where?'

'The Barbican Estate. We're going to talk to Frank.'

Morton pulled the car over and swung into a space barely larger than his car. Paddy Malone lived alone in a one-bedroom flat paid for by the state. He was allegedly unemployed, but had been in prison as recently as a few months ago. He'd been let out early on licence, despite being a repeat offender. The prisons were simply too full to waste the space on a low-level drug dealer.

Morton stepped out of the car, and led the way down a narrow alley. Halfway down, he snapped a right-hand turn into an even narrower alleyway with steps climbing up a level towards Malone's flat block.

The building was a brutalist, concrete monstrosity, one which had at some point become a listed building. Morton jogged into the foyer, pausing to call over his shoulder: 'Come on, fortieth floor. You ready for the climb?'

'You've got to be kidding, boss.'

'Luckily for you, I am. The lifts are in order today. Last time I was here, all three were out of order. We only had to go as far as the eighteenth floor then, but I thought I was going to have a heart attack by the time we made it.' Morton hit the call button, and the middle lift doors pinged open.

They rode in silence, their noses scrunched up to avoid inhaling the smell of urine in the lift. The longest sixty seconds of his life later, Morton darted onto the fortieth floor's landing, and inhaled deeply.

'Wow. Look at that view.' Ayala pointed out of a large window facing south across the City of London. People could be seen scurrying around ant-like, unaware they were being watched from above. At this height,

London seemed serene, almost peaceful. In the sunlight, even the other two concrete towers that made up the Barbican Estate looked relatively attractive.

'Where's the probation officer?' Ayala asked.

'You tell me. You called him.'

'I only got his secretary. He's supposed to be meeting us here.'

One of the lifts pinged behind them, and a tall woman in her mid-thirties stepped out. She was attractive and Morton sensed from her confident gait that she was the sort who could easily handle herself. He'd seen her loitering in the lobby on the way in.

'Are you gentlemen here for me?' she asked.

Morton shot a glare at Ayala. 'Ashley Rafferty?'

'That's me. I'm Ashley Rafferty.' Ashley offered a hand in greeting. Her grip was as firm as any man's, but much softer too.

'I'm DCI Morton. This is Bertram Ayala. Unfortunately my colleague was under the impression you were a man.'

'So that's why you flew past me on the way in. Not to worry. I get that a lot. Shall we get going? He's the seventh door on the right.' Ashley pointed down the corridor.

They marched in step to Malone's front door.

'Francis Patrick Malone! Police.'

A sing-song voice answered groggily. 'Show me the warrant. Shove it under the door.'

'We're just here to talk.'

'Feck off then. I don't have to talk to you.'

'No, but you do have to talk to *me*, don't you Paddy?' Ashley said. 'Open up. Now.'

Morton smiled. She really could handle herself.

Chains jangled and then Paddy's door opened. He shuffled sideways, careful not to open the door too far and risk giving the police a glimpse inside. He shut the door behind him.

Patrick, like Ellis, was thirty years old. Tattoos, sufficiently amateur that Morton suspected they might be prison tats, snaked up and down his exposed forearms. He wore baggy jeans with his hands thrust inside his pockets. Cheap cologne hit Morton immediately. It seemed that Patrick had no appreciation of the concept that less is more.

'Oh no, mister. We're not having this conversation out here. Open the door, or else.'

'I've got company,' Paddy lied.

'So get rid of them. Or we can take you back to Pentonville now if you'd prefer. I don't need to remind you that it's part of your licence that permits inspection of your residence on request.'

'Fine.' He opened the door reluctantly. The inside of the flat was breezy and spacious with much more room than most London flats. Paddy led the way inside and sat down in the living room. A patio door was open out onto a concrete balcony where clothing hung on a washing line.

'You going to take a seat, or are yous waiting for an invitation?'

'Nice try, Paddy. Let's have a quick look around first.' Ashley made a beeline for a door at the rear of the flat which evidently led through to Paddy's bedroom.

He shot up and ran after her. 'Hey! Miss Rafferty. Don't go in there. I said I've got company.'

She ignored him, and knocked on the door. 'Anyone in there?'

When there was no reply, she opened the door. A musky, dank smell wafted out immediately. Ayala and Morton followed closely behind.

'You, stay by the doorway,' she said to Paddy.

'What are you looking for?' Ayala asked.

'What do you think I'm looking for? He's a drug dealer, and I'm his PO. I'm checking to make sure he's got clean bed sheets,' she said sarcastically.

'No need to be rude,' Ayala replied.

'And there was no need for you to assume I was a man either. Want to call it even?'

Morton looked on bemused. Then he spotted something. 'Ashley. Look inside that pillowcase. That looks awfully lumpy to sleep on.'

'You've a good eye, DCI Morton.' Ashley picked up the pillowcase, then turned it inside out. A small plastic bag, the kind used to keep sandwiches fresh, fell out. It was full of pills.

'What have we got here?'

'That's not what you t'ink it is,' Paddy declared.

'It looks like Miaow to me.'

'Naw, it's Bubble. Perfectly legal.'

Ayala looked at Morton quizzically who replied under his breath: 'It's basically mephedrone. The law hasn't caught up with all the legal highs yet. Miaow was banned a few years back but Bubble hasn't been.'

'It's not a crime, all right?' Paddy looked anxiously from Morton to his parole officer.

'If it is what you say it is, then maybe it isn't a crime. But it is a violation of your parole. Francis Patrick Malone, you are under arrest, and will be recalled to prison for a fixed period of 28 days.' Ashley turned to Morton. 'Sorry, DCI Morton, but your interview will have to wait. He'll be processed in about four hours and back in his cell at HMP Pentonville by tea time if you still want him.'

Thirty seconds later, and they were gone. Morton and Ayala found themselves back outside having wasted a trip.

'Did she just nick our suspect?'

'Yes, Bertram. I think she did. Of course we now know where to find him. Can you sort out a Prisoner Production Form for Mr Malone, then get it over to the Governor at Pentonville?'

'Sure thing.'

They headed for the alleyway back to the car.

'Where we going next, boss?'

'I've got Lord Culloden's address in the Sat Nav but I think that'll have to wait 'til tomorrow. It's a fancy place way out in the country. For now, it's back to base to sort some of the paperwork we've got piling up and then we'll head up to the prison.'

'Via a sandwich shop?' Ayala asked hopefully.

'Fine, but it's your turn to buy.' They rounded the corner into the final alleyway, and the car came into sight.

A bright yellow and black parking notice was affixed to the wind-screen.

'Not again!'

Chapter 8: HMP Pentonville

MONDAY APRIL 7TH – 17:15

It was still daylight when Morton and Ayala arrived at Her Majesty's Prison Pentonville. Despite its name, the prison wasn't really in Pentonville. Instead, it was about a mile north, almost equidistant between Caledonian Road underground and Caledonian Road & Barnsbury railway.

They parked up in Wheelwright Street around the corner, prayed that they wouldn't return to another parking ticket which, while they'd never pay it, would mean extra paperwork to get it cancelled, and then headed around to the main entrance.

'This your first time to Pentonville, Ayala?' Morton asked as they neared the entrance.

'Yep. Impressive entrance.'

The doorway was a tall, thick, wooden door set into a whitewashed Victorian building dating back to 1842.

'It's not half as impressive as Wormwood Scrubs. That's a prison entrance to brag about. They've got a door just like this one, but guarded by two huge towers,' Morton said.

They walked in, and Morton paused before they reached security. 'Got your papers?'

Ayala nodded. Morton had forced him to pick up photographic ID and proof of address from his flat on the way up to the prison.

'Great,' Morton said, then strode for the security desk. He pressed his forefinger against the guard's biometric reader and the light pinged green. Morton nodded to the guard, and proceeded through the metal detector.

'Hey! Wait up!' Ayala called out. Morton pretended not to hear him, and went around the nearest corner to pick up a coffee from the vending machine hidden there.

Eventually, Ayala caught up with him. But not before being finger-printed, photographed and entered into the prison's biometric system.

'Hey, you could have warned me!'

'And miss all the fun? At least you only have to go through that once,' Morton said then added under his breath '...per prison.'

'Which way?'

'Down the hallway,' Morton said with a smile. There were seven residential wings in four buildings coming off the main entrance hall. Francis Patrick Malone, or Prisoner A7745BW as he was known inside, was still in the A-Wing where all new arrivals went for their first night in Pentonville or, in Paddy's case, his first night back.

The prison housed nearly thirteen hundred inmates, though it was rated for only nine hundred and thirteen. Overcrowding was a perpetual problem, as were rats.

'Funny. Quit messing with me, would you? This places gives me the creeps.'

'Fine. Got a quid I can borrow?'

Ayala dove into his pocket and pulled a handful of shrapnel. He picked out a solitary pound coin and handed it over.

'Cheers. I need it for the lockers. All personal belongings – your phone, your wallet, your keys, they all need to go in a locker. The mech-anism needs a pound coin.'

Ayala pouted. 'But you just took my only pound coin!'

'Yep. I guess we're sharing,' Morton said.

Once all the formalities were out of the way, they were escorted to an interview suite where a tape recorder and two sealed blank tapes sat on the desk waiting for them along with a pencil and notepad. The note-pad looked like it had once been spiral-bound, but someone appeared to have taken the precaution of removing the metal rings that held it together.

Paddy was led in a few minutes later, shackled and looking dejected. He sat down opposite Morton and Ayala and immediately slumped in his chair like a sullen teenager.

Morton unwrapped the tapes in front of Paddy, and began to give his usual spiel about why he was taping the interview.

'Yeah, yeah I've heard it all before. I've got the right to remain silent, blah blah. This ain't my first time at the dance. What the feck do you want?' Paddy demanded.

'Before we begin, I must advise you that that–'

'That I'm entitled to a lawyer. Don't want one. How about a hooker? Can you do me one of those?'

'Very droll. Am I to assume then that you're happy to talk to us without a lawyer?'

'Yup. I ain't done shit, so you can't pin it on me. I've been strip-searched, offered rehab, and then you pigs come right on dinner time. It's getting cold in my cell right now, and if I don't get back soon my new cellmate will eat it. It's pie and mash night. Five o'clock. Every night. Why you gotta come at just after five?' Paddy whined.

'Ellis DeLange. You were at her thirtieth birthday party.' It wasn't a question.

'So? It was a deadly party. Loads of us were there.'

'Not everyone at the party has a rap sheet for dealing.'

'Some gobshite say I was supplying? 'Cause I wasn't. Hump off and find some other patsy.'

'Did you see Ellis that night?'

'Duh. It was her birthday,' Paddy said.

'And when did you leave?'

'Dunno. Late.'

'Anyone see you go?'

'Yeah, Gabby. We were together the whole time.'

'Run us through the last bit of the party. The few minutes before you left.'

'I was in the kitchen, getting bladdered and playing poker with Kal when Gabby came running out, crying about something. Kal scarpered, leaving me with her. Then that posh twat–'

'Lord Culloden?' Morton interjected.

'So he says. He came out to talk to Gabby. Seems it was him that upset her. I told him where to stick it, and we left. That was that.'

'Where did you go?'

'Walked to Richmond Station, grabbed a taxi and came here.'

'And where was the birthday girl during all this?'

'Upstairs. She'd been doing shots since seven, and headed to bed early.'

'You didn't see her on the way out?'

Paddy shook his head.

'Or anyone else?'

'Nah. Just Kal, Gabby 'n' me and the prick. That was it.'

'And you didn't notice anything unusual?'

'Nope. I had a few drinks, played cards and came home with Gabby, the hottest girl at the party. Didn't see nothing, don't know nothing.'

'You know Ellis is dead.'

'Yep. I didn't do it. Got me an alibi. I gotta tell you that feels good. I shouldn't have to prove I didn't do nothing, but today I can. Ask Gabby. Now if there's nothin' else, I'll be having my dinner.'

Morton hit the button to end the recording, handed Paddy the information notice he was obliged to give him and then watched as Paddy immediately crumpled it up and tossed it on the floor, and then he was gone.

'So what do you think of his story?' Ayala asked.

'Malone's a natural liar. I'd bet my pension he's still dealing. A bit odd that he volunteered an alibi so easily. But his story isn't going to be hard to verify. Richmond Station is CCTV central, so if he didn't get a cab there, it was a stupid lie to tell.'

'And if he's not lying?'

'Then we've got a conundrum, because his story puts Ellis DeLange alone in her house at the time of her death.'

'What if Lord Culloden didn't really leave? Or Kal? Just because Paddy thinks they left, doesn't mean that they did.'

'Right you are. Nothing to prove Paddy didn't double back either. But right now, they all seem to agree that they left and our victim was alive when they did. Anyone could have left and come back.'

'They could all be in on it?'

'Possible but not likely. Can you imagine a good reason that a dealer, a peer, a model and a television presenter would decide to murder a friend?'

'OK. Someone else then? Vladivoben?'

'Possible, but we've no evidence to indicate that. It's also possible that Kal killed her and then just moved the body later. So far no one is claiming to have seen our victim since she went up to her room.'

Chapter 9: The Culloden Estate

Lord Culloden's address was listed as The Culloden Estate, Shirley Hills, Croydon. It was a thirty-five minute drive from New Scotland Yard, and about the same distance from Richmond in quiet traffic. Once past zone one, the roads were plain sailing and they made it out to Croydon only marginally slower than the Sat Nav's estimate.

Culloden Manor was situated off a private road, a few minutes from the A232. When Morton and Ayala arrived, they were greeted by a thick stone wall and an impressive security gate at the foot of the driveway. Morton was surprised to see an elderly guard sat in a hut just inside the estate. When the guard saw Morton pull up the driveway, he shuffled from his seat and walked with a limp towards a pedestrian gate off to one side.

Ayala leaned in conspiratorially. 'He doesn't look like much of a security guard, does he? One good chase and it'd be all over.'

Morton scowled. 'If you think being old counts you out, I'll find you a transfer to another department tomorrow.'

Ayala fell silent.

The elderly guard rattled a great key ring full of keys, eventually found the right one and then unlocked the gate before ambling over to Morton's to rap on the driver's-side window. Morton slid it down with the touch of a button.

'Good afternoon. I'm Detective Chief Inspector Morton, and this is Detective Inspector Ayala. We're here to see the Lord of the Manor.'

The old man frowned, as if trying to work out if he had forgotten an appointment.

'Is he expecting you?' he asked.

'We don't have an appointment. Would you be kind enough to phone up and ask if he might be able to see us?'

The old man limped off, and Morton watched him return to the guard hut. He spoke animatedly on the telephone. When he'd finished, he hit a switch which opened the main gate.

'Straight up the driveway. The main house is about a mile down. You'll be met at the front door. And mind the daffodils. Someone's already run over one of the beds this year, and his Lordship wasn't best pleased.'

Morton nodded. The drive was lined with oak trees whose branches entwined overhead, causing dappled light to splay across the gravel driveway. It really was quite pretty, and made a pleasant change from the drab grey of inner-city London.

About halfway down the road, Morton passed an access road going off into the woods. Eventually the drive ended in a great circle that stopped in front of an enormous oak door guarded by a pair of stone gargoyles stationed either side. The Manor was a grade one listed building with stone parapets that loomed overhead. According to Morton's research, the Manor was the site of a minor skirmish during the War of the Roses. He imagined archers lining up at the narrow windows to rain death down upon those assaulting the Manor.

Just as the guard had promised, a man waited for them on the front steps. He was a short, grey-haired man who had to be at least sixty.

'Lord Culloden, I presume?' Morton said.

'His Lordship is not at home at present. I am merely the butler. Lady Culloden asked me to see you through to the living room, if you'd care to follow me.'

He swept through the doorway with Morton and Ayala trailing in his wake. They strode briskly along the hall and into a sitting room blessed with a double-height ceiling and enormous bay windows opening out onto the rear of the property. The gardens were as grandiose at the back as they were at the front. A gardener perched on top of a step-ladder dangling over a hedgerow. He hoisted a pair of hedge trimmers that looked like they could decapitate a man. As Morton watched, he struck the hedge quickly and several branches fell to the ground leaving behind a level top. There was something to be said for working outdoors, especially in the springtime.

A floorboard creaking snapped Morton out of his reverie, and he turned to see a young lady enter. Morton glanced at Ayala, who flashed a cheeky grin. If this was Mrs Culloden then Mr Culloden was surely the luckiest pensioner on the planet.

'Lady Culloden?' Morton said.

'Indeed. I am she.'

'You're Lord Culloden's wife?'

'Correct. To what do I owe the pleasure?'

'We were hoping to speak with your husband.'

'That, my dear, was readily apparent. However he is not here, as you can plainly see. Perhaps I can assist you?'

'This is a matter of some delicacy, My Lady—'

'Please, call me Harriet. Lady Culloden makes me sound like an elderly lady who lives in a great big house with a dozen cats, and I hate cats.'

'At least you've got the big house,' Ayala said.

'Quite.' Harriet turned up her nose at Ayala and sniffed.

Morton continued gingerly: 'As I was saying, we'd like to talk to your husband about a party he attended in Richmond on the night of Saturday the 30th March.'

'The 30th of March you say? This year? There must be some mistake. We were in Venice for the weekend. I can send Grant to fetch our plane tickets if you so wish.'

'That would be helpful.'

Harriet picked up a small glass bell from a side table that Morton hadn't previously noticed, and rang it once. A high-pitched ring echoed throughout the room and the man who had greeted Morton and Ayala at the steps reappeared.

'You rang, m'lady?'

'Fetch me our plane tickets from his Lordship's study. The ones from our trip to Venice last month.'

'At once.'

Grant spun on his heel and disappeared. Footsteps echoed down the hallway. Silence ensued as the trio waited for Grant's return. When he did, he appeared with a small silver platter atop which sat an envelope. Harriet took it from Grant, nodded her thanks and handed it to Morton.

Morton upended it, and two return plane tickets spilled out. First class. Harriet and Lord Culloden were indeed out of the country over the weekend of Ellis DeLange's birthday.

'Harriet, why do these tickets say Mr and Mrs Culloden?'

'My husband's title is a manorial one. Technically, he is Mr Culloden,

Lord of the Manor of Culloden but that's such a mouthful. Everyone simply calls him Lord Culloden for convenience. I'm sorry to say such titles carry little weight with the sort of riffraff who run airlines.'

'Do you know Miss Ellis DeLange?'

'The photographer? The one who the papers say was murdered? Heavens no. We would never consort with anyone like that.'

Morton wanted to curse. He knew the papers would report the death, but he didn't think it would be quite so quick. Not only did they now have an impostor pretending to be an elderly landowner to track down, but now the press would be breathing down his neck. Instead, he forced himself to smile politely.

'Thank you for your time, Lady Culloden.'

Chapter 10: Missing Something

By the time Morton and Ayala arrived back at New Scotland Yard, Mayberry had assembled the press clippings from the daily newspapers and placed them on Morton's desk. It wasn't as bad as he'd feared. The same large photograph of Edgecombe Lodge, no doubt taken through the gaps in the gate using a long-range camera lens, was splashed across the front pages of all of the major daily newspapers. A tiny caption in the corner of the image credited the copyright to Rafe Soros Photography.

So far all the papers were taking the same tack. Ellis DeLange had been found dead and the famed DCI Morton had picked up the case. A few of the sleazier tabloids made reference to an old article about Ellis. Back then it had been her fall from grace that had interested the media. One day, Ellis had been the darling of the fashion world. The next, she was its scapegoat. Drugs were involved, but she was never prosecuted. Morton made a mental note to find out why charges had not been brought.

'Look at this. Three days from being discovered dead to hitting the front page of every major newspaper. We've got a fairly artsy piece in this one talking about her photography. Apparently some schmuck thinks he's a millionaire after putting an original print on eBay and seeing it sell for a cool one point two mil. As if the buyer is ever going to pay up!'

'Ayala, get your nose out of the gossip column. Unless the papers know something we don't, we'll ignore them as long as we can. Is Purcell still in the Incident Room? Good. Go get him.'

Morton watched as Ayala left, then pulled out a notepad and began to jot down what they knew so far. The victim had died at home on the night of her thirtieth birthday during a celebratory party which had been attended by numerous guests. She was alive after most of them were gone, but had spent the majority of the party sulking after a fight with her equally famous boyfriend which he claimed was about money. By the end of the night, she had just six people in the house including her: her boyfriend, her sister, her best friend, the mysterious impostor, and her alleged drug dealer.

Five suspects. One argument. One multi-million-pound property in Richmond. One career criminal. And one complete unknown.

The door to Morton's office creaked as Ayala returned with the Chief Scene of Crime Officer, Stuart Purcell, trailing in his wake. Where Ayala was exceedingly tall, chiselled and overdressed for the office, Purcell was the polar opposite. His chubby cherub-like features belied a seriousness and attention to detail that Morton admired – and he had a box of doughnuts tucked under one arm.

Purcell set the box on the edge of the desk where it perched atop a pile of old files. 'Help yourself, gents.'

Ayala waved off the offer of a doughnut.

'Counting calories again?' Purcell asked with a grin.

'Nope. Just not piling them on like there's a shortage on. Some of us actually need to be able to run after criminals.'

'Touché. I'll stick to the better-paid, safer work that comes with doughnuts. Speaking of food, did you guys spot the pizza boxes all over our victim's house?'

Ayala nodded, not removing his gaze from the box of doughnuts. 'Hard to miss them. They were from *Trattoria Da Mondo*. Tiny place, a few doors up from Richmond Station. I called them up. Evidently, Miss DeLange was a fan. They don't normally do deliveries, but she's only five minutes around the corner and she tips well so they make an exception if it's quiet enough to spare someone for five minutes.'

Morton tapped his fingers lightly on the desk. 'Did they deliver on the night of the party?'

'The guy I spoke to didn't know. Apparently three brothers own the place, and they alternate which nights they work.'

'Hmm. It's probably not important. She could have picked them up or sent someone else to pick them up or they could be from a month ago. There's so much junk you'd never be able to tell. Send Mayberry anyway.

Visiting a pizzeria should be just about within his sphere of competence. What have we got in the way of DNA, Stuart?'

The tech swallowed a mouthful of doughnut. 'Hundreds of samples. We don't have the time to test everything, but I think we can make a good start by looking at a couple of the more relevant samples.'

'Such as?'

'Such as a toothbrush with male DNA stored in the en-suite to the master bedroom—'

'Which probably belongs to the boyfriend, Kal Fielder,' Morton said.

'That was my thinking too. That sample's donor has been all over the house so it's a fairly safe assumption. I found seminal DNA from another donor—'

'In her bedroom?'

'Actually, no. We haven't finished processing the bedroom yet. It was on a towel caught on a rosebush outside.'

'Our mystery nudist.'

Purcell's eyes flew wide open. '*Nudist?*'

'Yep. We've got a witness who saw a man fleeing the scene in the buff after midnight.'

'That doesn't seem like much of a getaway plan for a murder. If it were me, I'd wear dark clothing and sneak away.'

'Quite. If he isn't Kal Fielder then we've got two other male suspects. Door number one, Paddy Malone, convicted drug dealer. Door number two, our impostor Lord Culloden.'

'Or it could be a third person entirely,' Purcell suggested.

'I doubt it. We've got the victim plus five others in the house when she died, as far as we know. We know this DNA is male, and we think it isn't the boyfriend. Process of elimination says our most likely suspects are Malone and our unknown male.'

'There's nothing to suggest the DNA was from that night.'

'The towel was outside. If it had been there for longer, why wouldn't she have brought it back inside? It fits with the timeline – a man flees the house wrapped in a towel which gets caught on the rosebush. He then jumps the fence and disappears into the night,' Ayala said.

'I don't buy someone committing murder but not having the faculties to get dressed before fleeing. And where did the clothes go? I didn't see any trousers or shirts on the scene. Did you?' Morton asked, a flash of a lost suit jacket flitting briefly into his mind. The orphaned jacket had to come from somewhere. Morton pushed the thought away. The presence of a suit jacket alone was immaterial. It could have been left by any of the guests who attended earlier in the evening.

'Nope. No men's shoes, shirts or trousers at all. Not even an overnight bag for the boyfriend,' Purcell said.

'Then someone else took them, which presupposes someone else being in the house, alive, after our nudist – which means he isn't the killer. And five become four.'

'The partygoers aren't our only suspects. What if the neighbour, Vladivoben, killed her?'

'Over a simple noise complaint?' Morton countered. 'Why not simply phone us? As motives go, that's weak. What about money? Who gets the house? That's got to be worth a good three million.'

'We didn't find a copy of Ellis' last will and testament anywhere in the house, though there was a safe stacked with £20 notes hidden inside. And yes, they did all end up in the evidence log. Ayala watched me count them into an evidence bag,' Purcell said.

'No will means the sister gets the lot. Three million quid buys a lot of motive.'

'If Ellis had money then why would she have been arguing with the boyfriend about money? And she could have a will in a bank deposit box or with her solicitor,' Ayala said.

'Then find out. Call her bank and her lawyer. If there's a will, I want to know about it. What else did we find?'

'Plane tickets for Heathrow to New York, and a receipt showing Ellis made a payment to the USA's Electronic System for Travel Authorization website. It confirms Kal's story and explains why no one thought she was missing.'

'That's pretty convenient timing. Who would have known about her travel plans, apart from Kal?'

'She could have told anyone at the party. Who hired her for the New York gig?'

'We don't know. The details are probably on her laptop, which needs to be decrypted. It's in the queue.'

'Bump it to the top.'

Purcell shook his head. 'No can do. You're not the only Murder Investigation Team, and this isn't exactly crucial.'

Morton glared. 'What can you give me then?'

'I can give you a thermostat. Ellis had a fully automated system which was designed to save energy by only heating rooms that are in use or are going to be in use. In theory it could have cut her energy bills by at least–'

Morton glared again. 'Anything useful? Like evidence I can actually use?'

'N-no… I suppose not.'

'Then get going and see what you can do to expedite my DNA.' Purcell bit his lip and nodded sheepishly before scooping up the leftover doughnuts and scurrying from Morton's office as fast as his stubby little legs could carry him.

Once Purcell was gone, Ayala said: 'That was a bit harsh, wasn't it?'

'We don't have time to dawdle here. The press are only going to get more voracious and we'll come under scrutiny. Better he hears it from me than the Superintendent next week.'

'You think this is the Matthews case all over again.'

'No… It'll be worse. Our victim is famous. Thank God the press haven't caught wind of our fake Lord of the Manor yet. That sort of scandal mixed with violence and new money would have the journos from *The Impartial* frothing at the gills.'

'Any clue who he is?'

'I think there's a work connection. How else would she have come into contact with him? If Purcell can get that laptop open then we can find out who she's been working with.'

'Maybe the sister would know? We've got to speak to her again to find out about her inheritance.'

'Right you are. Go call our victim's bank now, and see if you can find out who her solicitor is. I'll meet you at the car in ten minutes.'

'Where are you going?'

'To send Mayberry out on a wild pizza chase.'

Morton found DS Mayberry in the Incident Room, poring over a whiteboard adorned with the names of party attendees that Brianna had printed off of her social media account.

Mayberry had drawn a crude mobile phone to the right of each of those he had managed to contact, and a red X against those who had been due to attend but had been no-shows on the night. About half the list had such an X.

'Mayberry, do you have a minute?'

'Y-yes, boss,' Mayberry stuttered. Mayberry had a speech impediment. Occasionally he stuttered. But he often used the wrong word, which sometimes had unintended consequences.

'How's the canvass going?'

'Pretty well. We've been out on the paths of Richmond all week. Lots of… home… home…'

'Homeowners?' Morton prompted.

Mayberry nodded vigorously. 'They knew Ellis lived in the local area, but none of those we spoke to were on smiley terms with her. W-we did learn that our naked man was sawn–'

'Seen,' Morton corrected automatically.

'–throughout Richmond. He was spotted r-running along the high street.'

'Drunk?'

'We don't think so. He was sawn–'

'Was seen!' Morton corrected, again.

Mayberry screwed up his face, apologised, and continued: 'Sawn in the darkness heading up towards Richmond Park by a few of the homeless folks that sleep near there. The main gates are locked at dusk, but pedestrians can get in around the clock. We think he slept in the park because the next sighting was him coming back out of the park and heading down Church Road at about six.'

'Anyone snap a photo?'

'N-no. I'm trying to find somewhere along the road with, erm, moving v-video thing.' Mayberry frowned as he searched for the right phrase.

'CCTV?'

'Yes. To get a picture. All we know is he's white, about six foot tall and in his late thirties to early forties.'

'Well, that narrows it down to about three hundred thousand Londoners… Good work, Mayberry. I've got another job for you. At the crime scene we found dozens of pizza boxes from *Trattoria Da Mondo*. I need to know if they delivered to her on the night she died, and if so at what time.'

'I'm on it… and boss?'

'Yes.'

'Thanks for giving m-me another chance.'

Morton nodded, spun on his heel and headed for the car park. Mayberry might be a halfwit, and he might be the Superintendent's future son-in-law, but he was a half decent halfwit.

Chapter 11: Walworth Veterinary Clinic and Pet Hospital

TUESDAY APRIL 8TH – 15:00

It was nearing three o'clock by the time Morton and Ayala made it to the Walworth Veterinary Clinic and Pet Hospital where Brianna worked. As soon as they walked into the clinic, a particularly aggressive Dachshund began to yip and pulled on its lead. Ayala leapt away in surprise, eliciting a wry smile from the older officer.

'Down!' The Dachshund's owner grunted. 'Sorry 'bout that. He's not used to strangers.'

'Nor, it seems, is my detective,' Morton said before heading for a small hatch at the back of the reception through which a secretary could be seen tapping away at a laptop.

'Afternoon. I'm Detective Chief Inspector Morton. Is Miss Brianna Jackson available, please?'

'She's in the back cleaning out the cages. Go on through the door to your left then all the way down the hall to the back. I'll buzz you in.'

The secretary pressed a button under the desk and the door buzzed loudly. Once on the other side they proceeded as instructed and found Brianna on her hands and knees with a sponge in one hand and a bucket of soapy water next to her. A strong odour of wet dog pervaded the air.

At the sound of their footsteps, Brianna looked up.

'Detective Morton! Did we have an appointment? I'm afraid I'm about to finish for the day.'

'We'll keep this brief then. Firstly, have you seen your sister's will?'

Morton was careful to avoid letting on that, as far as he knew, there wasn't one.

Brianna's eyes widened. 'Her will? No... Am I a beneficiary? Shouldn't her lawyer be telling me this?'

'We haven't discovered one. Our inquiries lead us to believe your sister died intestate, which would mean that her immediate family will inherit – subject to inheritance tax of course.'

'Knock me down with a feather! I'm all she had. I get everything?' Brianna smiled toothily then suppressed her greed the moment she saw Morton's revolted glare.

'As I said, we can't confirm the absence of a will, but if she doesn't have one then yes, I suppose you do. I need to ask you a few questions.'

'Ask away!' By now, Brianna's gaze had drifted off to the side dreamily. Morton supposed she was mentally spending her sister's estate.

'Do you know Lord Culloden's full name?'

'Beats me. I only met him a few times. We aren't on first-name terms. Ellis worked with him, I think. Or for him, maybe?'

'Do you know where he lives?'

'Nope.'

'Or anything else?'

'He drives a Mercedes. An old one, like forty years old. He always said it's a classic. Junker, more like it. The thing was a rust bucket on wheels. Ooh, do you think I could get me a new one of those?'

Morton ignored her. 'What colour was it?'

'Black... No, dark blue... or black. I don't know. It was dark.'

'Anything else you know about him?'

Brianna cocked her head to one side. 'He's banging that little tart Gabby, Eli's model friend.'

'That would be Miss Gabriella Curzon?'

Brianna nodded. 'That's her. She worked with Eli too. Used to be a model, see.'

'Used to be?' Ayala asked.

'Yeah. She went back to university last year. Now thinks she's all high and mighty.'

'What's she studying?' Morton said.

'Law. She'll never make it. Not unless blowjobs count as oral persuasion.' Brianna laughed heartily at her own joke.

'And where does she live?'

'Tottenham Court Road. I went there once. Quite nice, but oh so loud! I can't imagine sleeping with that noise roaring below. I suppose you want her address. I've got it in my phone. I suppose I'll be getting a new phone soon too!'

Brianna pulled out her phone, and typed in her PIN carelessly. 5051. Morton made a mental note, just in case.

'Aha, here it is. 1 Eastcastle Place, Bernard Street. It's right bang in the middle of Fitzrovia.'

Ayala leapt into action, dutifully scribbling the address into the notebook he kept stowed in his jacket pocket.

'Save your paper, detective. I know where it is.' Morton turned to Brianna. 'One last question: do you use pentobarbital here?'

Brianna's jaw went slack for a split second, but she covered up her surprise quickly. 'Of course we do. This is a veterinary clinic and it's sometimes necessary to put animals to sleep.'

'Thank you for your time.'

On the way back out, Morton said under his breath: 'I guess we now know where Ellis was getting her pentobarbital fix.'

'Maybe. Just because she had access, it doesn't mean she's dealing.'

'Are you really that naïve? Get a sample from the receptionist.'

Morton lengthened his stride as soon as they were back into the reception area, and made for the exit.

'Hey! Where are you going?'

'Home. It's late. Get me that sample. See you bright and early.'

Morton knew something was up the moment he walked through the front door. Tuesday was his night to cook, so the sight of Sarah wearing an apron made him suspicious.

'What'd you do?' he asked knowingly.

Sarah turned away from the stove to flash a smile, then said, 'Nothing… yet.'

'Is that what I think it is?'

'Chateaubriand with Béarnaise sauce and hand cut French fries. There's been a Barolo airing on the dining table since first thing. Would you mind pouring while I plate up?'

Morton picked up the bottle, and wiped dust from the label with a napkin to reveal it was a 1985 vintage: the good stuff, which Morton never thought worth buying for himself, but which they inevitably got given by Sarah's side of the family every Christmas.

'Now I know you want something! Tuesday the eighth…' Morton murmured to himself, trying to work out if he'd missed a special occasion.

He poured the wine, allowing himself a generous glass, then swirled it around before inhaling deeply. Notes of pepper, dried berries and chewy tannins hit him immediately.

'Wow.'

Sarah leaned through the doorway. The apron was gone, revealing a slinky black dress. 'I told you it'd be worth the wait.'

'You certainly are. The wine isn't bad either.'

Sarah chuckled. 'You old charmer, you.'

'So, what is it? Did I forget something or are you after something?'

They both knew it was the latter. Morton's memory was virtually infallible – for things he considered important anyway.

'Just a second.' Sarah disappeared back towards the kitchenette. Morton heard the clang of cutlery as dinner was served, and she reappeared a minute later. After setting the plates down and lighting a candle in the centre of the table, Sarah sat down and took a sip of wine. Morton looked on expectantly, his food untouched.

'You know you keep saying no to retiring,' Sarah began but was cut off.

Morton flared up. He couldn't help but raise his voice. 'How many times do we have to discuss this? A man doesn't hit fifty and immediately lose his marbles. I'll keep going until they won't let me any longer.'

'Whoa! Slow down. That isn't where this is going. And don't let that get cold.'

Morton bit his lip sheepishly. 'Sorry,' he mumbled.

'So you should be. As I was saying, you're not giving up anytime soon, and the kids have long since flown the nest. I've been thinking – if you're not on the scrap heap just yet, then I'm not either.'

Morton took a bite of the steak, chewed and then swallowed. 'You want to go back to work?'

'Back? I'm not sure I got a great deal of work done in the first place.' Sarah gave him an accusatory glare.

'Hey! That took two to happen. It wasn't all my fault.'

'I want to go back to university,' Sarah said. 'I don't know what I want to study yet, but lots of people our age are going back to it.'

'Yes.'

'It's only part-time, and we can definitely afford it. I've been talking to the admissions officer at Brunel, and she told me I could qualify for any one of a number of master's programmes.'

'Yes.'

'I know I'm too old really, and that I probably won't go back to work after, but it would be great to get out and learn something new.'

'Sarah… I said yes. Twice. I think it's a great idea. You don't need to sell me on this. What do you fancy studying?'

'I was thinking that I might look into journalism or maybe criminology. Speaking of journalism, have you seen today's paper?' Sarah shifted uncomfortably in her seat.

Morton sighed. 'Don't tell me. I'm in it.'

'No, but your victim is.'

'Where'd you hide our copy of *The Impartial*?' Morton rose, as if to go look for it.

'It's in the recycling box in the kitchen–'

Morton stomped off to find his newspaper.

She called after him: 'David! Leave it! You haven't finished your steak yet.'

But he was long gone. He found the newspaper right at the bottom of the recycling box. Sarah was always so predictable. It wasn't his first time to the media circus rodeo.

He flattened the newspaper out on the sideboard, and flipped quickly through the pages. He didn't have to look too far. Ellis DeLange's death had warranted a two-page spread on pages eight and nine. Morton ignored the blown-up pictures of Ellis which compared her picture at twenty-five with the most recent picture they could find, as the reporter had come to the same conclusion Morton had. Ellis had not aged well.

'Damn!' Morton exclaimed. Two paragraphs in, Morton spotted his worse fears.

'*Ellis had allegedly been abusing pentobarbital. More commonly thought of as the drug which will put down a sick dog, pentobarbital can be abused to induce euphoria.*'

Sarah appeared behind him, and lightly touched his arm.

'They know about the drugs, even down to the specific type taken. That shouldn't have hit the newspapers yet!'

'I'm sorry.'

'You know what this means? There's got to be a leak in my department.'

'If there were, wouldn't they know more? I've read all the papers today. None have said anything about a naked man running from the scene in the dead of night, and you know that would be front page news,' Sarah argued.

'I suppose you're right. But we only just found out about the pentobarbital.'

'So someone in Ellis' life spilled the beans. Money is a formidable temptress.'

Morton crumpled up the paper, and threw it back in the recycling. 'It's got to be the sister.'

'Maybe. You can find out in the morning. I've got a movie in. Come take the evening off. I even made dessert.'

'You really did think I'd say no. I would never do that to you. It's your choice what you want to do with your days.'

'Well then, I choose a quiet night in with my husband.'

Morton smiled. The question of who was selling details of his investigation to the press could wait.

He wouldn't have to wait long.

Chapter 12: Wake Up Britain!

Kal wasn't doing his normal breakfast segment. The fifteen minutes normally allotted to discussing who might win in the Wednesday evening Premier League fixtures had been ditched in favour of what the viewers really wanted to hear about: the murder of Ellis DeLange.

It was an open secret at the studio that Kal and Ellis had been an item, so when the producers had been offered the opportunity of an exclusive interview with the dead girl's little sister, she had immediately roped in Kal to round out the show, and so Kal sat not on the presenter's sofa on the *Wake Up Britain!* set but on the guest sofa instead. Kal would have preferred to have stayed in bed, but orders were orders, and at least this way Brianna wouldn't be able to stab him in the back.

Brianna sat to his right looking every bit the grieving sister. Her mascara had been artfully smudged to give the appearance that she simply couldn't hold back the tears and she clutched a box of tissues in her left hand.

Kal's co-host, Meredith Creswell, sat forward on her sofa to listen to Brianna speak.

'Growing up with my sister was… Do you have a sister?' Brianna asked.

Meredith nodded. 'Two.'

'Then you know what it's like. She annoyed me constantly. We competed over clothes, jewellery and boys. She could be incredibly frustrating. She had to win at everything, and everything had to be done her own way. She was so smart. Twelve 'A' grade GCSEs. Our parents always said she could have done anything. But Ellis didn't want to be a lawyer or doctor. She chose photography. On her eighteenth birthday, she packed her bags and moved to a squat in Covent Garden with an older man. The rest, as they say, is history.'

'She sounds like a real free spirit.'

'She was. But she always had time for me. When I needed to talk, she was there. And when our parents died…' Brianna said, then paused to sob. She dabbed at her perfectly dry eyes with a tissue, and when the camera panned back, Kal could see she had brushed the corner of her eyes with artificial tears.

Brianna huffed, then pretended to pull herself together with a shudder. 'It's been just the two of us for a while now. Our parents died a few years back, and Ellis, well, Ellis didn't take it too well.'

Meredith shuffled forwards to the edge of the sofa, and leant towards Brianna. 'That's an understatement! I remember she was all over the papers back then.'

'Our parents' demise started her on a downward spiral. They weren't exactly old.'

'It was a car crash, wasn't it?'

'Yes. One night the roads were icy, and Daddy lost control. Mummy died within minutes. When Dad found out she didn't survive the crash, he became despondent. Three days later, he was gone. It was like they were soulmates and couldn't survive without each other.'

'Did you sister ever stop taking drugs?'

'I hope so. I never saw her take them. She was always careful to hide that part of herself away from me. Whenever I was around, she was the perfect big sister. But the police say she still had some in her system on the night she died.'

'What happened that night?'

'I don't know. It was her birthday. The big three oh. We had a party at her home in Richmond. The last time I saw her, she was arguing.' Brianna shot a nasty glance at Kal.

'With who?' Meredith stared intently. Apparently, she had not been primed to expect this titbit of information.

Brianna waited for hush before she turned the knife in. 'Kallum Fielder,' she whispered softly, just loudly enough for the microphone attached to her lapel to catch what she was saying.

A gasp rose through the audience as they collectively contemplated that the murderer might be in their midst. A silence fell as everyone in the studio turned to Kal for a response.

Kal exhaled deeply. He knew it would come out sooner or later, but he didn't expect the accusatory glances he got when he replied. 'It's true. We did argue–'

Before Kal could finish his sentence, the screens around the studio cut suddenly to black. Meredith placed her hand to her ear as she strained to hear a voice over her radio.

'We've cut to previews,' Meredith said. 'You've got a two-minute reprieve, Kal.'

A producer bolted forward from the back, and waved a warm-up artist into action. The man, who was paid to keep the audience in a ready state, leapt into action and began talking to the audience.

Kal pulled his microphone off, and gesticulated rudely towards the producer. 'What the hell, Si?' he asked the man. The producer was Simon Keller, a legend among the crew of *Wake Up Britain!* Kal had known him for years.

'You know what's up. If you're about to admit something, you need to talk to legal first. Don't do something stupid here.'

'I'm not. Eli and I argued. It wasn't serious. Couples argue.'

Simon looked doubtful. He glanced over at Brianna, who was watching Kal with an expression of curiosity.

'Si, I didn't kill Eli. Let me clear my name. I know you want the ratings,' Kal implored.

'Thirty seconds!' a stagehand yelled out. Kal began to tuck his microphone wire back underneath his shirt.

Simon nodded briskly, then stepped back off the stage just as the cameras began rolling again.

The stagehand held up five fingers then began putting them down one by one. 'Three…two…one!'

Meredith smiled. 'Our apologies for the interruption, we had some technical difficulties for a moment there. I'm here with Brianna DeLange and Kallum Fielder discussing the death of Ellis DeLange. Kal, you were just saying how much you regret your last interaction with Ellis.'

'I do. The night she died we had an argument. It wasn't a big argument. It was one of those small arguments that every couple has. We'd had a few to drink, and ended up arguing over nothing at all. One insult led to another and before I knew it, we'd dragged up every problem we've ever had. She gave me the rollicking of a lifetime, and went to her bedroom to sulk. I wish she hadn't. I never saw her again.'

'Do you think things might have turned out differently if you'd stayed?'

'I don't know. I guess I never will. Maybe whoever broke in would have left if they'd seen me first.'

'I'm sure they would have!' Meredith said. 'You're what, six foot three?'

'Six four actually.'

'You think it was a burglary gone wrong then?' Meredith asked.

'It wasn't a burglary!' Brianna cried out in a shrill voice. 'Nobody broke in that night. When I left, she was alive – and he was still there!' Brianna jabbed a finger towards Kal.

'It wasn't me. I left not long after you.'

'Who was there then?'

'Eli. Paddy. Gabby... And Lord Culloden,' Kal spat.

'*Him*? He's not even really a Lord! The police said so,' Brianna said.

Meredith looked gobsmacked. First the argument. Now an even more juicy rumour. Her ratings would be through the roof.

'Who are we talking about?' she asked.

'Some friend of Eli's who was at the party. He calls himself Lord Culloden, but apparently he's been using a fake name all along.'

Behind camera number four, Simon Keller was waving furiously. The conversation was skirting the bounds of defamation, and the producer knew he couldn't get away with cutting to pre-recorded trailers again so soon. Meredith spotted his frantic attempts to curtail things and took control quickly.

'There we go, ladies and gentlemen. A famous face that fell from grace. An argument with a lover, and an allegation of fraud. Let's take a look back at the life and work of Ellis DeLange in this video montage of her greatest work.'

The camera cut away, and a video showing Eli's photography began to play.

Chapter 13: Sources

Morton hit pause. They'd watched the *Wake Up Britain!* video three times in quick succession. He was in the Incident Room with his laptop hooked up to a projector so that the rest of his team could watch. Bleary-eyed officers sat around a large table drinking enough coffee to wake someone from a coma.

'She's got to be the one leaking details to the press,' Ayala said. 'She could certainly use the money.'

'Unfortunately, our wonderful courts have seen fit to protect journalistic sources. I don't think mere curiosity counts as an overriding public interest, so *The Impartial* will never admit it and it doesn't prove anything other than she's got fewer scruples than the Prime Minister,' Morton said.

Ayala slouched in his seat. Shot down again.

Morton saw his disappointment, and decided that team morale was worth letting Ayala waste an hour or two. 'But see if her bank will release her statements. They'll probably say no, and we don't have enough for Kieran to force them to comply, but it won't hurt to ask.' Morton referred to his pet prosecutor, Kieran O'Connor.

Ayala regained his enthusiasm almost instantly. 'Will do! And what about this fight? He tells us it's about money, then tells the world he can't remember. What's up with that?'

'Not everything is a conspiracy. Perhaps he simply wanted to avoid tarring her memory. The dead cannot rebut accusations, so the living should refrain from making them. If he loved her, it doesn't matter whether or not she spent his money.'

'You're buying the money bullshit? We found ten large in the safe!'

'Which we have no reason to believe he had any knowledge of. Let's assume he was telling the truth, just for a moment. He leaves when Culloden and Gabby burst into the kitchen where he's drinking with Paddy Malone. At this point, our victim is upstairs fuming at her boyfriend. Again assuming no one else entered the house, what happens next?'

'In that case, two options. Either Gabby and Malone leave together, and Culloden kills Ellis, or Culloden leaves and Ellis is murdered by both Gabby and Malone,' Ayala ventured.

'We're assuming that they did stay together.'

'CCTV proves it. At 02:17, they approached Richmond Station. On the tape it looked like they saw the shutters down over the ticket office and turned around. They then flagged a taxi down right in front of the station.'

Morton stroked his chin thoughtfully. 'They actually approached the ticket office? When did it shut?'

Ayala fell silent, and avoided eye contact. The other junior officers around the table did likewise, as if they collectively found a sudden interest in studying their nails.

After about a minute, Stuart Purcell, who was hovering near an evidence board near the back of the room and helping himself to the detectives' coffee, spoke up: 'Half past nine.'

Morton glanced up. 'How'd you know that?'

Purcell held up his smartphone. 'Google.' He grinned.

'Well then,' Morton said. 'If Detective McGoogle is correct then they'd have had no reason to approach the ticket office at all. It had been closed for hours.'

'They could have been drunk. It certainly looks like she's leaning on him on the tape,' Ayala said.

'They could have been pretending to be drunk. The CCTV camera is right above the ticket office plain as day.'

'You think it was an attempt to set up their alibis?'

'It seems awfully convenient that they flagged down a taxi right in front of a camera.'

'Boss, you're being paranoid. There are cameras all over the place.'

'If there are cameras everywhere, then find me one which shows what happened to our papier-mâché peer, because if Paddy and Gabby are innocent then our prime suspect is a nobody who has disappeared into the wind without a trace.'

Mayberry stood and raised his hand.

'Yes, Detective Sergeant?'

'Did our v-victim re-join the, the, the, dancy-music?'

'The party?'

'Yes.'

Morton paused. None of their witnesses had actually seen Ellis return to the party.

'You think she was already dead before the end of the night, and that she was dumped in the pool later?'

'Y-yes sir.'

'That means any of the guests could have done it,' Ayala said.

'That seems unlikely. We had no sign of a struggle upstairs. Presumably someone checked on the birthday girl during the night. She had friends there, and she'd just argued with Kal. Do we really think he killed her, came down to play poker and then left without anyone noticing him doing clean-up in the room? I'm not buying it. One of our five is the killer. Unless someone here can prove otherwise?'

Purcell cleared his throat. Everyone turned expectantly, expecting another insight from Detective McGoogle. 'The thermostat–'

'Not the thermostat again. I'd rather you told me you had made it into her laptop.'

'Yes, the thermostat. And no, I haven't made it into the laptop. It's a smart thermostat. To save energy, it turns off radiators when people have left the house. There isn't much point heating empty rooms. This is a crude system. The more expensive ones control homes on a room-by-room or zone-by-zone basis. This one just turns the heating off when everyone leaves.'

'So we calculate the drop in temperature between the time the party ended and when we got there?' Ayala asked.

'Don't be daft, Detective. It would have hit ambient temperature fairly quickly, and we'd be basically guessing. We also know someone entered Edgecombe Lodge before we did.'

'Who?' Ayala demanded.

'Whoever called you lot in. Someone found the body and unlocked the house.'

Presumably the same person that called in the anonymous tip. 'So how does this thermostat help us, Stuart?' Morton asked.

'Simple. It logs when the systems turns itself on or off. On the hour, every hour, it checks with a set of heat sensors to see if anything in the house is within two degrees either side of thirty-seven Celsius.'

Ayala looked on blankly.

'People,' Purcell explained flatly. 'People have a body temp of around thirty-seven. If the sensors don't detect heat signatures belonging to people, the system assumes the house is empty and turns off all the radiators.'

'You said sensors plural. Does that mean we can track where in the house people were on each hour by where the heat signatures were?' Morton asked.

'Sadly, no. That data isn't recorded. It's a binary set-up. Either people are there or they're not. It isn't a surveillance system.'

'It should be!' Ayala said. 'It would double up nicely. So when did the system turn off the heating?'

'Two o'clock in the morning.'

'Which means the house was empty by two,' Morton said. 'The station isn't far from Edgecombe Lodge, so it's consistent with when they left.'

'Which doesn't help at all, boss. Either it confirms they left just before two and were the last people in the house and thus have to be the killers, or it confirms someone else came in between them leaving and two o'clock.'

'Or that someone else never left. What it does confirm is that by two o'clock in the morning, Ellis DeLange was dead.'

Chapter 14: Pied-à-Terre

Morton and Ayala's next port of call was the final suspect that they had an address for. Gabriella Curzon lived in the centre of Fitzrovia. Her one-bedroom apartment was three floors above a flower shop in a pretty old redbrick building.

'Nice building,' Ayala commented as the pair ascended towards Gabriella's front door. 'Shame about the noise though.'

A constant hum of traffic went by below which hadn't subsided by the time they reached the top floor. The door of Number One Eastcastle Place was open by the time they reached it. Morton knocked on the door anyway. They entered a small hallway with another open door at the end of it. Through the doorway, Morton could see a sofa upon which a woman was sitting. She beckoned them in with a slender finger. They followed the hallway into a huge living area lit with floor-to-ceiling windows through which bright sunlight beamed.

'Miss Curzon, I presume.'

Gabriella, like Ellis, sported dyed-blonde hair. But unlike Ellis, she bore no tattoos. Where Ellis looked every bit of her thirty years and then some, Gabriella appeared to be almost effortlessly youthful with high cheekbones and a warm complexion. She had a smartphone in her hand and was busy tapping away at the screen.

'Gentlemen,' she greeted them without rising from the sofa. 'Welcome to my home. Do have a seat. Would you care for tea? The pot on the table is camomile, but if you would like something else then I shall fetch it for you.'

Morton sat down, glad to have the harsh sunlight behind him rather than blinding him. He shifted until comfortable then produced his notebook and a pen. Ayala did likewise.

'No thank you, Miss Curzon. Tell me about your relationship with Ellis DeLange.'

Without so much as putting down her mobile, Gabriella answered without looking up: 'She was my best friend. We've known each other forever. I became a model when I was seventeen–'

'How old are you now?'

'A lady never tells. Just kidding, I'm twenty-four. As I was saying, I had a scholarship to a boarding school when I was sixteen. Back then, Eli was the 'it-girl' of the fashion world and I was lucky enough that she came to speak to our six-form about the challenges of fame. I was picked to be photographed as part of a demonstration she did. We were all amazed at how good a photograph from a digital camera could be, but Ellis was such a sweetie. The moment she saw how my picture came out, she positively squealed with delight. She passed it on to a magazine. They didn't want the photo, but they loved me. A few weeks later I dropped out of formal schooling, came down to London to crash on Eli's sofa and never looked back.'

'What sort of modelling did you do?'

'I modelled clothes mostly. I did a few artsy shoots including a few with Ellis but everything I ever did was tasteful. Some of the girls I knew back then ended up doing less-than-savoury work. It was very competitive, and none of us ever made very much.'

'And what do you do now?'

'I still model, mostly catalogue shoots.' She hit a few buttons on her phone and brought up an image of her dressed to the nines in a studio shoot. She flashed the phone at the detectives so they could see for themselves. 'But I'm also studying. I won't be pretty forever.'

'Did you ever work with Lord Culloden?'

She recoiled slightly at the mention of Lord Culloden. 'Oh yes. He's a manager for a catalogue company. Alex often hires both Eli and me. Well, he did anyway.'

'Alex? Is that his name?'

'Alex Culloden. That was what he told me to call him in private.'

Something about her familiarity made Morton suspicious. None of their other suspects seemed to be on first-name terms with the mystery man.

'How would shoots with him work?'

'Oh, he almost never comes to the shoots, silly. I only ever see him socially. But he'd usually have someone call, and fly me out to wherever the shoot was. I go wherever designers need me: Paris, Milan, Sao Paulo, Berlin, wherever.'

'New York?'

'Sometimes.'

'With Eli?'

She nodded. 'It wasn't always Eli. She's been doing more for him lately than she used to. It's funny how it goes. She used to be too busy for mere catalogue photos. Now I am.'

'What are you studying?'

'Law. At Birkbeck.'

'That's got to be convenient.' Ayala said. It wasn't untrue. Birkbeck's campus was less than ten minutes away.

For the first time in the conversation she turned her attention away from her mobile and became animated. 'Very! I never have to go too far for the library, I've got boutique shops and nightclubs within a hundred yards and–'

'Tell me about the night of the party,' Morton said in an attempt to wrangle the conversation back towards the investigation.

'I got there at, like, eight. Eli was a great host. She passed out glasses of champagne, and we made the most of the garden as it was unseasonably warm. A few of us went in the pool.'

'You took your swimming costume with you?'

Gabby gave Morton a sly smile. 'No...'

'Ah. When did Eli go upstairs?'

'About half past ten, I think. It can't have been much later. We had a few pizzas–'

'From *Trattoria Da Mondo*?'

'Yes! I love their Pizza Florentine.'

'Did Ellis go to get those?'

'Oh no. Paddy volunteered to walk around. It was supposed to be Brianna's turn to buy, but she's... she forgot her purse that night.'

Morton scribbled a note down in his pad: Brianna's financial problems appeared to be common knowledge among the group.

'Are you friends with Paddy?'

'Well, one can't be too careful about who one is seen with. Paddy is... a little rough around the edges. It isn't proper for one who aspires to the practice of law to keep such company in public.'

'But you did sleep with him,' Morton said bluntly.

Gabby flushed red. 'Mr Morton, I cannot see how that is relevant to your investigation.'

'Did you or did you not leave the party in Mr Malone's company?'

'I did.'

'Thank you. When Brianna left the party, where was Ellis?'

'Upstairs still, with Kal, I think.'

'Was anyone else upstairs?'

'No,' Gabby said. 'The party was all on the ground floor that night. There are a couple of bathrooms downstairs so no one had any reason to venture upstairs.'

'So you don't know why she didn't come back down?'

'I heard them screaming at each other. We thought it impolite to say anything. Kal came back down on his own.'

'Did you see Ellis at all after that?'

'I went up to check on her after the fight. Brianna did too. She told us she was fine, but wanted to be left alone for a bit. You don't think Kal killed Ellis, do you?'

Morton ignored the question. 'How well do you know Mr Fielder?'

'He's been with Eli for six or seven years now. He's nice enough. And you can't deny he's sexy. But he's as dumb as a post really. His posh accent can make him seem smart, but he's not. I think he must have taken one too many blows to the head back when he played football.'

Morton couldn't help but agree with her assessment. 'Tell me what happened immediately before you left.'

'I had a few drinks with Paddy while we played gin rummy. I won, of course. And then we left.'

'Before that. He said you came out of the guest bedroom crying.'

'I suppose I did. If I tell you why, you won't think too badly of me, will you, Detectives?' She fluttered her eyelashes at Ayala.

'What happened?'

'I had an argument.'

'With Alex Culloden,' Morton murmured as he realised why she was on first-name terms with him.

'How did you know? Have you spoken to him?' Her surprised tone suggested to Morton that she didn't think it was possible for the police to have spoken with Alex.

'He's not in London, is he?'

Gabriella was stunned. 'No.'

'Where is he?' Morton asked, though he thought he knew the answer.

'New York,' Gabriella confirmed.

'On the trip that Ellis was supposed to have gone on?'

'Yes.'

'You were sleeping with him, weren't you?' Morton asked.

She nodded. Morton felt bile rise in his throat. Two men in one night. 'But you left with Paddy Malone?'

A tear rolled down her cheek, and she nodded once more.

'Where did Culloden go?'

'I chased him. He, err, wasn't dressed when I did so. He grabbed a towel and fled out the back door.'

'What happened then?'

'I ran after him. Paddy stopped me at the back door. Kal left, and we had a few drinks until I'd calmed down. I guess I felt fond of him by then.'

'What sort of time was this?'

'Most people went before the last tube, so I know it was a bit after midnight. I don't know how much. Maybe half past twelve.'

'And how did you leave?'

'We staggered towards the centre, and had to flag down a taxi.'

'One final question, Miss Curzon. When does Alex get back from New York?'

'He said he'd be back tomorrow. He gets in at Heathrow a little after lunch.'

Chapter 15: Finders, Keepers

WEDNESDAY APRIL 9TH – 13:00

The mobile phone used to place the anonymous tip was turned back on at 13:00. The number was unregistered, which meant it had a pay-as-you-go SIM card inside. It wasn't requesting Internet or GPS data, which probably meant a 'dumb' phone.

Upon getting the news, Morton headed in search of Purcell, whom he found in the cafeteria at New Scotland Yard. He saw Morton approaching and tried to hide behind a placard advertising a new bicycle-marking initiative that Morton knew would be a complete waste of time.

Morton sat opposite the Chief Scene of Crime Officer.

'Afternoon!' Morton said cheerfully.

'Hullo. Can't you see I'm eating?' Purcell's tray had two empty pre-packed sandwich wrappers on it together with an uneaten Twix.

'Looks like you're almost finished. I got your message about the phone. Do you know where it is?'

Purcell took a bite out of his chocolate bar, chewed for a moment, then gave up. Morton wasn't going anywhere.

'No. It's not responded to my ping.'

That confirmed Morton's theory that it was a dumb phone, without GPS functionality.

'Can't we just triangulate its position?' Morton asked. Triangulation would mean using the location of nearby telephone masts to determine how quickly the phone responded. The lag would tell them how far away the phone was from each tower. It was then a simple matter of drawing a circle around each mast based on distance and seeing where the circles met.

'After lunch. It was turned back on somewhere in central London. There's no reason to suspect it'll leave the county in the time it takes me to finish eating.' Purcell finished the first half of his Twix.

'If you want it that way.' Morton picked up the other half of Purcell's Twix and quickly consumed it.

'Happy now?' he asked.

'Hey! You can't do that. I'll… I'll–'

'Tell the police?' Morton smirked. He knew he shouldn't bait the man, but Purcell certainly didn't need the calories and Morton did need to know where the phone was.

'Fine. I'll find your phone. But you owe me a chocolate bar!'

Morton considered his request. 'Half a chocolate bar.'

'Cheapskate. I'll call you when I've got a location for you.'

Chapter 16: #RichmondStreaker

The press beat Morton's team to finding CCTV of the naked man. *The Impartial's* website ran a grainy black and white photo as breaking news at about two o'clock in the afternoon. By half past, it had been viewed over a million times and #RichmondStreaker had begun to trend on Twitter.

Morton dispatched Mayberry to find the source of the image. It wouldn't be too difficult, so he was confident that he'd manage it. He simply needed to compare the CCTV from the newspaper with the road to see which bit of Richmond the CCTV was pointed at, then work backwards to find the camera itself. It was plainly a very wide road with space for parking either side, which reduced the search area to 'A' roads between Edgecombe Lodge and Richmond Park where passers-by reported seeing an early-morning streaker. It was then further narrowed down by the presence of shops, which probably meant central Richmond between the Station and Richmond Park. It wasn't a particularly interesting task, but it needed to be done.

That didn't mean Morton was off the hook. For him, the afternoon would become a special kind of torture. The task he had set for himself came second only to the monotony of paperwork and once again the vultures were circling. Journalists had beaten his team to key information, television presenters had aired the DeLange family's dirty laundry over breakfast, and key individuals had taken to trying to turn the whole sordid affair into an opportunity to make a quick profit.

It was time to go on the offensive. A press conference had been called for three o'clock, which approached far more quickly than Morton anticipated. He chose to forgo any kind of notes. He knew his memory, which had taken on a reputation of its own among the force for outstanding recall, would serve him well when the time came.

At five to three, he peeked through the window of the conference room to find it was packed to the rafters. As he had requested, BBC News had been given space front and centre to film. Every medium and venue had been accommodated. From major television to the daily papers, from vloggers to crime-awareness websites with only one amateur reporter, all had been invited.

At one minute to the hour, he entered the conference room from the rear door and approached the lectern which had been set up for him. The room's attention fixed upon him and fell deathly silent.

'Ladies and gentlemen. Before we begin, I'd like to ask for your co-operation. I know that many of you will have questions for me. I will answer as many of those as I can, time permitting. Before that I would ask that you allow me the chance to give you an overview. I would also appreciate it if you could identify yourselves and who you work for when you ask a question.'

Morton surveyed the room. Every pair of eyes stared back at him ready and waiting for their scoop. He saw Ayala standing at the back of the room, hiding behind the slew of journalists who had not come early enough to bag a seat. Ayala nodded encouragingly, as if to endorse Morton's kids-glove approach to handling the media.

'On the night of Saturday 29th March, Ellis DeLange turned thirty years of age. By the end of the night, we believe she had been murdered. The facts as I am able to report them at this time are as follows. Miss DeLange was celebrating with friends on the night of her death. By all accounts, she was alive until after midnight. She was due to fly out to New York the next morning on business but never made it to the airport.' Morton paused to watch the journalists' reactions. So far, he had not revealed anything that hadn't already been reported. He was hoping to find a look of smug satisfaction among the crowd, a hint that they had uncovered something else that he could use.

'We found no evidence of forced entry at the premises. At the time we discovered Ellis' body, the house was unlocked, as was the front gate. We cannot definitively rule out the involvement of an intruder, but as we have found no signs of third-party involvement our investigation has focussed on those who were in attendance at the party and stayed until after midnight.

'It would be improper for me to comment on any particular individual at this time as we have yet to discern the exact involvement of all parties. I am sure many of you will want to know how our investigation relates to the so-called 'Richmond Streaker'. While I can't show any stills or footage at this time, as it is evidence needed to allow our investigation to proceed, I can confirm that the Streaker is of interest to our investigation. We are investigating his identity to the best of our ability and we will release that information as soon as we have been able to ascertain the extent of the Richmond Streaker's involvement. If any members of the public who are watching this have any relevant information pertaining to the Streaker please call our tip line, which I trust will be displayed at the bottom of your television screen.'

Morton paused for a sip of water. The heat from the lighting rig that the film crew had rigged up was almost intolerable. 'I'd like to invite questions at this time.'

The room interrupted into an incomprehensible din as every journalist shouted out at once. Morton pointed to the nearest one, then waited for silence.

'Sally Morgan, Federated News Co. Who was at the party?'

'Miss DeLange had a number of attendees. So far we have identified a handful who stayed until after midnight including her boyfriend, her sister, a school friend and two work colleagues.'

She followed up with another question. 'Was one of those individuals convicted drug dealer Paddy Malone?'

Morton leaned forward into the microphone. 'Yes. Could we please keep it to one question per attendee for the rest of the session? We have a limited amount of time today.'

Hands leapt into the air as journalists jostled for position. Morton pointed to a lady in the front row, but an obese gentleman in an ill-fitting suit pushed his way forward and shouted: 'Were drugs and alcohol involved?'

Morton took an immediate dislike to the man. 'Who do you work for?'

'Bill Bryerson. *The Daily Roundup*.'

'Is there a reason you didn't hear my instruction to identify yourself before asking a question? Next.'

'Like Bill said. Were drugs and alcohol involved?' The man next to Bill echoed his question.

Morton gave up. If he pulled the same stunt again, it would look like he was evading the question. 'We can confirm that the victim had been drinking on the night she died and that alcohol was made available to her guests. We cannot say to what extent any individual partook of that drink.'

'And the drugs?'

'The victim's toxicology tests showed that the victim had pentobarbital in her system. Now, I missed the lady at the front before. I'm sorry about that. What was your question?' Morton asked. He spotted Ayala nodding approvingly again. Perhaps the media awareness and sensitivity training that Human Resources had foisted upon the team hadn't been such a waste of time after all.

'Emily Landhurst, *Richmond Neighbourhood Watch*. Why didn't you call a press conference sooner?'

'While it is unfortunate that speculation has run rife in the last few days, we need to be able to conduct initial investigations free from prejudice and outside influence. Our department is committed to unprecedented transparency in both process and outcome, but we have to be free to complete the investigation unhindered in order to discover the truth. Justice demands that we avoid contaminating the potential jury pool, so it is our duty to report only the facts. I think that is all I can give you today. Please feel free to contact our Press Office with any further queries. Thank you very much for coming, ladies and gentlemen.'

Chapter 17: Computer Down!

Stuart Purcell didn't really report to Morton but somehow the policeman always managed to get under Purcell's skin. Of course he could triangulate a mobile phone! Any one of his team could do it. The computer did everything... Or it would normally.

In theory it was so simple. High signal strength meant quicker responses when a phone was close to a tower. By comparing the lag between tower and phone, the distance could be calculated between a given mobile phone and the nearest masts.

London had no shortage of towers. They varied in height, which meant the calculation was a little more difficult, but nothing that would have made the computer sweat. But the computer wasn't working; he had to do it by hand.

The problem there was the phone kept on moving, pinging different towers every few minutes. It was clear as day that it was being driven around London. Every time Purcell worked out the phone's location, it had already moved. It was travelling too fast to be in a pedestrian's pocket. The phone was still pinging towers, which meant it wasn't underground, and the route didn't match any of London's overland train or bus services. Whoever had the phone was driving around with it.

CCTV was no good either. Trying to find the phone by whatever vehicle it was travelling in meant trawling a dozen local authority CCTV cameras with spotty coverage. The temptation to simply call the phone and see who answered grew stronger with every passing hour.

When the signal finally came to a stop, Purcell felt himself give a great sigh of relief. It had landed, at just gone six thirty, in a residential street in Upper Norwood.

Purcell victoriously snatched up his mobile and dialled Morton's mobile. He answered after two rings.

'What?' Morton demanded grumpily. 'I'm about to have dinner. This better be important.'

'I've got your mobile.'

'Nope. Fairly sure I'm talking to you on it.'

'Very funny. Your anonymous tipster's phone is active at an address in Upper Norwood. Want me to text it to you?'

Morton's didn't immediately reply. Though Purcell was miles away, he imagined Morton staring longingly at a whiskey decanter he had just set on the coffee table in anticipation of a drink after a hard day. For just a moment, he hoped Morton was about to say, 'No, come pick me up.'

Instead Morton answered in the affirmative. 'Don't forget the postcode,' Morton chastised before ringing off.

So near, but so far. For Stuart Purcell, it was time to call it a night and head home.

By day Upper Norwood might have been quite attractive, but by the time Morton arrived the sun had set and torrents of rain poured from the sky, giving the neighbourhood a gloomy appearance. Two nineteen-eighties council blocks loomed large in the sky to the east.

Purcell had supplied grid co-ordinates rather than a full postal address. When Morton arrived, he found that the location housed a semi-detached three-story Victorian-style house with a balcony over the main doorway.

He parked up, squeezing in behind a white van marked '*DMC Electricals*'. He strode briskly towards the door to avoid getting too wet and was presented with two doorbells: one for the upstairs flat and one for the downstairs flat.

He took a gamble and hit the button for the ground floor flat first. A young man answered. He couldn't have been more than nineteen or twenty and seemed perplexed to find Morton on his doorstep.

'What you want?' He demanded. It wasn't an English accent, but Morton couldn't place it.

'I'm Detective Chief Inspector Morton. I'm looking for the person who has a mobile phone with the number 07500654091.'

'It mine.'

'Did you place a call to the emergency services last Sunday?' Morton knew the answer. It wasn't the same voice as the recording on DS Mayberry's call.

'No,' the man said. 'I just get phone.'

'Where did you get it?'

'It gift.'

'You got a decade-old mobile phone as a gift?'

'I told to bin phone. I kept it.'

'Why?'

'Had credit. Also, I like Snake.'

'The game? But…' Morton felt himself trip over his tongue.

'I go now?' He turned as if to retreat back inside the house.

'I need to know where you got the phone.'

'My boss. He give me. Say to bin it.'

'Why would he ask you to bin a mobile phone?'

'I say enough. Can I go?' The man was shifting his weight from left to right foot and back again restlessly.

Aha! He thinks it's nicked, Morton thought. 'I'm afraid you and the phone need to come down to the station.'

'That what I was afraid of. I get shoes.' He turned again and went to close the door, and Morton had to quickly jam a foot just inside the door. The man seemed surprised but shrugged and went off to pull on a pair of filthy old trainers.

The man with the phone was Sergei Krasnodar. It turned out that the white van Morton had parked next to belonged to him. Sergei was weeks away from finishing his electrician's apprenticeship, which was due to finish on his nineteenth birthday. Morton watched him through a one-way mirror. He was slowly chewing his fingernails and glancing around nervously.

Thank God he's eighteen, Morton thought. He'd had enough of dealing with minors on his last case. Morton was about to go into the interrogation suite when a voice called out down the hall.

'DCI Morton! W-wait up!' DS Mayberry came jogging down the hallway.

'Mayberry, you're here late.'

'So are you. I p-passed Purcell as I was leaving. He told me you'd gone to find the guy so I thought I'd wait. C-can I sit in on the interview?' He looked up at Morton hopefully with big puppy-dog eyes.

'Fine,' Morton said. Then an idea popped into his head and he added: 'But do one thing for me first.'

'Anything.'

'Take this.' Morton handed him Sergei's mobile phone, which was wrapped up in an evidence bag. 'Get them to run the IMEI, prove that it is stolen.'

Mayberry took the phone, and trotted off down the hallway to carry out Morton's bidding.

That ought to keep him busy for half an hour. Morton headed into the interview suite.

'Sergei. Tell me about your job.'

'I fix electrics. Most days I fix lights.'

'Do you like doing that?' Morton tried to build a little rapport with his suspect.

'Yes. It tiring. Long hours. But I like know do good job.' Sergei smiled and nodded enthusiastically.

'It can't pay well though.'

'True.'

Morton met his gaze. 'So how do you afford to live alone in London?' Sergei broke eye contact. 'I live Norwood. It's not expensive.'

'How much do you make?'

'Fifteen thousands.'

Not enough to easily afford a one-bed apartment, even with housing benefit.

'Do you do any other work?'

'No.'

'You don't, hmm, get rid of mobile phones in return for money?'

'That one-time thing.'

'It was stolen, wasn't it?' Morton put it to him.

'I didn't steal phone.'

'I didn't say you did. My colleague has gone to find out if that phone has been reported stolen. What's he going to find out?'

Sergei shrugged.

'Let's wait and find out, shall we?'

'I need lawyer?'

'You tell me. If you want one, I'll get you one. But if you're dealing with stolen goods, I'm not interested in that. I need to know if your boss might have stolen it.'

Sergei hesitated and then said: 'It's possible.'

'Were you working last Sunday?'

'No. Just weekdays.'

'When did he give you the phone?'

'Monday. After work.'

'And you've used it since?'

'No. I had to buy charger.'

That explains why the phone has been off for most of the week, Morton thought. Morton strained to think of anything else he needed to ask Sergei. DI Mayberry's return saved him from having to come up with anything. Mayberry slid an IMEI report across the desk as he sat down.

Damn. Not stolen. Looks like the kid gets to skate on handling stolen goods.

'Sergei. We're going to have to talk to your boss about this. Could you write down his address for me?' Morton handed him a pen and paper.

'Thank you. Once you're done with that, you can go. You can't tell your boss that we talked to you though, otherwise we can charge you with perverting the course of justice. Do you understand?'

'Yes. No tell boss. I keep phone?'

'I'm afraid we need to keep hold of it for the moment. You'll get it back when we're done with our investigation.'

Sergei finished writing the boss's address down in loopy handwriting. *DMC Electricals* was owned by Mr. David McArthur of Oak Cottage, The Close, Potter's Bar, North London.

Chapter 18: Late To Bed, Early to Rise

Despite Morton's late night tracking down the mobile phone he still made it into the office by eight o'clock the next morning. The first task of the morning proved to be a fairly simple one. Chiswick had readied the body of Ellis DeLange to be released to her family. Her body bore few visible signs of the damage inflicted during the post-mortem examination. Morton pinged off a quick email to Ayala to let him know to call Brianna.

The case had made the morning news again. *The Impartial* had run with the headline *Underwear Salesman Caught Short!*

The Impartial had reprinted the CCTV picture again but this time they had added a paragraph underneath.

'Aleksander Barchester, CEO of popular women's clothing company Wiles is thought to be the Richmond Streaker. Barchester had been attending the birthday party of murdered fashionista Ellis DeLange the night before his sojourn through Richmond in the buff. Is this a sign that the once-revered businessman saw something terrible that night and snapped? Turn to page 14 for the full story.'

'Damnit!' The journalists had beaten them to identifying the Richmond Streaker. It seemed they knew far more than the police. Though they had yet to connect Barchester with Brianna's claim that he had been illicitly using the name Lord Culloden.

'Barchester is currently en route back from New York after an extensive photo shoot for the new Simply collection that will appear later this year in

the Summer Wiles catalogue. For that reason we were unable to reach Mr Barchester for comment.'

Morton had been assuming Brianna was leaking information to the press, but as far as Morton knew, Brianna was clueless as to the whereabouts of Aleksander Barchester. She didn't even know his name. Morton had learned about the trip from Gabriella Curzon. It looked like he had two witnesses selling information to the press.

On the upside, the fact that the press hadn't reached Barchester meant that Barchester remained blissfully unaware of the publicity surrounding him. He wouldn't be in at Heathrow for a couple of hours yet so Morton still had time to ambush him at the airport.

Chapter 19: Homeward Bound

The trip from LaGuardia had been exemplary. Aleksander Barchester kicked back in a reclining chair in the first class cabin. His in-flight table was stacked with copies of every major paper, which he had perused while supping Dom Perignon. Unfortunately for Alex, he missed the mention of the Richmond Streaker tucked away on the middle pages of the morning edition of *The Impartial*. He even missed the knowing giggle of the lady seated three rows back, mistaking her curious gaze for attraction.

Alex enjoyed flying, but it had to be first class. First class meant no tussles over legroom with the row in front bashing his knees. It meant free drinks all the way through the flight, and it meant no screaming children. Alex couldn't even complain about the Foie Gras which, while tasty, hardly lived up to the experience of the same at a decent restaurant. There was something about flying which made food bland. Alex supposed it was the pressurised cabin or something.

After seven and a half hours the seatbelt sign pinged on and a voice crackled over the plane's intercom system. 'Ladies and gentlemen, we're experiencing mild turbulence this morning. We expect to land in the next fifteen minutes, so please place your seats in the upright position with the tray folded up and ensure that your seatbelts are fastened.'

Alex picked up his glass of champagne, his fifth of the flight, and downed the last few drops before handing it to an air hostess who seemed to spring out of nowhere to take the empty glass. Alex watched her walk away, admiring her ample buttocks as they swayed. Then she stumbled slightly. The turbulence was picking up. Alex gripped his armrest with a ferocity unbecoming such a frequent flier. This was the part he hated. As the plane descended it swung to the right in alignment with Heathrow Runway Two. The pressure built up slowly as they descended. With his free hand, Alex tore open a pack of sherbet lemons and popped three in his mouth at once. They didn't help.

By the time the plane landed, Alex could feel his ears had gone funny. When the cabin door opened to the waiting umbilical corridor of the airport, they popped gently and Alex finally let go of his armrest.

The pilot's voice crackled over the sound system again. 'Welcome to Heathrow. It's sixteen degrees and balmy outside, so put away your brollies, ladies and gents, you won't need them today. The local time is ten fifteen. Thank you for flying with *Imperial Airlines*. We wish you a safe onward journey.'

The seatbelt indicator light switched off, and Alex released his seatbelt, then stood to stretch his legs. It felt good to finally be on the ground. He was about to join in the dash for the exit in the hopes of getting to the front of the customs line when the air hostess picked up his hand luggage for him.

She smiled but it was forced. Her eyes revealed a look of concern. 'Allow me, sir. We have a complimentary escort waiting for you in the terminal.'

They were met at the door by a gentleman in a suit. If Alex hadn't been on the champers, he might have noticed that the man wasn't wearing the corporate blue of *Imperial Airlines*. He blindly followed the man off the plane and into Heathrow. He didn't even notice when they sidestepped the immediate queue of passport control in favour of a small door to one side, which the man opened with a swipe of a key card from his jacket pocket.

The hallway behind the locked door led to another door, which again opened at the touch of the man's key card.

'Can I get me one of those?' Alex joked. It was only when he saw the stark grey metal walls of the interview room that Alex realised he wasn't being given preferential treatment.

A middle-aged policeman sat on one side of a desk in the centre of the room. He had a microphone in front of him, and a pen in hand. Alex sat down.

'What's going on?' he demanded.

⚖

'I'm Detective Morton. And you are?' Morton omitted his full title deliberately to avoid giving away the reason behind being at Heathrow.

'Aleksander Barchester. That's Alex with a 'KS', not an 'X'.'

'Unusual spelling.'

'My mother was Russian.'

'Ah. Now the other formality – I need to confirm your address for me please.'

'It's The Culloden Estate, Shirley Hills, Croydon.'

Morton pretended to mishear him. 'Culloden Manor, Shirley Hills, Croydon.'

Barchester didn't correct him.

'Doesn't that land come with a manorial title? My apologies for addressing you as Mr Barchester before.'

Culloden smiled, puffed up his chest and held up a hand as if to wave away Morton's apology.

'Is it Lord Culloden then? Or Lord Barchester of Culloden?'

'Either is fine.'

'Really? That's strange. My sources tell me the actual Lord of the Manor of Culloden is in his eighties. I wouldn't have guessed you were much past fifty.'

'I'm forty-seven!' Culloden retorted. A split second later he realised his mistake and added, 'And that's my father you're talking about.'

'If I call him, will he verify that?' Morton reached into his pocket for his phone.

'Wait!'

'You're not Lord Culloden.'

'No...'

'And you don't live at Culloden Manor. Give me one good reason I shouldn't have you prosecuted for attempting to enter the country under false pretences?'

'I do live on the Culloden Estate. I live in the servant's cottage on the eastern perimeter, OK? And I never lied about my name. I just didn't say anything when you got it wrong.'

Morton smiled pleasantly. 'Passport please.'

Barchester fished in a pocket for a moment then handed it over. Sure enough it read 'Aleksander Barchester, Lord of Culloden' in the name field.

'See?' Barchester asked.

Morton continued to look through the passport. He flipped to the observations page where 'THE REFERENCE TO LORD IS TO THE HOLDER'S NAME AND NOT THE HOLDER'S TITLE' was printed in bold.

He turned it around so Barchester could see. 'If you really held the title it would say that the holder is also known as the Lord of the Manor of Culloden. Why are you impersonating the Lord of the Manor?'

'I'm going to decline to answer. I'm a British citizen. Either charge me with something or let me go.' He stood, as if to make his point.

'There's one door out of here, and it's locked. Stop posturing and sit back down before I do something you'll regret.'

He sat.

'Tell me about Ellis DeLange.'

'That useless bitch? Is that what this is about? What does she say I've done now? I waited a full three days before I hired a replacement. If she'd only answered her bloody phone!'

'Whoa, whoa, whoa. Hold up for second there. Let's go back a minute. You hired her. What for?'

Barchester looked at Morton as if the detective were an idiot. 'To take photos.'

'For your catalogue business?'

'That's right. We're shooting pictures for the Summer Wiles Catalogue, which comes out in July. It's got to go to print by the end of the month. I'm sorry if Ellis has been telling tall tales here, but I had to hire a replacement when she didn't show up.'

'In New York?'

'Yes, in New York! Are we or are we not sat in an airport?'

'She's was murdered the night before you fled the jurisdiction,' Morton said. 'Did you kill her?'

'No! Wait. I need a lawyer.'

'You only need a lawyer if you killed her. But as you wish.' Morton reached for the tape recorder. 'Interview terminated at–'

'Stop… I'll talk to you. Alone. On one condition.'

'The police don't usually make concessions to criminals.'

'I'm not a criminal. I need you to promise me, man to man, that you won't tell the Board of Directors about me using the title.'

Morton gave Barchester a thin-lipped smile. There was no downside to agreeing. Brianna had already told the world on *Wake up Britain!*

'Deal.'

'What do you want to know?'

'What happened on the night of the party?'

'I got there late. I'd been out of town all week working so I slept through much of Saturday. I drove the Merc down at about ten thirty. I never saw Ellis that night. When I got there, everyone was talking about the argument.'

He's awfully quick to point the finger at Kal. 'Who did she argue with?'

'Her boyfriend. That awful bore Kallum Fielder. He's got two topics of conversation – football and women. I don't know what they were arguing about. It was probably the usual.'

'The usual?'

'Money. Kal gambles. He earns well. Perhaps not as well as Ellis, but that's only because I'm a sucker for a pretty face. She says he spends every penny, won't stop asking me for a raise every time.'

It sounds like he's been played... Unless he's hiding her drug addiction. 'Did you ever witness the gambling?'

'Never had reason to, my good man. We weren't friendly. I tolerated him for Ellis.'

'Who came to the party?'

'The usual crowd. Gabby was there, of course. She and Ellis are inseparable. Vladivoben. Patrick Malone.'

'Vladivoben?' *He didn't mention that when we interviewed him.*

'Eli's next-door neighbour.'

'Why was he there?'

'Same reason as everyone. He seemed to be having a wonderful time. Why, I even saw him leave with a very handsome young man.'

'No noise complaints then?'

'Not to my knowledge. We were pretty loud, but it's a big house and *The Old Coach House* is quite a way away.'

'OK. Tell me about the end of the party.'

'I went to sleep about midnight in the guest room, and then drove home the next morning about six. I never saw or heard anyone else, but I thought people might be sleeping.' His eye twitched as he spoke.

'Uh-huh. That's not what our other witnesses have told us. Patrick Malone says you left some time after midnight.'

'Does he now? Well, that little berk is a lying toe rag. And he owes me money. I paid for pizza when I arrived. He took two hundred quid. I never did get any change.'

'Miss Curzon and Mr Fielder confirmed what he said.'

Barchester's face drained of what little colour it had left. 'You spoke to them too, did you?'

Morton nodded. 'We did. Tell us about the fight you had with Miss

Curzon. What was it about?'

'It's not about anything illegal. It's not relevant.'

'I'll be the judge of that, Mr Barchester. If it isn't illegal and doesn't impact on this investigation then it won't leave this room, I promise.'

'She's pregnant. She said it's mine.'

A gorgeous twenty-five-year-old sleeping with this washed up forty-seven-year-old man? Beer googles and money can perform miracles. 'But you don't believe her.'

'Would you believe an addict? She wanted money. I know I'm not the only one she's been sleeping with. I asked for a prenatal DNA test to prove it. She went ballistic.'

'Because you didn't believe her or because you demanded an invasive test with a chance of miscarriage?' Morton asked, his voice full of scorn.

'Oh, come on. Junkies don't worry about their unborn babies. She was drinking all evening. Good mothers don't do that. She just wanted my money.'

'Who else is she sleeping with?'

'How would I know? I just know she is. She's gorgeous and she's a student. I'm not soft in the head.'

'So what happened next?'

'She physically attacked me. I ran from the room and then left. I went home.' His left eye twitched again.

'If you're going to keep trying to conceal the truth, I'm going to have to break my word and call your board of directors. Tell me what really happened.'

'That's it, I swear it.'

'So you didn't run out the back door then.'

'Fine. I did. I came back.'

'Forgot something, did you?'

'My… My wallet. I left it in the bedroom.'

'Together with all your clothes?' Morton said.

'Yes, if you must know. That's how crazy she was. I couldn't even get dressed.'

'So you thought you'd spend the night in Richmond Park.'

'No! I told you. I stayed in the guest room.'

'No one was in the house. Edgecombe Lodge has a smart thermostat. It turned itself off at two o'clock. Besides, you were caught short on camera all the way to the Park and back. Did you come back for your clothes or did you come back to cover up a murder?'

'I think I'll have that lawyer now.'

'Fine with me. But first, I'll let immigration process you. Thank you for admitting you've been in contact with drugs. I'm sure immigration will need to, ahem, check you over for any you might be carrying.'

Chapter 20: Peek-A-Boo

Mayberry squinted through the darkness. It was a quarter to six o'clock, and thanks to the combination of darkness and poor weather, visibility was minimal. No shops were open, not even the mini-supermarket by the station; it wouldn't open for another hour.

Traffic was light. Morning bus services had begun and a few weary commuters seemed to be heading towards central London for the day. Jogging naked down the high street from Richmond Park would have attracted a fair bit of attention despite the early hour.

The still image of the Richmond Streaker published in all the papers had been taken from a low-resolution CCTV camera feed. Mayberry held a copy of *The Impartial* in one hand and lifted it to compare with his view of the road. *There! That looks like the picture.*

There was a phone box with a basket full of flowers hanging nearby illuminated by the lights from an estate agent's window. The same phone box was in the corner of the CCTV image, but the rest of the scene didn't match up. Mayberry moved closer.

Then it hit him. The CCTV footage was from the other side of the phone box. Mayberry jogged along the pavement until he was twenty feet the other side of the phone box, then held up the newspaper again.

Yes! The scene from the newspaper was laid out in front of him. He looked around, searching for the CCTV camera, and there it was sandwiched between the awning over a greengrocer's and the drainage pipe a few inches above. A thick cable ran down towards the awning then disappeared through the wall into the grocer's. He'd found it.

Mayberry earnestly jogged towards the grocer's. A black and white 'Closed' sign hung just inside. The shop's opening times were listed underneath. It wouldn't be open for two more hours. Defeated, Mayberry slumped against the door, then slid down until he was sitting on the step into the shop. He would just have to wait.

After a few minutes, Mayberry felt himself wanting to sleep. The lack of caffeine was getting to him. He was beginning to drift off when a gruff voice demanded to know what he was doing outside the grocer's.

'Oi! What are you doin' on my bleeding step? We're not open so sod off.'

'Umm, err, I'm Detective Sergeant Mayberry. I'm here about the Richmond Streaky Bacon. No! Streaker.'

The grocer looked at Mayberry like he had something wrong with him. 'I already gave you lot a copy of the tape. Did you lose it or sum-mat?'

'Us lot? You spoke to a p-p-please man?'

The grocer went inside to grab a tray full of vegetables, and started to unload them onto the display in front of the grocer's. 'Policewoman. Little lassie. She came in a few days, all sweetness and smiles. I thought she was a hooker to be honest. Then she said she was plain clothes. I felt like a right pillock.'

'What did she say her name was?'

'Officer Byrnes.'

Mayberry cursed. Gifford Byrnes was a reporter for *The Impartial*. No wonder they beat the canvass team. 'Did you see any sort of photo badge?' he asked.

'No. I didn't think to ask. Lass said she was plain clothes. Do plain clothes carry badges? I've never had one come in before. There were coppers up and down the road. I assumed she was with them.'

'Do you still have the original v-v-video tape?'

'Nope. That's long gone. We cycle them every forty-eight hours.'

Mayberry cursed. 'S-sorry. That sort of slipped out. I really need some sort of v-video tape. My new boss has been on my back about that tape.'

'If it helps, I saw the willy-whacker go by.'

Mayberry burst out laughing. 'The what?'

'It's what me mam used to call 'em, streakers. He jogged on by, plain as day. Funny sod had his hands over the front as he walked towards me, then the back as he walked away. He even said good morning!'

'Did you get a good look at the suspicion, sorry, suspect?'

'Unfortunately. That sight will be burned into my eyeballs 'til the day I die.'

'Did you tell Miss Byrnes about that?'

'Nope. I don't need to be going down to the station to identity a streaker. I've got better things to do.'

'We wouldn't need you to come in. We can do a v-v-v–'

'Video?'

'Yes, v-video identification parade right here. It's incredibly simple. We play you a v-video with nine people in it; the guy we think it is and eight m-more. You tell us which one you saw. It'll take three minutes, max.'

'My name's not Max,' the grocer joked. 'But if it's three minutes then no problem.'

'The video will be about three minutes. You'll have to watch it twice. We'll also have to invite the defendant's lawyer to attend plus one of my colleagues from the identification unit.'

'I'm here working 'til five. If you can do it on my bosses' time then I'll do it, but you get to explain why I wasn't working if any customers complain.'

'Great. I'll go get that set up and I'll be back here before bananas.'

Chapter 21: Hook-A-Duck

Morton was impressed. Mayberry's video identification parade had confirmed that the Richmond Streaker was Aleksander Barchester, which gave Morton the ammunition he needed to bring him in.

Barchester's Friday afternoon meeting was interrupted by uniforms coming to arrest him on the charge of indecent exposure. It was unlikely he'd ever get time for mere nudity. He'd probably get away with community service or even just a fine. As if a few grand would make much difference to a man of Barchester's wealth. But while Barchester wasn't likely to be bothered by money, he did care about his reputation.

Morton made sure Barchester was brought in the front of New Scotland Yard, right past the journalists camped outside. If the case had to be in the news, it was best for Morton's team to be seen to be doing something. Once inside the building, Barchester had been hastily escorted to a holding cell while awaiting his lawyer.

His lawyer was well known to Morton. Elliot Morgan-Bryant of Cutler & Kass had crossed Morton's path on more than one occasion. He was expensive, sharply attired and as dirty as they came. On Morton's last dealing with him, Morgan-Bryant had been representing a man connected with the notorious Bakowski crime syndicate, whose boss was still at large.

'Ready to begin?' Morton asked once the lawyer and his client had been offered time to confer. They nodded and Morton started recording the interview.

'You seem to be becoming the man of many names,' Morton quipped once the formalities of time and parties in attendance had been committed to tape. 'Aleksander Barchester, Lord Culloden and, perhaps most famously of all, The Richmond Streaker. Which one shall we use for today's interview?'

'Let's start with my client's name, shall we?' Elliot said.

'If you insist. Mr Barchester, witnesses have testified that you were running through Richmond naked on the morning of Sunday 30th March. Were you?'

Morgan-Bryant raised a hand. 'Don't answer that.'

'If he doesn't answer, we can infer guilt from his silence. We have CCTV footage and an eyewitness. If your client wants to minimise his sentence, now would be the time to start doing something about that.'

'I was naked,' Barchester said, much to the chagrin of his lawyer, who fixed him with a stare. 'But I wasn't streaking. I didn't intend to cause any offence. I just… lost my clothes,' he finished lamely.

'Lost your clothes?' Morton repeated disbelievingly. 'How did that happen?'

'I had a few too many to drink that night.'

'Such that you misplaced your clothes? And where perchance did you lose them?'

'Edgecombe Lodge, as you well know. I told you before, I was sleeping with Gabriella Curzon.'

'In the downstairs guest bedroom?'

'Yes.'

'So it'll be your DNA on the sheets. Would you care to volunteer a DNA sample?'

The lawyer interjected: 'I don't think he will.'

'OK. I'll put it another way. We know your semen is on the sheets. Will we find that DNA anywhere else in the house?'

Aleksander grimaced. Morton had him and he knew it.

'On a towel perhaps? But then you wouldn't be too worried about that. We know you fled out the back door. So where else will we find your DNA?' Morton smiled. 'Sleeping with Ellis?'

'Fine. Yes, I was sleeping with Ellis.'

'Blimey. You are doing well for a man of your, ahem, *size*.'

Aleksander blushed. 'You can't say that! You're a policeman!'

'You noticed!' Morton mocked. 'I certainly can say that. I don't *need* to but I can. On record in court if it'll help.'

'Enough!' Morgan-Bryant snapped. 'Just what do you want out of my client, Morton?'

'I want the truth,' Morton said. 'I want him to tell me exactly what happened on the night Ellis died. I also expect your client to plead guilty and pay whatever fine he gets for the nudity.'

'And in return?'

'In return I'll make sure that *as little as possible* detail is contained in the court record. I see no need to bring this up with your Board of Directors. Anything civil is no concern of mine. Is that fair?'

The lawyer turned to his client, who nodded. 'I'll take the deal.'

'What really happened that night?'

'I slept with Gabby,' Barchester said. 'She did tell me she was pregnant. But she also said she was going to get rid of it. I offered her money not to. I don't know if it's mine or not. She inferred that it is. She turned me down, said that I was pathetic and that she'd be ashamed if any child of hers bore even a passing resemblance to me. I slapped her. Open-handed. I shouldn't have, but she kept pushing my buttons. She mocked me. Then she bit me.' Aleksander rolled up his sleeve and held out his arm for inspection.

Morton looked at it. He could see a very faint impression of a bite mark. 'Go on.'

Barchester withdrew his arm, and rolled his sleeve back down. 'We fought. I wasn't wearing anything. She had on a t-shirt and trousers. Before I knew it, she'd gone out of the room screaming. I thought it was a shakedown. I went after her to try and stop her, with just a towel around me. She just wanted Kal and Paddy to see her as the victim. Of course, they did. What man wouldn't try to protect a beautiful damsel in distress? They threatened me. I fled out the back door. It was dark and I tripped. My towel caught on a rosebush and down I went. I knocked the bins over as I did so. Instinct took over and I ran.'

'And?'

'And I didn't stop running. I went to the park because I knew it was open. I thought I was going to freeze to death. The next morning I went back.'

'How did you get in?' Morton said.

'I climbed the back fence and went through the kitchen door. The same way I left. It was still unlocked. It was still early, about six. I nabbed my clothes, got dressed and let myself out the front gate.'

'Did you lock it?'

'Didn't need to. It clicked shut behind me. As did the front door.'

'And then what did you do?'

'I went back to my car. I got in, and drove to my office. I had enough time for a quick scrub in the bathroom, and then grabbed my suitcase from under my desk. I got my flight and headed to New York for the shoot. I was supposed to meet Ellis there, as you know.'

'What did you do when she didn't turn up?'

'I called. No answer on the landline and her mobile was off. I figured she blew me off because of Gabby. They're best friends, so I was never going to win that one. Then you had me stopped coming back.' Aleksander glared at Morton.

'You're welcome. I think that covers what we need. I will ensure our deal is honoured, but I can't guarantee our prosecutor won't be adding fraud charges for pretending to be Lord Culloden.' Morton rose as if to leave.

'Wait!' Barchester gestured for him to sit back down. 'I wasn't being dishonest. My mother worked as a servant on the Culloden estate in the late sixties. She had an affair with the Lord of the Manor. Lord Culloden is my father. It's why I use his name. It's also why I moved into the Servant's Cottage. I never had much of a family growing up... I suppose that's also why I snapped at Gabby that night. Children aren't pawns to be traded.'

'Interesting. But it's not a defence to fraud. I'll leave you to talk to your solicitor about that one.' Morton stood, and headed for the door.

'Wait!'

Morton turned. 'What now?'

'Thank you.'

'For what?'

'For not ruining my life.'

Chapter 22: Money, Money, Money

Morton managed to make time for a wonderful Friday night out with Sarah on the town, but his Saturday was more than boring enough to make up for it. Armed with only a headache, he was in work by eight o'clock. The building was quieter than on weekdays, yet still it hummed with a quiet efficiency. Crime didn't sleep and neither did Scotland Yard.

Unfortunately, the same wasn't true of those in the banking system. It was a minor miracle that Morton got a response over the weekend at all. Warrants had been obtained and served on some of the city's biggest banks in order to obtain the financial details of Morton's five primary suspects: Brianna Jackson (née DeLange), Aleksander Barchester, Gabriella Curzon, Kallum Fielder and Patrick 'Paddy' Malone.

Those details didn't arrive until shortly after nine, by which time Morton had been joined by DI Bertram Ayala, who came in toting a bag full of bagels and two large cups of fancy coffee from the bakery down the street.

'Look at this. They're all bloody broke. Patrick Malone doesn't have two pennies to rub together on paper. The only cash he's got going in comes from the taxpayer.' Morton pushed a stack of printouts towards Ayala.

After an interval Morton said, 'Hello. What do we have here? Our friend Mr Barchester might not be a Lord, but he is worth a few quid. Nearly half a million in cash on deposit with a private bank,'

Morton said.'

'Isn't that the minimum deposit for Coutts?' Ayala asked.

'No idea. Look at Barchester's last three bank statements. It looks like he's been transferring £1,500 a month to Miss Curzon. Every month on the third. I wonder what that's for.'

'Charity? She is a student and we know they've been sleeping together. Or money for sex. Sounds like prostitution.'

'Sounds like being married… Though perhaps without the sex,' Morton said with a chuckle.

'Gabriella isn't the only one getting handouts. Look at Brianna's bank statement. Two grand a month coming in from our victim.'

'In one lump sum?'

'No. Dribs and drabs throughout the month, but always adding up to about two thousand. Is that relevant, chief?' Ayala asked.

'It's certainly curious. That would be a good reason not to kill her.'

'Unless she's been getting greedy.'

Ayala flipped through Brianna's bank statements. 'The amounts haven't changed, boss. Two grand a month give or take a couple of quid going back for years. Why now?'

'Good question. And what of our victim? She's giving away two grand a month, but barely keeps the same again for herself. I know I'd do anything for family, but that seems rather extravagant. Ellis had to have much higher outgoings than her sister. There's a big difference between paying rent on a place in Southwark and maintaining a huge house in Richmond.'

'But she was making it. She's just about stayed in the black.'

'What's the estate worth? Check with the Land Registry and see if there's an outstanding mortgage on the house.'

'I already did, boss. The house has a charge registered in favour of Aleksander Barchester Holdings Limited.'

'Her boss lent her money? That's insane. Why not just go to a bank?'

'Yes, but it's recent. She had the whole thing paid off ten years ago then remortgaged Edgecombe Lodge a few months ago. Perhaps that's when the money from her days as a big shot ran out.'

'If I suddenly ran out of money, I'd come clean and stop giving away what I had left,' Morton said.

'Would you though? Wouldn't pride come into it? If you've been seen as the family provider for years, and suddenly you can't contribute, are you sure you'd never be tempted to fake it? Ellis might have assumed she'd be back in the big leagues sooner rather than later so it didn't matter if she gave away the money. By the time she realised that wasn't going to happen, it was too late. She'd committed, and to pull out months or years after the fall from grace could have been too much to bear. She gave away the money not out of sisterly love, but to save face.'

'That's certainly possible. In which case, where did the £10,000 in the safe come from? There's more to the money than meets the eye.'

'What's our next move, boss?'

'We find the man that called in the anonymous tip. It's time to pay a visit to Mr David McArthur of *DMC Electricals*.'

Chapter 23: The Thief

Potter's Bar was a commuter haven. Located just off the M25, and with a local train and tube station nearby, living in Potter's Bar was a nice compromise between the City and the country. It was technically in Hertfordshire, which meant Morton was on borrowed turf. He'd pinged off an email to a colleague with Hertfordshire Constabulary as a courtesy before he and Ayala left, which was acknowledged while they were on the A1 headed towards the home of David McArthur, owner of *DMC Electricals* and the boss of Sergei Krasnodar.

McArthur lived in a detached property with a generous garage which doubled up as his home office. *DMC Electricals* had been incorporated and the shares in the company were split between McArthur and his wife, presumably to maximise their combined tax allowances.

The company had showed a healthy gross profit of two hundred thousand in the last year accounts had been filed. The net was less than a third of that, which immediately put Morton on edge. Few electricians owned such well-proportioned homes. Oak Cottage, as McArthur had named it, in 2007 had cost him a cool £950,000. It was possible that McArthur had inherited money, but Morton thought it more likely that McArthur was doing work off the books. It wasn't illegal to take cash payments for work, but it was illegal to fail to declare them.

As they approached the door, a homemade "*Beware of the Dog!*" sign came into view.

'That's got to be to scare off salesmen, right?' Ayala asked.

'One way to find out.' Morton knocked the door, and the sound of barking erupted from the hallway inside. They heard a man's voice, the same South London accent as on the call recording, as he tried to hush the dog.

The door swung open, and a scruffy nose tried to press its way between its owner and the door. The man pushed the dog back inside and opened the door. The dog sat behind its owner and eyed the detectives warily.

'Don't mind him. He's a big softie really.'

'What kind of a dog is he?' Morton asked.

'German shepherd–malamute cross. The best alarm system money can buy. What can I do for you, gents?'

'We're investigating the murder of Ellis DeLange.'

'Lass in the news this week?' McArthur said. 'Wish I could help you, but Richmond is a million miles from Potter's Bar. You'd be better off canvassing there.'

'You didn't call in a tip to our hotline then?'

McArthur paled, then clenched his jaw. 'Why would I have anything to do with it?'

Morton pulled his phone from his pocket and hit play. The recording blared out, '*Dead body. Edgecombe Lodge. Richmond. Doors open.*'

'That sounds an awful lot like you, Mr McArthur.'

'That's much too deep for my voice. Besides, it sounds an awful lot like a lot of men in London, Mr…?'

'Morton. DCI Morton. Not all men in London give the phone that made that call to their apprentices–'

The door slammed shut.

'Quick!' Morton yelled, 'around the back!'

Ayala sprinted to the side of the house and out of view. Morton eyed up the door, swore under his breath then charged at it. At the last second, he threw his right leg out towards the right-hand side where the door was locked, and slammed his heel into the door. His momentum carried him forward and his foot collided with the door with a loud crack. The door splintered immediately, but didn't collapse. He pulled back, steadied himself so that he could aim again, being careful not to hit the lock itself, and then kicked again.

The door swung inwards, leaving a chunk of wood attached to the lock on the right-hand side. The dog was waiting for him just inside, but scarpered when the door came crashing inwards. Morton spotted light at the back of the property, through the kitchen. The door to the back garden was already open.

Morton ran. His legs ached from the exertion of taking the door down, but he powered through the house as quickly as he could. He raced past the stairwell, through the hallway into the kitchen and towards the backdoor. He just reached the back door when he heard a floorboard creak above him.

McArthur was trying to double bluff them. Morton doubled back, then darted up the stairs. At the landing on the first floor, he paused for a second. Ayala had gone around the back. If he were McArthur, he'd be trying to get out of the front of the house.

The garage! The double garage was beneath a bay window, the perfect escape onto the street. Morton turned and vaulted back down the stairs four at a time, and emerged from the front of the house just as McArthur dropped from the roof of the garage to the ground outside with a 'whoomph'.

Morton dived towards him, using his weight to pin the suspect down. 'Mr McArthur! You're under arrest on suspicion of handling stolen goods.'

Ayala reappeared from around the side of the house.

'Been for a nice stroll, have you, Bertram? Help me get this heffalump into the back of the car, will you?'

Before McArthur could be brought into an interview suite, he demanded to speak to a lawyer. McArthur was turned over to the Custody Sergeant and processed. The search of his person turned up an iPhone, a wallet and a set of car and house keys. He was then photographed and swabbed, and his DNA sample sent for urgent comparison to the samples on file for the DeLange murder.

McArthur wasn't in the system already. He didn't have so much as a speeding ticket to his name. He didn't have a go-to lawyer, which meant he got stuck with whoever happened to be the duty solicitor for the day.

Unfortunately for Morton, the duty solicitor was a little more competent than average. Genevieve Hollis was a direct access barrister, and an advocate for criminal rights to boot.

'And on a Saturday too. Don't lawyers have social lives?' Morton bemoaned his misfortune.

'She can't be any worse than that snake, Elliot Morgan-Bryant,' Ayala replied.

'Oh, yes, she can. She's *honest.*'

An hour later, and Morton and Ayala were seated opposite Ms Hollis and the suspect in Interview Suite One. McArthur had been given plenty of time to consult with his lawyer, and looked visibly more relaxed than he did in Potter's Bar. He leaned back in his chair and smirked at Morton.

'Let the tape reflect that Mr McArthur is smirking in response to my last question. I'll ask you again, Mr McArthur, was the voice on the tape you?'

'It doesn't sound like me, does it?'

Morton produced an evidence bag which contained the Nokia 3310 that Sergei Krasnodar had had on his person. He then placed McArthur's own iPhone next to it, and began to tap away at the screen.

'I think, Mr McArthur, that the reason it sounds slightly different is that you used an app to modify your voice. This app in fact.'

Morton turned the phone around so that McArthur and his lawyer could see it. The iPrankCall app was open on screen.

'Mr Morton! You had no right to search my client's phone.'

'I disagree. He waived any expectation of privacy when he failed to set a simple password. Besides, we would have unlocked it anyway. It's not unreasonable to suppose this phone might have been stolen–'

'So run an IMEI check,' the lawyer suggested.

'Or,' Morton continued, 'that the phone might contain evidence like the contact details of your client's fence. And what's this? An audio file within the app? Let's just play that back.'

'*Dead body. Edgecombe Lodge. Richmond. Door's open,*' echoed throughout the interview suite.

'That's pretty damning if you ask me. Clever too. I assume you played the distorted voice back to your simple Nokia to avoid detection.'

'So I went to the house,' McArthur said. 'Big deal. I didn't steal anything.'

'You didn't steal anything. Really? And what exactly were you doing there then?'

'Looking. Don't you ever get curious about what a rich person's house looks like?'

'You want me to believe that you just happened to trespass on Ellis DeLange's property the day after she was murdered.'

'Doesn't matter what you believe, Mr Morton.' McArthur grinned and jerked his head towards his lawyer. 'She says trespass ain't a crime. It's a tort. So tell me what you think I stole, Mr Morton.'

'Did you break in?'

'Nope.'

'So you're now saying you just happened to trespass on the property of a famous photographer on the day after she was murdered, and that the house was unlocked. That's pretty far-fetched.'

'Truth can be stranger than fiction, can't it?'

'You smug git. I put it to you that if you're willing to break into a house then you were there to steal. Do you deny it?'

'Categorically.'

'Then our search of your home won't turn up anything, will it?'

The smile from his face vanished.

'I'd like to speak with my lawyer.'

'Fine. Interview terminated at 13:04.'

At half past two, DS Mayberry returned with the search team. Mayberry seemed to be walking a little taller when he led the team into the Incident Room where Morton and Ayala awaited their return.

'That dog is v-vicious!' Mayberry stuttered. He thrust his arm towards them; a minor mark could be seen on his forearm.

'The dog's got nothing on that front door. I practically dislocated my hip getting in,' Morton quipped. 'Don't keep us in suspense. What did you find?'

Mayberry whistled loudly, and a WPC trotted into the room carrying a pink suitcase, the wheeled kind popular with travellers who only take carry-on. It was in an oversize evidence bag and the label read '*Oak Cottage, 13:35, April 12th*'.

'Nice work. Chain of custody paperwork complete?'

'Y-yes, sir.'

'Impressive. Let's have a look inside then.'

Mayberry laid out a polythene liner on the table and proceeded to decant the contents of the suitcase.

'Clothes?' Morton said.

The suitcase was full of women's clothing. Underwear, trousers, three blouses, a skirt and a gown were inside together with a hairbrush and various toiletries.

'Looks like about a week's worth.' Ayala said. The case was about two thirds full.

'And we're sure it belongs to Ellis?'

'She's a size six. So are these clothes. McArthur's wife wears a fourteen. It fits.'

'See if we can get DNA samples from the hairbrush and toothbrush to be on the safe side. Good job, Mayberry.'

'Th-th-thanks, boss.'

'Interview resumed at 15:16. Present are Mr David McArthur, Ms Genevieve Hollis, Detective Inspector Bertram Ayala and DCI David Morton.'

Ayala held up the suitcase.

'Do you recognise this, Mr McArthur?' Ayala asked.

'Should I?'

'It was found in your house.'

McArthur shrugged, as if to suggest that suitcase could be his.

'Do you regularly wear women's clothing, Mr McArthur? No judgement if you do,' Ayala said.

'No!' McArthur spat.

Morton smiled. Nothing like pride to elicit a reaction. 'Then to whom does it belong, Mr McAthur?' he asked.

'Ellis DeLange. I… borrowed it.'

'You borrowed it?' Morton mocked.

'Yes. I'm a fan. I was always going to give it back. I had no intention of permanently depriving Miss DeLange of the goods.'

'Her estate you mean. And I'm fairly certain your lawyer told you to say that. So now your story is that you found an unlocked multimillion-pound house on the day the celebrity owner of the home died, then borrowed her suitcase unilaterally before phoning us using a voice-modifier app? That's one heck of a tall tale. You ever thought about writing fiction, Mr McArthur?'

'My client has already answered you, Mr Morton. Unless you can prove intent to steal, this interview is over.'

Why would anyone steal clothing? Morton wondered. Unless… they wouldn't. There was one thing Ellis wouldn't go on a business trip without.

'Mr McArthur, what else was in the bag? Did it contain all of Ellis DeLange's photography equipment?'

McArthur turned to his lawyer and whispered in her ear.

'Mr Morton, my client is a Good Samaritan. He went out of his way to call you to notify you of a murder that you had no idea happened. Can we put our cards on the table here?'

'By all means.'

'If, and this is hypothetical of course, my client were to admit to stealing camera equipment, would that confession be enough to get him a deal?'

'Stolen goods don't interest me, Ms Hollis. If your client tells us everything in writing – including how he knew the house would be empty – then he walks out of here a free man. Do we have a deal?'

McArthur nodded.

'The recording can't see you nodding, Mr McArthur.'

'Yes, we have a deal.'

An hour later, Morton was back in his office clutching a written witness statement. He placed it on his desk and turned on his desk lamp, then began to read while Ayala peered over his shoulder.

WITNESS STATEMENT OF DAVID MCARTHUR

On the morning of March 30th at around eleven o'clock in the morning, I went to Edgecombe Lodge in Richmond. The homeowner, Ellis DeLange, was previously known to me as she hired my firm, DMC Electricals, on multiple occasions. On the last occasion we were hired to install a Smart Thermostat in her residence.

When I set up the system, I demonstrated the 'Holiday' feature to Miss DeLange. It allows you to tell the system when you will be away from the house for a protracted period. I set up the system so that it emailed me a notification whenever this feature was used.

Miss DeLange had entered a holiday into the system from the 30th of March so I knew the house would be empty. I went to the house, alone, and let myself in (I installed the gate for Miss DeLange on a previous occasion). I began to explore the house. I was drawn to the swimming pool in the back of the house, as it is the only domestic pool I have ever seen.

When I entered the pool area, I saw her floating face down in the pool. I assumed she had drowned. I fled Edgecombe Lodge, snatching up the suitcase on the way. It was packed and ready to go in the hallway, otherwise I wouldn't have bothered.

I then phoned the police anonymously to tell them about the body, and I sold everything I could that was in the bag.

I make this statement in exchange for full immunity from prosecution.

'Blimey. Purcell was right. Nobody tell him or we'll never hear the end of it.'

'Too late, boss. Look who's standing outside.'

Sure enough, the plump technician was in the hallway. Someone had given him a heads up.

'Let him in.'

Ayala opened the door and Purcell bounded into the room like an overgrown puppy.

'Stuart, I'd like to congratulate you on realising the importance of the thermostat,' Morton said through gritted teeth.

'Thanks,' Purcell said modestly. 'But that isn't why I'm here. I got a copy of your witness statement, and we're totally wrong.'

'Excuse me?'

'I said we were wrong. All our times are off.'

'How so?'

'Your thief. His deal is contingent on telling the truth, right?'

'Yes.'

'He says he went to Edgecombe Lodge at eleven o'clock.'

'That's right.'

'The thermostat showed he came in at ten o'clock.'

'He could have got the time wrong.'

'I thought so too. Until I took another look at that thermostat. It isn't programmed to take into daylight savings. It never made the switch to British Summer Time. It should have gone forward an hour at one o'clock that morning and it didn't. McArthur was right and the thermostat was wrong. All of our assumptions, all of our timings, they were off by a full hour.'

'Which means any of our suspects could have done it.'

'I'm afraid so.'

'Fuck.'

Chapter 24: The Wedding

Sunday went by in a blur for Morton. He had hoped for a well-earned lie-in, perhaps with breakfast in bed. Unfortunately for him, one of Sarah's myriad of cousins, Jennifer or Jaina or Jessica, something beginning with the letter J anyway, was getting married.

Morton was therefore up at the crack of dawn like the dutiful husband he was. For reasons Morton could barely comprehend, the invite was for traditional morning dress.

'What's wrong with a plain old suit?' Morton complained. Sarah had laid out his attire for him: a grey morning coat, striped trousers and a double-breasted burgundy waistcoat with matching tie. 'I'm going to look like an idiot.'

'Nonsense. You'll look very dapper.'

'I'll concede the morning coat, as long as I can put it on once we get there. But sod wearing that waistcoat.'

'You'll wear it, and you'll smile. You'll even like the wedding cake. This is my side of the family so it's my say, capiche?' For comic effect, Sarah picked up the striped trousers and held them against her.

'Very funny. Fine,' Morton said. 'But why won't I like the wedding cake?'

'She's vegan.'

'That's it. I'm not going. It's the FA Cup on this afternoon. You go on without me.'

'You're not going to win this argument. If you keep arguing, I'm going to double the gift we're giving Jane and Humphrey.'

'Jane!' Morton cried.

'You forgot, didn't you? I think that's just doubled it to £100.'

'Oh, come off it. That's not fair! Besides, we barely know them. And asking for cash gifts only? How cheeky is that? We barely got a toaster and we had to be grateful for it. I'm not going.'

'£200, and don't push me, David, I will keep going.'

'No. I'm putting my foot down.'

'£400.'

Half an hour late, dressed to the nines, they were in the car.

Chapter 25: The Father

Security stopped Morton on the way into New Scotland Yard that Monday morning. It was barely nine o'clock, late by Morton's standards but perfectly reasonable considering the long day he'd had with Sarah at her cousin's wedding. A guest was waiting for him, but had been detained in reception.

Morton turned around, and headed for the waiting area. It was almost like a doctor's waiting room. There was a pile of magazines, mostly out of date, and a child's play area with toys neatly stacked in plastic boxes.

Three men, four women and one child were in the waiting area. All looked up when Morton appeared, hopeful, almost expectant. One, an elderly white man in a three-piece suit, immediately rose from his rickety seat and made a beeline towards Morton.

He was an older man, perhaps in his seventies, but looking good for it. He wore a comb over which had gone almost entirely grey but had a few traces of brown still visible. His skin bunched around the eyes, as if he had spent a lifetime smiling. And but for a small skin tag on his left cheek, he was much as Morton imagined Aleksander Barchester would look if aged up twenty years and had he also lost three or four stone.

'Mr Morton?' the man said.

'Lord Culloden, I presume.'

The elderly man looked delighted to be recognised. 'My boy, how did you guess?'

My boy? Morton thought. He hadn't been called anything like that in years.

'Deduction,' he quipped.

The real Lord Culloden laughed heartily. 'Is there somewhere we might talk?'

Morton looked around. None of those in the waiting area were paying the slightest bit of attention to them. He shrugged, and nodded. 'We have a conference room upstairs. It should be empty this early in the morning.'

He beckoned Lord Culloden to follow him, and then nodded at the security guard to buzz them through. A guest pass was hastily affixed to Lord Culloden's overcoat, and then they made their way to the lifts.

Culloden looked around in wonder as they made their way to the conference room. 'I haven't been here in years.'

'Perhaps you should commit a few more crimes then,' Morton said.

Another booming laugh. 'My boy, you really should be a comedian.'

'Uh-huh... This is us.' Morton unlocked the conference room door with a swipe of his police ID, and then held the door open for his guest. Once they were settled, Morton looked on expectantly.

'I surmise from your knowing who I am that you also know why I'm here.'

'Aleksander Barchester using your name?'

'That... But not in the way that you think,' Lord Culloden said. 'My wife, Harriet, whom I believe you met, is my second wife. My first died many years ago. The one thing I always regretted was my indiscretion. As a young man I was very much driven by hormones.'

'You slept with another woman.'

'Quite. My maid, Aleksander's mother, was quite something. I regret it to this day, but my fidelity wavered.'

'And you're telling me this because…?'

'I believe Aleksander is my son. If that is true then he hasn't committed fraud by using my name, has he? I need a favour.'

'You want a DNA test.'

'Sharp as a tack, my boy, sharp as a tack. So can you?' He leaned into the conference table, looking imploringly at Morton.

'No.'

'Excuse me?'

'No chance,' Morton said. 'This is a police station.'

'If it's about money, my dear boy, then I can certainly solve that issue!' Culloden beamed, and put his hand into his pocket as if he were about to pull out a chequebook there and then.

'Lord Culloden, I think you may be misunderstanding me here. I cannot run a DNA test for you. Nor can I accept your money, for obvious reasons. It would be wholly improper. If you want to run a DNA test then find a private laboratory.'

'Mr Morton, please. I need your help. Are you a father?'

'I am. Did you want one of mine? I'd be prepared to sell one.'

'Ha. I'm not sure if you know this, but Aleksander and I are already close. He lives on the Estate in my old Servant's Cottage. I let him have it for peppercorn rent years back. We speak all the time while in the gardens. He told me something, something in confidence.'

'And?'

'He's expecting a child. I have not met the mother, but if that is my grandchild then I need to know. I have no other children, and Harriet doesn't wish to bear me any.'

Morton frowned. He knew about the child, but Gabriella told Aleksander about the baby only on the night of the murder, or so they claimed.

'When?'

'Nine months, I suppose.'

'When did he tell you?'

'A couple of weeks ago.'

Interesting, Morton thought. *More lies.*

'And who is the mother?'

'Aleksander said her name was Gabriella. Pretty name, isn't it?'

Morton made a snap decision. 'I suppose so. Lord Culloden, we'll do it. I'll need a DNA sample from you, of course.'

'Outstanding, my boy!'

'On one condition.'

'Anything. Just name it.'

'Stop calling me "my boy".'

Chapter 26: Where There's a Will, There's a Way

Morton's Monday morning started out strange, but it wasn't until eleven o'clock that he got a bolt from the blue. He was just finishing up signing off on the paperwork Forensics had sent over for the DeLange residence. They'd released the property the previous Friday, so it was no longer a crime scene. DNA analysis was underway, but Morton needed to cajole exclusionary samples out of the rest of his suspects. Morton pinged off a quick email to delegate the task to Mayberry.

He was running over the timeline in his head, trying to work out who might have benefitted from an extra hour in their window of opportunity, when he got a call from Dr Larry Chiswick.

'Larry. What can I do for you?'

'Morning, David. I've got a Kallum Fielder on the other line. He's demanding a medical death certificate. But I've already told him I've sent the usual paperwork over to next of kin.'

'Strange. The only reason he could want that–'

'Is to get a death certificate from the registrar,' Chiswick finished for him. Responsibility for registering a death fell on the next of kin, or the executor if there was one, under pain of criminal sanctions. To get the death certificate from the Registrar of Births, Deaths and Marriages, Kallum needed a medical death certificate.

'Which means he thinks he's the executor.'

'Exactly. But you haven't found a will yet, have you?'

'Nope. We called her bank, checked her home and talked to the lawyer she uses to manage her intellectual property. Nada.'

'What do you want me to do with him?' Chiswick asked.

'Tell me him he needs to come see you in person, this afternoon if you're free.'

'You know I'm not. But if you're planning what I think you're planning, that doesn't really matter.'

'Cheers, Doc. I won't see you at one.'

At precisely one o'clock in the afternoon, Kal Fielder appeared outside New Scotland Yard. He had an entourage in tow. The media had yet to let up, though social media engagement had begun to wane. Sooner rather than later the death of Ellis DeLange would no longer be big news. It was starting to happen already. Fewer journalists were calling in to ask how the investigation was progressing. Not that that would last should an arrest be made.

Morton watched as Kal entered the building. Security had been instructed to stop the media from following him in, and then take him through to one of the ground floor meeting rooms.

Morton let him stew for ten minutes, then headed down.

'Mr Fielder,' Morton greeted him. The former footballer looked even more tired than on their last meeting. His eyes were bloodshot, and his shirt was crumpled as if it had never seen an iron in its life. He had a folder on the desk in front of him which was unlabelled. He saw Morton looking at it and subconsciously pulled it towards him.

'Detective Morton. I didn't realise you did deliveries for the coroner.'

Morton pulled out a chair but didn't sit down, choosing instead to lean against it. 'You're here for a medical death certificate. What for?'

'I need to register Ellis' death of course.'

'Yes, but why you? You're not her next of kin.'

'Like hell I'm not. The law might say Brianna is her next of kin, but it's me left picking up the pieces.'

'But what, specifically, do you intend to do with a death certificate? I'm guessing you want to file probate.'

Kal's hand went to the folder again. 'That's correct, though it's none of your business.'

'May I see the will please?'

'It's none of your business, Mr Morton. This is Ellis' personal wishes.'

'You do realise that wills become public when filed? What have you got to hide?'

'Nothing, but–'

'Then you won't mind showing me.' Morton pursed his lips and held out his hand.

Kal sighed, and pushed the folder across the desk. Morton leant forward, picked it up and opened it. Inside was a crumpled, coffee-stained rag of a document titled '*The Last Will and Testament of Ellis DeLange.*'

'I found it like that. I guess she must have spilt coffee over it,' Kal said.

'Then crumpled it up before putting it in a nice new folder for safe-keeping? That doesn't sound like a sensible way to deal with such an important document.'

'The folder's mine.'

Morton flicked through the will, which ran to six pages. Ellis' assets were not specifically listed other than provision for everything to be sold off bar a few mementos, but – surprise, surprise – the remainder of the estate had just one beneficiary: Kallum Fielder. Two witnesses had signed it: 'Lord Culloden' and 'Francis Patrick Malone'.

'Where was this? We didn't find it at her house nor did her lawyer have it on file.'

'My safe. Eli always had guests around, so she keeps some stuff at my place. Can't be too careful.'

Morton glanced back at the will then arched his eyebrows. 'This is your idea of safe-keeping?'

'Like I said, it was like that when I got it. When she put it in my safe, I mean.'

'And which law firm prepared it for her?'

'She didn't use a lawyer. I think she used one of those DIY will kits you can buy on CD to print at home.'

'You seem to know a lot about this. Did you know you were the beneficiary?'

'Yes. But she's the beneficiary of my will too,' Kal said.

'The difference being that she was worth three million, and you barely have two pennies to rub together.'

Kal's expression turned stony. 'You background checked me? How dare you!'

'What do you think we do during murder investigations? Sit around and wait for the murderer to turn themselves in? You're damn right I background checked every person who turned up at the party.'

Kal turned away, then stared at his fingernails. 'I'm sorry,' he mumbled.

'I'm going to need a copy of this. I'll be back with the original in ten minutes. OK?' Morton headed for the door.

'But what about my death certificate?' Kal asked.

'Sorry. Can't help you with that.'

Chapter 27: The Cavalry

The last will and testament of Ellis DeLange was quickly photo-copied and handed to everyone on Morton's Murder Investigation Team. Morton even paged Kieran O'Connor to join them. The CPS lawyer swung by over lunch while Morton, Ayala and Mayberry were in the Incident Room.

'Kieran. Thanks for coming.' Morton said.

'Make it quick, David. I'm due back in court at three, and I'm starving.' Kieran eyed up the sandwich platter on the table.

'Quit staring at my lunch,' Morton said. He passed Kieran a copy of the will. 'Is this real?'

'It looks like it's been fished out of a bin. Where on earth did you get it?'

'One of our suspects. He stands to inherit three million and change in property, plus a portfolio of photographs the victim took.'

'It looks like it's been lifted straight from Parker's Modern Wills. I should know. I used it for mine!'

'So it's valid?' Morton asked.

'It's a little generic but it should pass muster,' Kieran said. 'I take it that it was drafted by a non-lawyer?'

'It's from a DIY will kit.'

'Ah. Plenty of pitfalls there, but this one doesn't seem too bad. She's got one beneficiary and leaves him pretty much everything. Very little room for dispute over the terms. I'm no probate lawyer, but it looks legally sound. I don't like the state it's in though. Are you thinking it's forged?'

Morton nodded. 'Can't prove it though. I'll have to have a specialist give it the once-over. I don't suppose you know anyone?'

'Sorry. Fraud is outside my bailiwick these days. I'll ask round for you though if you like.'

'Please.'

'Now can I nick a sandwich? I'd best be heading off. I've got to get all the way out to Snaresbrook Crown Court.'

'Go on then. But not the bacon sarnies. They're off limits.'

'T'anks,' Kieran said as he stuffed a sandwich in his mouth, then sprinted for the door.

'Lawyers,' Morton muttered. He turned to Ayala and Mayberry, who had simply watched the whole conversation. 'You two going to sit there like lemons or have you anything to add?'

'Don't look at me,' Ayala said. 'I'm on lunch.'

'Mayberry?'

'I…'

'Spit it out. We haven't got all day.'

'S-sorry. M-my aphai – aphai – aphai–'

'Aphasia gets the better of you, yes, we know.'

'The autographs.'

'Signatures,' Morton corrected.

'They're s-suspects.'

'Not this again. Ayala, have you been coaching him?'

Ayala looked up from his lunch. 'He's not wrong. They could all have done it.'

Morton shook his head vehemently. 'No bleeding way. This is not an Agatha Christie novel. One victim does not get murdered by an entire party full of people. You mark my words.'

'Then who do you like?'

'It's not Aleksander Barchester. It stretches credibility that he'd leave naked, come back and kill someone, then leave without his clothes again. Kal could have done it, but he'd have to have left and come back. Brianna likewise. Gabriella and Paddy are each other's alibi and the extra hour we gain from the clock change doesn't affect that. Both Kal and Brianna could have returned. They both live within a reasonable travelling distance, and both left early enough that they now have a window of almost three hours apiece.'

'The boyfriend and the sister. How do we tell which one?'

'Let's check the route between Edgecombe Lodge and the suspects' homes. We'll start with Kal as his place is marginally closer. That'll narrow down our timings.'

'And w-we can check for v-video t-tapey things on the way,' Mayberry added.

'Yes, Mayberry, we can check for, ahem, video tapey things too.'

Chapter 28: Walkies

They arrived at Edgecombe Lodge at 14:00. The plan was to travel from Edgecombe Lodge to Kal's residence in Twickenham. It was only a two-mile trip. Morton felt confident that a former footballer would be in good enough physical condition to complete a round trip of four miles in no time at all.

'Bets, gentlemen?' Morton asked.

'Half an hour for the walking,' Ayala said.

'And for the running team?'

'Ten minutes.'

'Excellent. I'll take eleven minutes and thirty-one seconds. Shall we say a pint for the nearest guess for each half?' Morton smiled. There was no way poor Mayberry would run it in under ten minutes.

'You're on.'

'Are we happy with our routes? We'll go out on the A305, and we'll come back on the A316. There shouldn't be much difference in times, but we need to check both routes for CCTV as Mayberry suggested. Make a mental note, and we'll circle back around again after doing the timings.' Morton referred to the two bridges that separated Richmond and Twickenham which were, rather originally Morton thought, called the Richmond Bridge and the Twickenham Bridge. Kal could have used either.

'In the car?' Ayala asked.

'Yes, in the car. We don't have all day. On your marks, get set, go!'

Three hours later, the three detectives were in the Orange Tree enjoying a much-earned pint. Morton's was paid for by Ayala, and they had taken to a table under a heater outside to watch the world go by in central Richmond. The afternoon was warm and only minimally breezy, so it was no surprise how quickly the pub packed out as the evening wore on.

It had taken Mayberry almost fourteen minutes to run the 1.9-mile route, and nearly seventeen coming back the other way, which was a hair longer at 2.1 miles.

At Morton and Ayala's more leisurely pace, the trip still only took thirty-eight and forty-three minutes respectively, and that was with traffic. If they'd needed to wait at lights then all the journeys would have been substantially quicker.

The conclusion was obvious: Kallum Fielder had more than enough time to make it home, and still be back in the window of opportunity.

Less fortunately, they had proved he made it home. CCTV on the A310 where it crossed the River Crane showed Kal going past at 12:42, eighteen minutes before the clock change.

'What that CCTV didn't show is Kal coming back,' Ayala said after he had drained his second pint.

'An absence of proof is not proof of absence. He could easily have come back another way. First thing tomorrow, I want both of you checking the backstreets for any routes he could have taken to get back. Ayala, you concentrate on finding CCTV-free routes from Edgecombe Lodge to the river. Mayberry, you get the other end.'

'Rightio, boss.'

'Next round is on me.'

'Really? I owe you another one from the bet.'

'Yes, really. I knew I'd win,' Morton said. 'I checked Google Maps for timings before I made the bet.'

Chapter 29: Jailhouse Snitch

TUESDAY APRIL 15TH – 10:00

On Tuesday morning, Morton got a call from Ashley Rafferty, the feisty parole officer who'd nabbed Paddy before Morton could interrogate him.

She insisted on a meeting that morning, and so once Morton had made sure Ayala and Mayberry were busy checking alternative routes, he headed to meet her on neutral ground. She picked the meeting place, a coffee shop tucked away behind Great Ormond Street Hospital.

Though he was early, Morton found her waiting for him with two empty mugs beside her.

'You been here a while?' Morton gestured at the coffee mugs.

'Nope. Not really. I had a meeting here half an hour ago, so it was convenient for us to meet here.'

'Convenient for you, maybe,' Morton said quietly as he sat down.

'Hah. I keep forgetting you're the boss around here. Speaking of which, did I hear there's an opening on your team?'

'That's why you called me to an urgent meeting? You want a job?'

'Nope. I like to kill two birds with one stone. I used to be a DS before moving into probation. I want back onto proper work. I want onto your team.'

'So do a lot of people. You're very direct, you know. Taking liberties with a DCI's time, then demanding a job takes some real cojones. What've you got to back it up?'

'Paddy Malone. He had a visitor yesterday.'

'Who?'

'Kallum Fielder.'

'Interesting. Not enough to buy you an interview, but thanks anyway.' Morton made as if to stand.

Ashley grabbed his arm. 'Sit.'

'This ought to be good.'

'For such a famous detective, you're a snarky bugger, aren't you? I'm not done. Mr Fielder tried to pass Patrick a mobile phone and a bundle of twenties across the visiting room table.'

'How'd he get those in there?'

'You ever heard of plugging?'

Morton shook his head.

'You don't want to. Just trust me, there are ways and means of getting things into Pentonville if you're willing to experience some discomfort. Unfortunately for Mr Fielder, one of the guards was watching him like a hawk.'

'Good to know we've got such attentive guards.'

'Sorry. I'm afraid not. The guy just wanted Kal's autograph.'

'Is that it?'

'That's it. Would you mind moving from that seat? It's just I've got a ten-thirty meeting with one of my parolees.'

Chapter 30: Secrets

The Old Coach House beckoned on Tuesday afternoon. Morton knew Vladivoben lied about not attending the party. The other attendees had put him there early evening, long before the murder took place. He wasn't really much of a suspect. By all accounts he left well before the other guests, with company which would presumably provide him with an alibi, and he had no plausible reason to have murdered Ellis DeLange. They'd argued about noise on occasion, but that had to come with the territory of living near a party-hosting neighbour. Perhaps they'd squabbled about Ellis' guests blocking up the road with their cars.

None of that was enough to kill over. But lies were only told by those who had something to hide.

Curiosity might have killed the cat, but then again it surely would have caught the cat's killer too. Ferreting out secrets was Morton's drug of choice, and he simply had to know why Vladivoben lied.

Maria answered the security gate and let Morton in. The sun was shining, and Morton was shown through to the rear garden where Vladivoben was reclining in a deck chair sunbathing, with a jug of iced tea and a trashy magazine set upon a low table next to him.

He sat up when Morton stepped onto the veranda, and squinted into the sunlight.

'DCI Mormon–'

'Morton. It's DCI Morton. And would you please put a shirt on?'

Vladivoben shrugged as if it was of no concern to him, and then pulled his shirt on.

'You lied to me, Mr Vladivoben.'

'I lie? About what?' Vladivoben played dumb.

'You said you didn't go to the party, and I believe you also disclaimed knowing Miss DeLange socially.'

'Is that a crime?'

'Yes. Obstructing my investigation is a crime, and I take it personally. Why did you lie?'

'It doesn't matter. I was there. I left. End of, yes?' He tugged at the collar of his shirt as if he was going to take it back off and return to his sunbathing session.

'No, Mr Vladivoben. It matters because you made it matter. What time did you leave?'

'Nine thirty, ten o'clock. Ask Maria.'

'Witnesses saw you leaving with someone else. Is that correct?'

'*Da*.'

'A man. Who was he?'

'I do not know.'

'You don't know? I'm not sure you're taking this seriously, Mr Vladivoben. This is a murder enquiry and you're making it very difficult to trust you. If you've been hiding something then now is the time to tell me. If it isn't illegal, it won't go any further than this veranda.'

'Promise?'

'Yes.'

Vladivoben looked anxious. He whispered almost inaudibly: 'In Russia, we do not have…'

'Men who like other men?'

'*Da*.'

'You're gay. That's what all this secrecy is about?'

'*Da*.'

'Then I shall leave you to your sunbathing. Thanks for your time, Mr Vladivoben.'

Lies were always suspicious. They get told for a myriad of reasons of which guilt is but one. This time, it seemed, the lie had been born out of fear not guilt.

Chapter 31: Authenticity

'He was hiding the fact he was gay?' Ayala asked incredulously. He and Morton were sitting in the Incident Room topping up on their morning coffee.

'Yep. Poor sod was tying himself up in knots over it,' Morton replied.

'I could have told you that a week ago. He's not exactly, well, subtle.'

'Well, when we next need a forensic gaydar, I'll give you a ring. Until then, have you found me an expert on forging wills?'

'Not wills specifically, but Kieran came up with a name for us. Radley Freeman.'

'Why do I feel like I've heard that name before?'

'He got convicted in the late eighties for printing his own £20 notes. Got out ten years later, and now works as an expert witness testifying mostly in civil trials. Kieran said he comes highly recommended.'

'Right. I guess we'll have to book him then.'

'Err...'

'You already did?'

'Uh-huh... He's waiting in the conference room for us now. And I've got the original will too. Picked it up from Kal myself first thing this morning.' Ayala puffed up his chest proudly, certain that Morton would be pleased. Instead, he was furious.

'You let an ex-con into the building without even telling me first? Are you insane?'

'But Kieran said–'

'I don't care what Kieran said. You work for me. If you want to stay second-in-command, you run things like that by me. Otherwise the new DI will also be your new supervisor.'

'New DI? You've hired someone?'

'I'm sitting on a CV.'

'Who?'

'Ashley Rafferty. I'm sure she'll have forgiven you by now for assuming she was a man…' Morton said.

'You can't hire her. She's a complete ball-buster. There's got to be someone else.'

'We'll see,' Morton said. 'Well, let's not keep our forgery specialist waiting.'

Radley Freeman was a big man with a booming voice that echoed around the conference room when he spoke. Morton supposed it worked well in court, but in the confines of the conference room it was practically deafening.

'Documents which have been forged tend to be flawed in some kind of way. You said this wasn't prepared by a lawyer, so presumably the content is of little assistance in discerning provenance,' Radley said.

'That's right,' Morton replied. 'It's from a fill-in-the-blanks will kit.'

'Then it'll look like every other will using that template, and if that template is cheaply available–'

'£14.99 at WH Smith,' Ayala said. He produced a printout of WH Smith's website showing the kit for sale.

'Then it's a forger's dream. Print it out, fill in the blanks. It doesn't need to be checked by a professional. It can be done at home. It's a bog standard generic will. Do you know how much probate fraud is worth every year?'

'No, but I gather you're about to tell me.'

'A hundred and fifty million a year. That's not chump change. I suspect that's a conservative estimate. If I was in the game, I could find an old lady with no family easily enough and switch out her will. Who's going to challenge it?'

'The courts?' Ayala suggested.

'Hah. No. Someone has to challenge the will. If there's no next of kin, and no named beneficiary to challenge it, then it's probably going to slip by. Think about this. I could pose as a will-writer going door to door in the suburbs during the day. That'll find me people without family and who don't have a lawyer's will already prepared. I ask them what they want in their will. Then I fill out the form on my laptop, bring it back and let them sign it. Then just forge a copy later on with me as the beneficiary. I could even charge them for the service and make a bit extra while I wait.'

'Don't wills need to be witnessed?'

'Yup. But who checks those? No one, unless there's something fishy going on. With no one to challenge the will, it's not hard to just put any old name on there. Or I pick another couple of old people as my witnesses. Chances are they'll have either died or gone senile between me picking the mark and the time of probate. It's almost the perfect crime.'

'You sure you're not still a criminal?'

'I'm just a consultant these days. My days of stealing from the unwitting are long gone.'

'How much are we paying you, anyway?' Morton asked.

'£850 per day plus VAT and expenses.'

'Bloody hell. You are a bleeding criminal.' Morton looked across at Ayala, horrified they were spending so much to get Radley's expertise.

Radley laughed heartily. 'I said stealing from the unwitting. I've no problem taking money willingly given.'

Morton had to give it to him. He'd found the perfect mark in Ayala. 'You said almost perfect. Why almost?'

'Yep. I could see a few forged wills being caught. If the marks've got distant relatives. If they promised money to someone, or a charity perhaps. Or if the forgery is just plain obvious.'

'Is this will obviously forged?'

'Nope.'

'It's not obvious or it's not forged?'

'Not obvious. Firstly, it's been crumpled up, a lot. Someone's spilled a liquid on it too. Looks like coffee. That means the fibre of the paper is damaged. You ever seen paper up close? Here.' Radley produced a microscope from his bag, then placed a small piece of A4 paper under a slide for Morton to look at.

'See how this is rough, textured and almost like interwoven fibres?'

'Yes.'

'Now take a look at the corner of the will.'

Morton peered through the microscope. 'It's flat.'

'It is. The crumpling smoothed out the fibres. It means we can't effectively use EDSA–'

'ESDA?'

'Electrostatic detection analysis. I'd normally look for impression marks in the paper to see if other documents were placed on top of it and pressure applied. It's a little more complicated than that but between the mishandling and the liquid, we'd be wasting our time. If it was in good nick, I could have compared the paper with manufacturer samples to tell you what paper was used and what ink.'

'Could we use that to link the will to the printer that printed it?'

'In theory, though it's not specific. The combination of high street generic paper and a common printer means we'd narrow it down but not definitively. I usually do civil cases, so I don't know how much good that sort of circumstantial evidence would be for proving a crime.'

'If not the paper, then what?'

'The signatures. Ideally, I'd have exemplars for all three of those who signed this.'

'Two of them are alive. We can get comparators.'

'If they're alive and willing to testify that they signed this, then they're a dead end forensically, as there's no reason to claim a forged signature.'

Morton frowned. Paddy had been paid off, he was sure of that. But why had Culloden signed? Did Kal have something on him to keep him quiet?

'Therefore,' Radley continued with a wave of his giant right hand towards the bottom of the document, 'this is the money shot. Look at Miss DeLange's signature. It's loopy, slants at about fifteen degrees. Quite girlish, and a lovely signature for autographs.'

'I agree. So how does it compare with the comparator?'

'What do you think?' Radley passed Morton the will and a copy of the exemplar, which was a photographic print belonging to Ayala.

'They look the same to me.'

'Exactly.'

'So it's real then,' Morton said.

'No. I said exactly. As in, they're exactly the same. Here,' Radley passed Morton a pen and paper. 'Sign this twice.'

Morton did, then looked closely at them.

'See what I mean? Similar, but not the same. No one signs documents exactly the same way every time.'

'It's been printed?'

'Again, no. The ink has made a bit of an indentation on the page, and it's not the same ink as the printer. It was done with a pen. It's not the same pen as the other signatures either.'

'How can you tell?'

'Her signature is in black. The other two are blue.'

'How is it so similar then?'

'My guess is an autopen,' Radley said. 'Your victim was famous. She obviously signed prints of her photos. Did you find an autopen in her house?'

'Ayala?' Morton turned to his deputy. It had been Ayala's responsibility to fill out the evidence logs for the crime scene.

'What does one look like?' Ayala asked.

'The smallest are about forty-five by forty-five centimetres, usually metal with a boxy end on one side and arms sticking out of it to hold the pen or pencil.'

'One sec.' Ayala dashed out of the room, then returned panting two minutes later holding a binder full of crime scene photos. Ayala flicked through quickly, then settled on one page. He turned it around so Radley could see it.

'Like this?'

'That's the boy. She's got a USB one port, so it's not massively new.'

'How would it work?'

'The signature is recorded, loaded onto USB or smartcard, then inserted into the autopen. Then it's easy to put the paper in the right position and hit the "sign once" button and you're done.'

'No PC needed?'

'Not if you've got access to the USB key with the signature on it. I can see it in the photo, so it looks like accessing it would have been relatively easy. Whoever did it might have needed a few tries to position the signature on the dotted line, but that's about the only complication.'

'And we've no way of knowing who used the machine.'

'You could dust for fingerprints. It wouldn't prove what it was used for, but it would show who had been near it.'

'Unless they took the obvious precaution of wearing gloves.'

'Like I said, it's the perfect crime.'

Once Radley was on his way out, Morton and Ayala turned their attention to the crime scene documentation.

'Damn!' Ayala exclaimed.

'What?'

'Purcell dusted the autopen already.'

'And?'

'He only found prints belonging to our victim. I guess our footballer is smarter than we gave him credit for.'

'Maybe. The will-writing software. How does it work?'

'You fill in the blanks, click export, get an RTF file–'

'A what?'

'Rich text file. It's a really common format for saving text documents.'

'When you save one, is it like when I upload a photograph to my computer?'

'What do you mean?'

'Is it date stamped?'

'Yes, boss, I suppose it is. It'd be stamped with whatever time the system is set at.'

'So if we find the computer that created the will, we'll be able to check the system time against the file's timestamp to see when it was created–'

'And if that time is after our victim died, we've nailed it,' Ayala finished for him.

'Then get me Kallum Fielder's laptop.'

'We'll need a warrant.'

'Go get it,' Morton ordered. 'And clear us going back to pick up the autopen from Edgecombe Lodge. We might need it to exhibit as evidence.'

'You got it, boss.'

Chapter 32: The Findy-Windy Thing

Kallum Fielder's Wednesday afternoon nap was cut short when DS Mayberry arrived on his doorstep. Sleeping in the afternoon was pretty normal for Kal. Filming from six every morning would throw anyone out of sync with their circadian rhythm, so it took a while for him to realise that there was a forensic team on his doorstep.

Mayberry was about to ram the door down when Kal finally answered, bleary-eyed and wearing only boxers and a t-shirt.

'W-we have a… a… f-findy-windy thing to c-come in.'

'Excuse me?'

Mayberry handed him a copy of the warrant, fresh from the magistrate's court. 'L-look at t-this.'

Kal squinted at the paper. He didn't have his contact lenses in. The words search and warrant swam into focus.

'What in God's name are you looking for?'

'It's in the… document. P-please step outside, s-sir.'

Kal stepped outside, then shivered. It might have been late April, but a chill wind cut through Twickenham. A blanket was hastily found, and Mayberry was able to lead Purcell and his team inside to search.

It was a beautiful home, rented according to the Land Registry, but certainly pricey. Kal had very few assets. Losing the rent on a detached house in Twickenham in favour of moving into Edgecombe Lodge was presumably a very appealing prospect to Kal.

The house was pretty empty. Kal had few personal knickknacks, and most of those he did own were football related in some way. He had old shirts hung everywhere. Some were his. Some had once belonged to players that Kal had played against on the pitch. One small shelf was dedicated to television awards. They all seemed to be from low-rent magazines rather than prestigious competitions.

Kal's prize possession was a television large enough to be used as a cinema screen. Mayberry found Purcell staring at it with wide-eyed admiration.

'It's a beauty, isn't it? Nine feet corner to corner. It's only 1080p mind you, but if you sit far enough back it'd be a beauty for watching films or sports on. And in the winter, it'll double up as central heating.'

'It's n-nice,' Mayberry said. He didn't see the point really. Surely you could just sit closer to a smaller television.

Kal's office was where Mayberry headed next. They were looking specifically for personal computers and laptops. There was only one in the house. It was a brand new Dell. The box was still on the floor underneath Kal's desk with the shipping label still attached.

Mayberry bent down to examine the label. It had been delivered the day before. He went outside and found Kal shivering. It had begun to rain.

'Y-your l-laptop. Do you have a-another?' Mayberry asked.

'Nope. Just that one.'

'D-did you?'

'I did.'

'W-where is the o-old one?'

'Sold it, I'm afraid. I've only got the one now.'

Mayberry returned to New Scotland Yard in dour spirits. He relayed the news over a pot of coffee in the Incident Room.

'It's got to be a cover-up,' Ayala said.

'That much is obvious,' Morton said. 'He's used the old one to prepare the will and ditched it before we could come at him.'

'What do you want to do next?'

'Pick him up,' Morton ordered. 'Make a splash when you do it. We need to be seen to be doing something. I want the media to know, but you aren't to tip them off directly. If he's the killer, great. We'll look like the poster child of good policing.'

'And if we're wrong?'

'Then we hit Kal for fraud. And we hope that Kal's arrest allows the real killer to sleep more easily. The more relaxed they get, the more likely they are to make a mistake which will let us catch them. Grab him first thing tomorrow morning. Do it on set at the BBC in the middle of filming. He'll be all over the news before breakfast.'

'Then what?'

'Then we watch and wait. Have someone stake out all our suspects, and call me if any of them starting acting strangely. I'll get Kieran to meet me here tomorrow morning so we can sweat Kal.'

Chapter 33: Making a Splash

Security at Broadcasting House weren't best pleased to see Ayala and a half-dozen constables walk into the lobby.

'Kallum Fielder. Where is he?' Ayala demanded of the reception staff, though he knew the answer. Kal was in the middle of filming on Studio One, which was being beamed live to the nation. Morton wanted a splash, and Ayala planned to give it to him.

After only the briefest of arguments, security escorted them through to the studio, where they found filming in progress. As soon as they made it into the studio the show's producer, Simon Keller, stepped forward. Ayala ordered one of his team to escort Keller out lest he repeat cut to adverts before Ayala made a splash.

Kal was sat on the sofa opposite a bungling would-be politician called Hudson Brown. He was a right-wing nut job who'd been getting airtime for his outrageous views. Kal's eyes flicked briefly in the direction of camera five when Ayala walked in, and his facial muscles twitched in recognition before he continued with his interview segment.

'Mr Hudson, if you were to come to power, what would be the first thing you would do?' Kal read from the teleprompter.

'British jobs for British workers. I would make it illegal to hire out if local talent could do the job. A booming economy starts with a booming Britain.'

'But how? Would you repeal our equality legislation?'

'Damn right, I would. If you're a white man, born here in good ole Blighty, then working here is your birth right. This country needs to forget political correctness.' Hudson stared pointedly at his host, knowing full well how offensive he was being.

'A white man?' Kal's nostrils flared. 'What difference does race make?'

'None if you're British. But my job is to protect British working class stock. I want to close the borders, reduce taxes and start making things here. We need to wean ourselves off the teat of cheap imported tat and get back to basics. My plan is simple: get Britain working and eradicate that which does not serve the greater good.'

Ayala looked on from the shadows, mesmerised. Hudson Brown genuinely believed in what he was spouting. It was time to put an end to the clown show, and take Kallum Fielder in for questioning. He waved his team forward and stepped in front of the camera.

Hudson Brown leapt to his feet. 'What's going on here?' he demanded.

'Sit down. We're not here for you,' Ayala said. He turned to Kal, 'Stand up and put your hands behind your back. Kallum Fielder, you are under arrest on suspicion of forgery.'

Kal stood slowly. He had known they were coming, and he was ready for it. He stared straight into the nearest camera, unblinking, as if the entire arrest were simply a scene in a daytime drama. 'Forgery? There must be some mistake.'

'No mistake, Mr Fielder.'

Chapter 34: The President of the United States of America
THURSDAY APRIL 17TH – 10:00

The same interrogation suite, the same lawyer. Upon arrival at New Scotland Yard, Kal had begun yelling for a lawyer. Not just any lawyer, but Elliot Morgan-Bryant of Cutler & Kass. Again. The same pie-in-the-sky-priced lawyer that represented Aleksander Barchester mere days earlier. It was no coincidence.

'Tell me again why you had Ellis DeLange's will,' Morton said. He had a copy of their last chat in front of him. The slightest slip, and Morton would nail Kal for the inconsistency.

'Safety,' Morgan-Bryant said. 'My client has a high-grade commercial safe installed in his home, while Ellis did not. While Ellis was a social, trusting woman, she was well aware of the footfall at her parties and felt that her documents would be safer with her long-term partner than out in the open for anyone to inspect.'

'Mr Morgan-Bryant, I would appreciate it if you let your client answer. Nice to see you again, by the way,' Morton added with only the barest hint of sarcasm.

'I will let my client answer when you ask a question that hasn't already been covered extensively.'

'Mr Fielder, did you forge this will?'

'No comment.'

'I'll rephrase. This will is forged. You claim to have been looking after it all this time. Ignoring the accusation makes you look rather guilty. Did you print and or sign this will yourself?'

Morgan-Bryant touched his client lightly on the arm, a subtle signal to shut up. 'What reasons do you have for questioning the document's provenance?'

'It's damaged from excessive folding. It has had coffee spilled upon it.'

'That isn't in the slightest bit suspicious. My client has already stipulated that he received the document in that condition. If anything, it goes to show that the decision to store the will at his residence was the right decision.'

'The witnesses then. You know them, do you not?' Morton asked.

'I do,' Kal said.

'Are you close?'

'I know them socially, through Ellis. I'm not on first name terms with either.'

'Names. Glad you brought that up. One of your witnesses is, according to the will, Lord Culloden. Doesn't that strike you as odd?'

'Why would it?'

'It's not his name.'

Kal's lip twitched. 'It's what I've always known him as.'

'Indeed. But I think Aleksander Barchester would probably sign a legal document in his real name, wouldn't he?'

'Kal, don't answer that,' Morgan Bryant said quickly. 'What are you getting at, Mr Morton?'

'I think your client signed the name.'

'I did not,' Kal said, but nobody in the room believed him. He stared at the table, afraid to make eye contact.

'Perhaps we could simply call Mr Barchester to verify his signature if there is a problem here?' Morgan-Bryant suggested.

'You're also Mr Barchester's lawyer, aren't you? Very convenient.'

'Just what are you implying, Morton?'

'It strikes me as awfully coincidental, that's all.'

'You'd best watch your tone, Mr Morton. I am a respected solicitor-advocate, and I will not stand for slander.'

The two stared in silence for a moment. Morton shrugged and took a sip of coffee. 'Besides, it's not just Mr Barchester. Did you forge Mr Malone's signature?'

'I did not,' Kal said again. He continued to stare at the table.

'Then perhaps you could explain why you visited Mr Malone in jail and tried to pass him money?'

'That's perfectly easy to explain. My client is friends with Mr Malone.

He knows how tough it is in prison. If you don't have money to buy basic necessities from the commissary then it is even tougher.'

'It wasn't a bribe then?'

'No.'

'You do seem to have an answer for everything. The third and final signature then. Did you forge that, Mr Fielder?'

'No.'

'You didn't use an autopen machine to place Ellis' signature at the bottom of the document?'

'No.'

'And you didn't prepare the will on your laptop?'

'Mr Morton, you seem to be badgering my client. For the record he has clearly said that he did not prepare, print, sign or otherwise have a hand in the creation of that document.'

'Did you own a laptop?'

'Yes.'

'Did you dispose of that laptop recently?'

'Yes,' Kal mumbled.

'To hide your forgery?'

'Mr Morton. This is getting very repetitive. If you think you have any sort of evidence, put it on the table and we'll explain it as best we can.'

'Your client is in possession of a will prepared without the assistance of a lawyer. I believe that will was printed on your client's old laptop, which he has now conveniently disposed of.'

'She used hers.' Kal said, his voice strengthening with renewed confidence.

'Ellis used her laptop? The pink one studded with diamante stones?'

'Yes.'

'No, she didn't. Our techs have examined that laptop thoroughly. The will was not prepared on her laptop.'

'Does it matter where the will was prepared? It could have been printed at a library. You have nothing to connect that will and my client.'

'Because he destroyed the evidence!' Morton said.

'You seem to be getting awfully close to slander again, Mr Morton.'

'She didn't make the will. It was signed by a convicted criminal and an impostor—'

Morgan-Bryant cut him off. 'Civil matters. The validity of signatures is for a probate court to determine. I'm sure my client will be able to produce the witnesses in question to validate those signatures.'

'—that you bribed, threatened or cajoled into hiding the truth. You hid key evidence.'

'Eli wanted me to have the money. She hated Brianna, and Brianna hated her. I'm not a criminal, Detective Morton. I just want to honour my dead fiancée's wishes.' Kal spoke forcefully, his eyes shining. For the first time in the interview, Morton believed him.

'Eli hated Brianna? Why?'

'They fell out when her parents died. They were wealthy, very wealthy. Eli was just beginning to come into her own as an artist. She'd just moved to Richmond. We'd been together for about a year. This was before her fall from grace.'

'You mean the drugs?'

'Yes. That all started when her parents died. A coping mechanism, I suppose. It wasn't her first time. She'd experimented as a teenager, but she wasn't famous as a teenager. The pressure was immense. Much like now, we had journalists following our every move. The starlet photographer and Fulham's star forward. We didn't ask for the attention, but we got it.'

Becoming a footballer isn't asking for attention? Morton thought.

'Her parents left behind a great deal of money,' Kal said. 'The girls had every privilege growing up. I suppose you need to if you want to pay for a drug habit.'

'Didn't Ellis fall out with her parents over that?'

'Sort of. They weren't best pleased, but really their disappointment was with her life choices. She turned down Cambridge for her art. It was risky. She could have had a comfortable professional life, but she gambled everything. It paid off. Her dad had begun to come to terms with it. They didn't see each other much, but the relationship was on the mend.'

'And then what happened?'

'They died. That one fateful December night their car went into the river. That was five years ago.'

'Wouldn't that have brought the sisters together?'

'Perhaps it should have, but for the money. Her parents left everything to charity. Their family home went to the National Trust. Their money went to charities for cats, dogs and the rainforest. All the girls got were their parents' personal belongings. Eli got her mum's jewellery. Brianna got the antiques.'

'Was the jewellery worth much?'

'Not really. Her parents were a real rags-to-riches story. Eli got the jewellery, which was sentimental. Brianna got more financially.'

'But she still wasn't happy with that?'

'No. She wasn't. She wanted more. She wanted to challenge the will. She even went to a lawyer about it. But Eli dissuaded her in the end. She agreed to help support Brianna financially.'

That would explain the monthly bank transfer. 'And did she?'

'For the most part. After the press ravaged her reputation, work became harder to come by. My football career ended when I busted up my foot. We've had a couple of lean years. Eli's photography is all free-lance. One month, we've got plenty. The next, it's beans on toast for tea. But she always made sure Brianna was taken care of, even if that meant hardship for her.'

'That's an interesting story. It doesn't verify who signed the will. Do you seriously want me to believe she signed a valid will using an autopen?'

The lawyer jumped straight in. 'There's nothing wrong with an autopen. If it's good enough for the President of the United States to sign a bill into law using one, then it's certainly good enough to authenticate how someone wishes to dispose of their assets. And again, Mr Morton, you're straying into a civil dispute.'

'Last time I checked, Kallum Fielder was not the President of the United States. Mr Fielder, this is only going to get worse for you. Right now you've forged a document. If you attempt to probate that will then you will be committing fraud. If you come clean now, I will ask the prosecutor to recommend leniency.'

'No deal, Mr Morton. You don't have anything on my client.'

'I think a jury will see it differently. I wouldn't want to be in your shoes, Mr Fielder. Famous men attract a lot of attention in prison. You might think you're the big name on campus when you're in the news, but inside you won't feel so lucky.'

Morgan-Bryant shrugged. He'd heard it all a million times before. Prison was bad, yada yada yada. His client was far more emotional. His knuckles tightened into fists of rage, and he looked like he was ready to explode. But when he spoke, it was remarkably calm and not at all what Morton was expecting.

'How dare you, Mr Morton. You sit there all high and mighty, but threaten me with prison. You insinuate that I'll be raped by other inmates, as if it were just part of the punishment. You sicken me. If I were a woman, you'd never ever dare threaten me with rape as way of coercing a confession. What makes it less abhorrent when it's male-on-male? Do I deserve it? Is that what you're saying? Our laws prohibit cruel and unusual punishment, don't they? No, Mr Morton, I will not give you the satisfaction of crumbling under such a threat. Get out of my sight. I have nothing more to say.'

Morton sat there, stunned. Kallum Fielder was not your typical ex-footballer.

Chapter 35: Thicker Than Water

THURSDAY APRIL 17TH – 20:00

Sarah brought coffee in to Morton at eight o'clock. He blearily took the mug, then excavated a space for it in the pile of paperwork which had become a mountain atop the dining table.

'Busy day?' Sarah asked. She slipped an arm around her husband's neck.

'You have no idea.' Morton continued shuffling through papers.

'Tell me about it.'

'My new Detective Sergeant, Mayberry, is causing me all kinds of headaches. The poor sod had a stroke a few years back and suffers from a speech disorder. He knows what he wants to say, but he ends up saying something different. I had him execute a search warrant this week. He called it a "findy-windy thing". Can you imagine it? Defence counsel is making a mountain out of a molehill and have filed a formal complaint.'

'Are you going to have to fire him?'

'I wish it was that easy. He's engaged to the Superintendent's daughter. Mayberry would have to do something extreme to get himself fired. But if he does, you can bet your bottom dollar that it'll be me that catches the flack for it.'

'What are you going to do about it?'

'I don't know. Yet. Take a look at his personnel file.' Morton handed over a thick file. It contained all of Mayberry's police test scores.

Sarah rifled through the file. 'Wow.'

'100% in numerical reasoning. 100% in verbal reasoning too – before his stroke of course. He even aced the written exercises. He clearly isn't stupid. But now he's a liability.'

'It sounds frustrating,' Sarah said.

'It is. Not nearly so frustrating as my case though. I've got a killer in the house at two o'clock in the morning, but every one of my suspects had either left well before then or has an alibi.'

'Then someone has to have returned, or the alibis are fake.'

'That was my thinking too,' Morton said. 'I'm so sorry. I've just realised we've been talking about work all evening. How was your day? Did you have lunch with Nick?'

'I did indeed. Your son says hello, and can he borrow a grand for a post-graduation blowout?'

'Hah. He wishes. What did you say?' Morton asked.

'I said he could have a grand towards doing a postgraduate degree instead.'

'Our money is as safe as houses then.'

'I don't know about that. If being a student for another year gets him a stay of execution on finding a real job, he'll jump at it in a heartbeat.'

'I guess we'll just have to hope no university is daft enough to let him in.'

'I saw Steven today too.'

Morton's expression darkened. His older son hadn't spoken to him voluntarily in almost a year. He'd barely had a text message from him despite attempts to reconcile.

'He's moving to Dubai, for six months.'

'Why on earth would he move to Dubai?' Morton asked, though privately he wondered what difference it would really make to their relationship.

'Why don't you ask him?'

'Maybe. Ask me again when this case is over.'

'Don't worry, I will. It's about time you two made up.'

Chapter 36: Got Your Back

Morton summoned a very nervous DS Mayberry to his office first thing the next morning. Morton felt like the living dead despite copious quantities of caffeine. He hadn't slept well at all. It seemed almost impossible to find a way to work with the younger officer without either of them ending up out on the street.

He was tempted to simply fire Mayberry. He'd risk the wrath of the Superintendent and Human Resources, and possibly even a lawsuit for discrimination, but it would put things back to normal.

That wouldn't be fair. Poor Mayberry didn't ask to have a stroke.

But then again, Morton didn't ask to have poor Mayberry join the team either. The other option was to keep him away from any suspects, which seemed less cruel but would still hamper Mayberry's career. What good is a policeman who can't go near a criminal?

His mind kept flicking back and forth. When Mayberry knocked on the door, Morton called out for him to come in.

'You a-asked to see me, s-sir?' Mayberry stuttered.

'I did. Mayberry, we have a problem. There's been a complaint made,' Morton began, being exceptionally careful to keep his language neutral and non-accusatory.

'By w-who, sir?'

'Mr Fielder's lawyer. He alleges misconduct when we searched his client's home. He claims that we tried to execute, and I'm quoting him exactly here, a 'findy-windy thing'. Did we?'

Mayberry's began to tear up, and he hung his head. 'Y-yes, sir.'

'I'm sure you can see my dilemma here. We can't risk recurrence here. We didn't seize anything of real value under this search warrant, so this time it's almost a case of no harm, no foul. But imagine if we had seized critical evidence. Poor Kieran would have had to spend many hours to try and fend off defence counsel. Not to mention the poor publicity.'

'Am I t-toasted?' Mayberry asked.

Morton stared at him for a full minute. When he spoke, he chose his words carefully. 'I will not be firing you for this. However, we need to find a way to make this work before it gets us both fired. Is there anything that helps with finding the right word?'

'Writing.'

'Then write. We don't mind it if you need to take a little time when you speak. We're a team here. But I also think it is best if we minimise your contact with suspects. Is that a fair assessment?'

Mayberry nodded.

'Then for now, I'd like you to do some investigative work for me. I need you to run down CCTV for me to find any hint of our suspects. At Richmond Station. Near the homes of suspects. Even night-buses in the area. I want no stone left unturned. Got it?'

'Yes.'

'And then I want you to sit in the Incident Room and draw a timeline of the night of the party. I want arrival and departure times. I want everything noted in both British Summer Time and Greenwich Mean Time. Colour-code it. Add pictures. I want a crystal clear display showing what our suspects were doing, when and where they were when they did it,' Morton said. It was make-work really but it ought to keep Mayberry occupied for a day or two.

'T-thanks, boss,' Mayberry said.

Morton rose, and offered a handshake to his junior officer. Mayberry looked at Morton's hand, but didn't take it.

Instead, he hugged him.

Chapter 37: Bad Blood

Mayberry's timeline display was beginning to come together by the time Morton assembled the team for their morning briefing. It was, by any standard, a distinctly masculine team. All of the senior officers were men. It hadn't always been that way.

Perhaps it's time to give some serious thought to bringing Ashley Rafferty on board. She was certainly competent enough, and she'd keep Ayala on his toes. But not now. It was too soon.

Morton pushed thoughts of team members past and present from his mind. He needed a clear head. From the corner of his eye, Morton saw Stuart Purcell shuffle into the room. The Chief Scene of Crime Officer lurked by the door.

'Stuart. How kind of you to join us. We saved you a seat.'

Morton waited for Purcell to waddle awkwardly towards the end of the conference table where there was an empty seat, and then began his briefing.

'Gentlemen. We're at a crossroads in our investigation. We began with five suspects who could plausibly have killed our victim. I think we can rule out only one. It seems highly unlikely that Aleksander Barchester, also known as Lord Culloden, could have been the killer. We have CCTV of him running along the high street towards Richmond Park and the corresponding return journey the next morning. We know our victim was dead by the time he returned. Does anyone disagree?' Morton looked around the room. Stuart Purcell looked blankly at him.

Morton noticed that the biscuit tin had mysteriously migrated from the side table to Purcell's end of the conference table.

Ayala put on a brave face. He always did when he was about to play devil's advocate in the full knowledge that Morton would ridicule him for it.

'What if–'

'He left, came back, left again, came back again but didn't bothered to dress in the interim?'

'Err, yeah. Pretty much. I know it's left field but picture this – the streaking is an attempt to set up his alibi. He could easily have returned via the back streets to commit murder. He was gone in the small hours of the night. Nobody would have seen him.'

'It's not impossible,' Morton conceded.

Ayala looked relieved.

'But it's not remotely likely either. If Maria's recall is correct, that means he would have had to voluntarily out himself as having a micropenis. It would have meant voluntarily sleeping in the buff in Richmond Park, and it gets seriously windy there at night. It would have meant committing one crime, and risking the embarrassment of being ridiculed in the press, just to hide another. The man is the CEO of a major company. You think Wiles like this publicity?'

'No, but–'

'But what? Tell me then: just what did Aleksander Barchester have to gain from killing her?'

'Maybe she was defaulting on the money she owed him?'

'So then he'd repossess the house. Barchester isn't short of cash. His bank account is flush. He hired one of the priciest lawyers in London. The victim died on her birthday. That can't be a coincidence. Everything about this murder screams that it's personal.'

'Maybe she knew about his fraud,' Ayala said.

'You think he told her on the night of her birthday? As far as we know, he didn't even speak to her that night. No. I'm not buying it. He was gone well before she died, a little after midnight by all accounts. Multiple witnesses saw him go. They were there for almost an hour after he went. We've got him on CCTV a couple of hours later coming back from the Park. There just wasn't enough time for him to get in, kill her and get out. If he wanted Ellis dead, he'd have many better opportunities at his disposal. Let's not forget that he tried calling her in New York. Angry calls. Emails. He left voice messages for her.'

Purcell raised a pudgy hand.

'Yes?' Morton said,

'He's not committing fraud. He really is the son of Lord Culloden. He's a bastard, but that's the least of his worries,' Purcell said.

'DNA came back positive? Good work. Let the real Lord Culloden know, and thank him for his assistance for me. Any other objections or can we rule Aleksander Barchester out?'

No objections were made, and Mayberry ceremonially picked up a red pen with which to strike out Aleksander Barchester's name on the white board.

'Kallum Fielder. Where are we?' Morton asked.

'He's on CCTV almost home at forty-two minutes past midnight, so he probably left less than ten minutes after midnight,' Ayala said. 'He was visibly drunk on the CCTV footage, and he was stumbling slowly. If he made it home for just after one then the clocks would have changed just as he got home. He got into work late that day, but only ten minutes late as he parked at ten past five in the morning. Thirteen miles in traffic is about an hour so he left just after four, suited and booted ready for work.'

'That gives a two-hour window in which he was either asleep or heading back to Edgecombe Lodge to murder the girlfriend we know he argued with. Let's keep holding him on the fraud for the moment. To my mind, he's unlikely to have made it back in that state with that sort of timeframe. If it took him an hour to stumble home then he'd have needed to sober up remarkably quickly to be a viable suspect. Keep looking for any sign of a return journey on CCTV between Twickenham and Richmond. If you don't find any, we'll rule him out. Next.'

Ayala volunteered again. 'Gabriella and Paddy alibi each other. At no point were either of them alone in the house–'

'As far as we know,' Morton said.

'We've got them leaving at about one. They're on CCTV by Richmond Station at 02:17 British Summer Time. We can clearly see them getting in a cab. I ran the plates, found the cabbie and called him. His GPS records show he took them back to the Barbican, though he doesn't remember them in particular.'

'Hmm,' Morton mused.

'What are you thinking, boss?'

'Two options. They both did it. Not impossible. Malone could probably be persuaded by a woman as beautiful as Gabby, but he was drinking heavily. We've got nothing to suggest they could have done it together.'

'Or?'

'Or they split up. Unless we can break their mutual alibis, we're going to have to strike them for now. Mayberry, would you mind putting an orange X next to them on the board? Thanks,' Morton said.

'Then we're only left with Brianna. She's the next of kin. If we're right about the probate fraud, and it looks like we are, then she's got three million reasons to want her sister dead. We know there was bad blood there.'

'The only problem is a complete lack of evidence. She left incredibly early. There's nothing to suggest she came back. Richmond is a long way from Southwark. After the tubes closed, it would have been pretty awkward getting back without taking a cab. Circulate her photo at the taxi rank by Richmond Station. See if any of the locals picked her up that night.'

'Where does that leave us, boss?'

'It leaves us up a creek without a paddle, that's where it leaves us. Find me something, anything. We need to close this as soon as humanly possible. There's an extra week's leave on the table for anyone who can break the case.'

The team rose as if to go about their business, but then Purcell raised a pudgy hand.

'Uh, chief?' Purcell said.

The team, as one, sank bank into their seats.

'What?'

'I still need comparators. You want your DNA evidence, I'll need something to compare it to.'

'Who are we waiting on?'

'I've got Paddy, Kal and Barchester from their arrests. But the girls are a blank, and we've got far too many samples on-site to sift through without reference samples.'

'What've you found so far?'

'Nothing. Nothing you don't already know, anyway. The towel confirms Barchester's story. Kal's DNA is all over the en-suite master bedroom. Beyond that, nothing incriminating.'

Morton turned to his second-in-command. 'Ayala, I want you to take point on this. Work with Kieran to compel DNA from them if you have to. But get it done today. Anything else, gents? No? Get to work.'

Chapter 38: Front and Centre

Kallum Fielder was trending all over the Internet after the Wednesday morning tabloids went out. Most of them ran him as their lead story, complete with a still of his arrest extracted from the morning footage of *Wake Up Britain!*

No doubt the story was selling papers up and down the country. A former football star, the man whom most Brits woke up to every morning, and a criminal too. It was an irresistible combination for any tabloid journalist.

Most celebrity crime involved the celebrity as the victim. There were countless stories of starlets being stalked by members of the public. But for one of the nation's most recognisable to be hauled off-screen live on breakfast television was a real spectacle.

A byline for *The Impartial*, the work of Gifford Byrnes, really stuck the knife in. They ran a six-page spread connecting the dots between Kal's arrest and the death of Ellis DeLange. They had a photograph of him in a casino, taken years before when he had been out with the lads from Fulham, and theorised that Kal was yet another gambling addict who would do anything for one more high.

They stopped short of actually labelling Kal the killer, but only just. The newspapers used euphemisms like 'Wanted in connection with the death of' in order to suggest it without crossing the line into libel.

The only person glad of the coverage was Aleksander Barchester. His Thursday morning was the best of his life.

He had been summoned to the main house by Lord Culloden for a late breakfast, something which had never happened before. On his arrival, the valet had shown him through to the dining hall, a resplendent relic of Victoriana with hanging chandeliers and brass candlestick holders strewn along an old oak table.

The men had eaten quietly, making nothing but small talk. The events of the recent past were buried, if only for a little while. Once they had finished their Omelettes Arnold Bennett, and a steaming pot of Earl Grey had been brewed, the conversation turned towards the reason for his summons.

'Aleksander, I didn't invite you up here just for breakfast,' Lord Culloden began. He watched his son carefully, studying every wrinkle and crease in his face. The similarities between the men seemed to have grown starker in the day or so since Culloden had found out that he had a son.

'I surmised as much. Why am I here?' Aleksander asked.

'There's no easy way to say this, but I'm your father.'

'I know,' Aleksander said simply. He'd known for a long time.

'You… you knew? How?'

'Mother told me, before she passed. I've wanted to ask you for the longest time.'

'I wish you'd said something sooner. I didn't know. I suspected. But I only found out for sure this week. I asked the police to test my DNA. They called last night with the news. Is there anything you wanted to ask me?'

Aleksander stared straight at his father, unblinking. There was one question, the burning question, the question which had been on his mind for many years. 'Did you love my mother?' he asked.

Culloden nodded. 'Yes, I did. And I'm sorry I let things end as I did. Can you ever forgive me?'

'I don't know. But I'd like to try.'

Chapter 39: If at First

Morton had a *Eureka!* moment during his lunch break. He had nipped out for a walk along the Thames, one of his favourite ways to think about the world. He found himself a bench in Victoria Tower Gardens with a view across the Thames, and watched as boats glided by on the water.

A few tourists, and more than a few office workers, meandered by. Many glanced up admiringly at the southern aspect of the Palace of Westminster.

Eventually, a woman approached and asked if she could sit on the other side of the bench. Morton obliged and went back to admiring the view. He closed his eyes and felt the sunshine, dappled by the trees hanging overhead, fall upon his brow.

When he opened his eyes, the woman was watching him. She had a notebook in hand, notes scribbled throughout it.

'Can I help you?' he asked.

'You're a cop, aren't you?' she said. 'You've got the same expression my father had, as if the weight of the world is on your shoulders.'

'Some days it feels like it is. But I'm sure Atlas had it much worse off. The biggest stress in my life is knowing something but not being able to prove it.'

'Don't you guys have DNA or fingerprints to do most of the work for you?'

'I wish. Sometimes there aren't any fingerprints–' Morton paused.

Sometimes there weren't any fingerprints. He stood straight up, almost knocking the notebook from the woman's hands.

'I'm sorry. I've got to run.'

He found Purcell in the Incident Room. 'Stuart!'

'Yes, Chief?'

'The autopen. You printed it when you searched the house.'

'Yes, boss. Just the victim's fingerprints.'

'Do it again,' Morton ordered.

Purcell held up his hands defensively. 'Hey, I did it right the first time. There's no need to do it all over again.'

'I'm not accusing you of anything. Just do it again.'

Purcell didn't look happy, but he fetched the autopen and his kit and began to dust.

'Nothing.' Purcell frowned. 'How can there be no prints on it?'

'He wiped it. We cleared the scene for him to go back – and Kal wiped it down after he used it. But we'd already printed it. He took the victim's prints off as well as his own. It was clean when we picked it up earlier this week as evidence of fraud. Stuart, I could kiss you!' Morton bounced on the spot like an excited schoolboy. There was nothing like the adrenaline high of a breakthrough.

'Please don't kiss me,' Purcell whimpered.

'We've got him. We've finally got him.'

'So you've got an autopen machine which has no fingerprints on it. Is cleaning a crime now?' Elliot Morgan-Bryant asked, as cocky as ever. His client sat next to him silence, his gaze flicking between his lawyer and Morton as if he were watching a game of tennis.

'It looks like obstruction of justice to me. It was the only thing wiped down. If I were cleaning up, I'd have probably dealt with the empty pizza boxes and beer bottles before dusting. It's pretty suspicious, when combined with your client's disposal of his old laptop,' Morton said.

'Is my client being charged?'

'Yes. Two counts of obstruction, one of attempted fraud, and one of forgery,' Morton said. He'd discussed the charge sheet with Kieran earlier in the day, and the tactic was simple: throw the book at him, and then offer to reduce the charges back down for a guilty plea.

'He didn't even probate the will.'

'Come off it. He attempted to obtain a medical death certificate to begin the process.'

'That is, as we lawyers like to say, not more than merely preparatory,' Morgan-Bryant said.

Morton gave the lawyer a tight-lipped smile. The battle lines had been drawn.

'The prosecutor disagrees. However, in the interests of expediency and seeing to it that the punishment fits the crime, he might see the light in dropping the inchoate offence in return for a guilty plea on the other charges.'

'No chance. If that were to become a guilty plea on forgery only, then my client and I might have something to discuss.'

'I'll have to speak to the CPS about that. Perhaps you'd like the room to talk to your client while I give him a ring?' Morton offered.

"No need,' Kal said. He turned to his lawyer, cupped his hands like a funnel and whispered in the lawyer's ear. They exchanged meaningful glances.

'And you'll drop any possible investigation into Messrs Barchester and Malone as they pertain to the will?' the lawyer asked.

Morton considered the request. Malone was already in jail, and with his history of dealing he was already headed for a life comprised of brief periods of freedom interspersed with progressively longer periods in jail, and an extra charge with little evidence would serve little purpose. Culloden would soon be joining him inside once his indecent exposure charges progressed to a trial.

'I'm not interested in them. They didn't forge anything,' Morton said.

'I'll take the deal,' Kal said.

'I'll make the call now then. One more thing.' Morton paused the tape recording. 'You made a complaint against one of my officers. I want it dropped, immediately.'

Elliot Morgan-Bryant's eyes sparkled. 'I see we're not so different after all, Mr Morton. You have yourself a deal.'

Chapter 40: Legal Extortion

Kieran quickly rubber-stamped Morton's informal deal with Morgan-Bryant, but he hadn't told Morton that yet. It was another easy win to his credit, saved the taxpayer the cost of a prosecution which was still somewhat circumstantial, and it landed Morton in his debt. To make the most of that debt, he decided to let Morton think the decision was still up in the air. They met in Morton's office where Kieran found Morton hunched over his laptop, with Mayberry perched at the end of the desk rifling through paperwork.

Morton looked up as Kieran entered. 'Afternoon. Court finished already?'

'Yep. No judge wants to finish too late on a Friday.'

'Nor me. To what do I owe the pleasure?'

'Do you still think Kallum Fielder is a viable suspect in the murder of Ellis DeLange?' Kieran asked. Personally, Kieran felt that Morgan-Bryant was too smart to plead out on the lesser charge if there was still a serious case for murder on the table.

'We don't think so,' Morton said.

'He didn't have t-time,' Mayberry stuttered. He pointed to his neatly drawn timeline that spanned an entire whiteboard.

'Mayberry is right. Once the clock change is accounted for, Kal got home after two o'clock in the morning. He appeared dishevelled and drunk on the CCTV footage we recovered of him walking home. He parked up in Portland Place at five past five, and was on-set ten minutes later.'

'How far is that?' Kieran asked.

'Thirteen miles, about an hour in light traffic at that time of the morning,' Morton said.

'And had he changed by then?'

Morton shrugged. Kal's attire was the least of his worries.

'Y-yes,' Mayberry said. 'On the way b-back from the p-party, he had on a t-t-shirt. H-he was wearing a penguin.' Mayberry furrowed his brow in consternation, and pulled out a moleskin notebook. He began writing and then corrected himself. 'S-suit.'

'Right. Then we've got a two-hour window for a clearly drunk guy to sober up, go back to Richmond from Twickenham, kill his girlfriend, return to Twickenham, put on a suit and get to work. How long did he take going from Richmond to Twickenham when he stumbled home?'

'About three quarters of an hour,' Morton said.

'So if he walked at the same rate then we've got about half an hour maximum for him to have committed murder,' Kieran said.

'It's less than that. We know that he got home at two or thereabouts. If he doubled back immediately, he'd have needed to take a longer route to avoid being on the CCTV on the way back, which means he'd have needed more than forty-five minutes.'

'Fine. Let's say he took an hour. Fifteen minutes is still enough to kill and run.'

'The heating at Edgecombe Lodge went off at three. That meant the house was empty at that point – and the victim's body had begun to cool enough not to register when the automatic thermostat checked for heat signatures. He'd have got back outside that window, unless he sobered up and ran, which it doesn't look like he was in any condition to do.'

'Then he's got either a very slim window or he's out. I don't like this. It's enough for any defence counsel to put doubt into the jury's mind.'

'Sorry, Kieran, but that's not our problem. We can only present you the facts as we find them. Maintaining your conviction rate is your own concern.'

Kieran paused to fiddle with his blackberry, then sighed. 'You just want me to approve your deal with Morgan-Bryant.'

'Damn right I do,' Morton said. 'We've got him on the substantive charge which, to my mind, is much better than our gambling on throwing everything at him. We've talked about this.'

'We did, but funnily enough you didn't mention coercing defence counsel into dropping a complaint against your team.' Kieran jabbed a finger at Mayberry.

'Leave him out of his. Are you going to approve this or not?' Morton demanded.

'I want something in return. I hear you've got FA Cup tickets for this weekend.'

'No! You git. You know how hard it is to get them.'

'That would be why they're worth something. Do we have a deal?'

'Fine. You know you're why I hate lawyers, don't you? And this is totally unethical of you.'

'Hah. It's not a legally binding deal. This isn't the USA. I'm simply choosing not to pursue a reckless criminal charge, which you'd know I already decided to do three minutes ago if you'd checked your email.'

Morton swore. 'You sent me an email after this meeting started, but before you extorted me? That is evil.'

'Yes, it is. Make sure they're on my desk by the close of business, please.'

Chapter 41: Video

Mayberry proved to be particularly adept at reviewing CCTV footage. After learning what Morton had done on his behalf, he had forgone Friday night drinks with the rest of the team and stayed late to review all of the footage the team had accumulated over the past week.

Morton found him the next morning, sleeping in the Incident Room. The diagram of the timeline had been finished with all the suspects and their movements plotted neatly.

Five suspects. Five timelines. Two had already been discounted. Kal and Culloden were gone at midnight or shortly thereafter, never to return.

That left the sister, the best friend and the drug dealer. The sister had the most obvious motive. Without a valid will, Ellis died intestate, which left Brianna with everything.

Ever since he had laid eyes upon Edgecombe Lodge, Morton's gut had been telling him that money had to be involved somewhere. But Ellis' murder felt personal too. The killer waited for her thirtieth birthday party, and killed her in her own home.

No murder weapon had been found. If it were from the house, there was no sign of something missing. If it were brought in from outside, then the kill was premeditated.

Then there was the timing. All the witnesses, and the victim, had been drinking and doing drugs. If ever there were a more lax set of witnesses to be found, Morton had yet to meet them. It didn't help that the clock change threw off the timeline and confused the already-unreliable witnesses.

Morton scanned the timeline. Kal was gone by about midnight, passing CCTV at 00:42, and getting in at just gone two once the clock change had been accounted for. A great red X had been placed next to Kal's mugshot.

Culloden was out too. He left within minutes of Kal, and didn't return until morning, when he collected his clothes. Ayala's nudity-as-reasonable doubt theory was pie in the sky. Morton snatched up the red pen from the table, being careful not to wake Mayberry as he did so, and placed an X next to Culloden. Morton smiled. Mayberry had placed a Post-it note over the CCTV printout of Culloden as a modesty guard.

Brianna was the obvious suspect. She had access to pentobarbital from her work as a veterinary assistant. She had money troubles. According to Kal, she hated Ellis too. Morton placed a question mark next to her. While she had the motive, she didn't have the opportunity.

'Morning, b-boss,' Mayberry said, stirring from his slumber. 'What time is it?'

'Just gone nine. Were you here all night? Go home. It looks like you need to sleep.'

Mayberry shook himself like a dog, and waved off Morton's concern. 'I'm f-fine. Do you l-like my drawing?'

'I do. It's helpful having a visual aid. What do you think of Brianna as a suspect? I don't think she doubled back. She'd have needed three buses to do so. Did you find any images of her on night buses?'

Mayberry shook his head.

'Did any taxi drivers identify her?'

'No... b-but...' Mayberry turned away from Morton and booted up a laptop. 'L-look here.'

Morton moved over to the conference table and pulled up a chair. Mayberry had a video open showing the platforms at Richmond Station on the night of the murder. Brianna Jackson was clearly visible getting on the district line heading east on a train bound for Upminster. Morton watched the train pull away. The video was time stamped for 23:45.

'What route did she take?' Morton asked.

'To get to Southwark? D-d-d… Green line to Westminster.'

'Right – so district line to Westminster and then change for the Jubilee Line. How long did that take?'

'I d-don't know. Forty-five minutes?'

'I don't need guesses, man. Get me the CCTV for Southwark.'

'I've asked for it. Not got it y-yet.'

'Then check the Oyster records. We can do that remotely, right?'

Morton watched as Mayberry rewound the CCTV at Richmond, then queried Transport for London's database to get Brianna's Oyster card details. She'd entered the station at 23:42. He typed in a query asking the database to spit out the details of where she 'touched out' at the end of her journey.

ERROR: NO TOUCH-OUT was displayed on screen, which meant she'd been charged the full daily fare.

'How the hell did she manage that?'

'B-broken b-barrier?' Mayberry suggested. 'A place with n-no b-barrier?'

'There aren't any places on the district line without a barrier. She could have jumped it, I suppose, but why bother? Touching out would have meant a single journey rather than paying the maximum possible fare. Barring some unusual equipment failure we're left with two scenarios. She either tailgated someone, which would be pointless for the same reason there's no reason to jump a barrier, or she left the underground network somewhere else.'

'O-OK…' Mayberry replied, unsure what Morton wanted to hear.

'What other stations are there on the district line? Get me a map up,' Morton demanded.

Mayberry did so. Morton squinted at the screen. 'There. Kew Gardens. It's the only station really close to Richmond. A little over a mile. That's pretty easy to manage on foot. I'm guessing we can't remotely access their CCTV?'

'N-no, boss.'

'Send in a request. Actually, scratch that. We can see journeys from Kew that used Oyster cards, can't we?'

'Yes.'

'Then check journeys at Kew after 23:42. They locked up for the night not long after, so I can't imagine there's be a lot of footfall.'

'W-what am I l-looking f-for?' Mayberry asked.

'I want to know if anyone went through a barrier at Kew using a ticket, either paper or Oyster, for which there isn't a station of origin. If there is any ticket showing a check-out without a check-in then it could well be the other half of Brianna's journey.'

Mayberry tapped away in silence for a few minutes. Morton began to pace up and down impatiently. He kept muttering to himself: 'Taxi,

Number 53, District Line, Richmond, Kew.'

'Got it! One journey terminating at 23:48 that didn't have a first arm,' Mayberry said proudly.

'First leg. But well done! We've just put Brianna back in the frame.'

Mayberry beamed.

'Get the CCTV and confirm it. We need to be sure. How long will that take?'

'P-p-probably Monday.'

'Right. I guess we're not going to get much help over the weekend,' Morton said. He turned his attention back to Mayberry's timeline display.

'And that leaves us with only the lovebirds. We've got them on CCTV getting into a taxi at 02:17 British Summer Time. It takes fifteen to twenty minutes to get from Edgecombe Lodge to the station on foot. That puts them in the house until just before one o'clock. We know the central heating cut out at three, so the house was occupied after two... That's pretty tight. If they left at fifty-nine minutes past midnight then we've proved someone was in the house after them. If they left one minute later, two o'clock accounting for the clock change, then the central heating system could have been responding to them.'

'But boss, if the th-th-ther–'

'Thermostat?'

'If it u-uses warmth then couldn't the v-victim–'

'Have triggered it? Yes, you're right. There's a margin for error there. If they killed her together at ten to the hour then perhaps her residual body heat could have keep the bloody heating on. But that requires two murderers, which seems unlikely.'

'B-but what if they s-split up?'

'They were together at Richmond Station.... But then they did conveniently put themselves in front of the CCTV.'

'B-before then.'

'At the house? We've no indication anyone left during the party. But what if they weren't together, even for a few minutes? Could someone have committed murder while the other was outside smoking a cigarette? I suppose so. If they left, as Paddy said before, after Culloden went running out... then we've got the better part of an hour unaccounted for. Fancy a trip to HMP Pentonville?'

'Y-yes, sir!'

'Good. But don't say anything. If you've got a question during the interview, for God's sake write it down.'

Chapter 42: Then I Got High

Saturdays were rarely the best time to question witnesses. Witnesses were prone to travelling around when they weren't working, and finding a witness in a crowded shopping street like Oxford Circus was akin to looking for an innocent man in HMP Pentonville.

But Paddy was still in jail. He had no right to refuse a visitor, as long as Morton kept the warden onside.

At the lockers with Mayberry, Morton checked his mobile. One new message. He thumbed the slider on the screen to unlock it, and the message pinged up.

'What a git.'

'W-who is it?'

'Kieran. He's sent me a picture of him inside the stadium. I'm going to have to get him back for this.' Morton turned the phone off, put it in the locker and put a pound in the locking mechanism. It was the same pound he'd liberated from Ayala on their last visit.

They quickly made their way through to the interview room to find Patrick Malone waiting for them. Paddy looked pale, almost dishevelled. His fingernails were worn down to the quick, and his hair was tousled and unkempt.

'Paddy, Paddy, Paddy. Prison doesn't suit you at all,' Morton said.

'It ain't prison. It's my new celly. The freak keeps doing *it*, all day long.'

Morton didn't want to ask what *it* was, though he had a fair guess. 'Then I expect you'd appreciate it if someone had a word with the

Governor about moving you.'

'What's the catch?'

'You answer my questions. Honestly. And you agree to testify to those answers in court should I need it.'

'Sod off. You'll have to do better than that. You shades are all the same. You think I'm an eejit.'

'Got something to hide?'

Paddy placed an elbow on the table and leant on it. 'Jaysus, what do you think? I'm a drug dealer. No sir, I don't have nothing to hide.'

'No need for sarcasm,' Morton said. 'I'm not interested in you, nor is the prosecutor. You're a small fry. Assuming you haven't killed anyone.'

'No, I bleeding haven't.'

'But you did take money from Kallum Fielder.'

'I would have,' Paddy said bitterly. 'If the guards hadn't stopped him handing it over. You don't know what it's like in here. One slip, one show of weakness… It don't end well.'

'You've only got three more weeks. You could always go into solitary.'

'Three weeks in the hole? I'd go mad. I'll take my chances.'

'Then talk to me. I'll get you moved. Besides, Kal already cut a deal. We know he forged Ellis' will, and paid you to say you signed it.'

'I ain't been paid nothing.'

'Right. Well, I don't care about that. But I do want to know what you did after Kal left the party. We know he left at midnight. Barchester fled at almost the same time. You didn't leave for an hour after that. Why?'

'We did leave,' Paddy said.

'We've got you on CCTV. And that's the last lie that I'll forgive. Another one, and I'll have you charged with conspiracy to commit probate fraud.'

'Fine. We stayed. We had a few drinks. So what?'

'Then why lie about it?'

'I don't know. I was drunk. Look, we had a few drinks while we played gin rummy. She won. Happy now?'

Morton flashed back to his meeting with Gabriella Curzon in Fitzrovia. 'That's exactly what she said.'

'See. Told you I wasn't lying.'

'No. That's exactly what she said, word for word.'

Paddy paled noticeably.

'You've prepared this. You split up that night, didn't you?'

'No. I just comforted her, and we played some cards, alright?'

'Which is it? If she was distraught and in tears, why would you play gin rummy? Paddy, you're digging yourself into a very deep hole. If you were apart, even for a cigarette break, then I need to know about it. Otherwise you could be facing accessory to murder charges.'

'Murder? You think Gabby killed Ellis? No way. They were tight.'

Morton smiled. If he had to defend their relationship, then it was obvious he knew that Gabby had the physical opportunity to commit murder. 'So you did split up. How long for?'

'Half an hour, but that's it.'

'Where'd you go?'

'No comment.'

'Right. Something illegal then. If it's unconnected to Ellis' death then I'll see to it that you get blanket immunity.'

'All charges? I walk out of here a free man?'

'All charges,' Morton confirmed. 'Once the prosecutor sorts the paperwork, you're a free man – unless you screw up again.'

'I won't,' Paddy promised. 'I went to see a client.'

'You were dealing?'

'Yes.'

'Where?'

'Just around the corner. Look, I was gone for half an hour at most. I got the text at twenty-five past midnight. I took the drugs around, got paid and came back.'

'What time exactly did you get back?'

'How would I know? Maybe five to one.'

Brilliant, thought Morton. Maybe it could have been five to the hour or it could be five past. Never before had such a tiny amount of time seemed so important.

'Then what?'

'I came back. Gabby was outside smoking a ciggie, waiting for me. We went into town to find a cab and went back to my place. There was no way I could have been gone long enough for Gabby to be involved.'

'She was outside the house? At one?'

'It's not like I checked my watch, but yeah, about then.'

'How can you be sure? You said you'd been drinking all night.'

'I guess I can't. But the tube was closed so I can't have been far out. I know we paid the night rate in the taxi too. That cost a bleeding fortune.'

'But you were flush from selling drugs, weren't you?'

'You obviously don't smoke. Fifty quid for a quarter of an ounce doesn't even cover a taxi trip from Richmond to my place.'

Don't smoke.

The words resounded in Morton's head. Why were they important?

'Paddy... Does Gabby normally smoke?' Morton asked. He didn't recall the smell of cigarettes pervading Gabriella's flat, though that wasn't conclusive of anything.

'Only when she's stressed. But she'd just argued with Culloden, sorry, Barchester I mean, hadn't she?'

'Right.' Unless she was stressed because she'd just committed murder. 'Are we done here?'

Mayberry tapped Morton on the shoulder, then pointed at his note-pad upon which he'd scribbled *'Why did she go home with him?'*

Morton nodded his thanks to Mayberry, and continued his interrogation. 'You can go back to your cell in a minute. You said you took Gabby home. Did you sleep with her?'

Paddy rolled his eyes as if it were a stupid question. 'Why else would I take her home?'

'But if you were drunk, as you claim you were, then, well, wouldn't your performance have suffered?' Morton said.

'Oi! Don't you insult me like that.'

'I'm serious. This doesn't have to leave the room, but she's miles out of your league. Had you been together before?'

'I, err... well... no.'

'So your first time was on the night one of your oldest friends got murdered, and you didn't think that was strange?'

'Look, she was upset alright. But that party was deadly. We had loads of drinks. Maybe I was taking advantage—'

'From what I've been told, you drank far more than she did. Let's move on. What time did she leave in the morning? Did she stick around for breakfast?' Morton asked. He was trying to discern if it were anything more than a drunken fumble.

'I don't remember.'

'You don't remember,' Morton said. 'That's bloody convenient. I think you're playing games here, Paddy. Unless you want our little deal to be taken off the table, you need to man up and tell me the truth.'

'Fine. I didn't sleep with her. Or maybe I did. I don't know. I woke up the next morning and she was gone.'

'What was the last thing you remember?'

'Meeting her outside the house.'

'You don't remember going to the station?' Morton probed. If he couldn't remember it, it clearly wasn't a deliberate attempt to set up an alibi – at least, not on his part.

'No.'

'Then she could have gone at any point after getting into the taxi. It could even have dropped her off somewhere else, couldn't it?'

'I guess so.'

'I think we're done here. Let's go, Detective Mayberry. We need to find that taxi driver.'

And then there were two.

Chapter 43: Sleeping Beauty

Mayberry was oddly talkative on the way back from HMP Pentonville. Whether it was the use of his notepad to write down what he wanted to say before he said it, or that he was beginning to relax around Morton, he seemed to be less affected by his aphasia and much more willing to discuss the case.

'Depending on the exact timing of Paddy and Brianna's departure, we've got two windows. Window number one – the time Paddy was out of the house. Number two, after Paddy left,' Morton said.

'Is h-half an hour enough?'

'It might have been. We think Ellis was asleep at midnight, so for her to have been murdered in the half-hour window she must have woken up. Otherwise, how did she get down to the pool?'

'The k-killer could have carried her?'

'Both our suspects are women. Neither is particularly stocky. I know our victim is pretty small, but a dead body isn't exactly ergonomic. The coroner didn't report any scrapes or nicks that would have occurred if she'd been dragged.'

'B-but there were scrapes.'

'From the side of the pool, yes. But nothing directional to suggest dragging. It's much more likely that our victim was killed in the pool area. Let's say she woke up exactly when Paddy left–'

'What if he s-slammed the window?'

'The door,' Morton corrected automatically. 'Plausible. OK. Two minutes to come downstairs. Then either she got changed, or the killer swapped her into a bikini, presumably to make us think she drowned. That's another five minutes at least. Dressing a body is no small task. Let's assume she changed voluntarily.'

'OK.'

'Then we've got a window of about twenty-three minutes to commit murder and get out. Ellis died from a single blow to the head. She could have been gone in a minute.'

'So she didn't expect to d-die.'

It was true. She had to have been faced away from her killer. That made an argument followed by a murder unlikely, again suggesting pre-meditation.

'Right you are. Do we think Brianna could have returned in that window?'

'Y-yes. What if she came in through the k-kitchen?'

'Through the door that Barchester left unlocked? Or perhaps she has a key. They are sisters after all. It seems unlikely, though, that Brianna could have returned without Gabriella noticing it.'

'Unless she was outside s-smoking?'

'Did we find cigarettes outside? I'm guessing we didn't look. If she'd gone out and chain-smoked, she could have got through a couple, which might explain the timing. Or there's the second window after Paddy left. We know Brianna doubled back. Gabby could have too. Was the CCTV footage of the taxi high enough resolution to get a number plate from?'

'It's part h-hidden.'

'Then check the bit that is in frame against the list of authorised taxis. It can't be a very long list. I also still need you to get the footage from Kew Gardens. If I drop you at the Hub, do you think you could sweet talk British Transport Police into getting us the footage today? Bribe 'em if you have to.'

'O-OK, boss.'

'Excellent.'

'Morton, what the hell do you want?' The voice of Dr Larry Chiswick sounded less than pleased to have his Saturday afternoon interrupted.

'Is that cheering I can hear in the background, Larry?'

'Yes, it damn well is. You know this is an emergency number, don't you?'

'Hang on. Are you watching the match with Kieran? He took you on my ticket?'

'So what?'

'So since when have you two been close?'

'Are you forgetting that I'm a lawyer as well as a doctor? We lawyers tend to stick together.'

'Git.'

'What do you want, David? It's almost half-time, and I'm dying for the loo.'

'Our victim. Could a woman have carried her in your opinion?'

'Theoretically, yes. In this case, no. The evidence doesn't support that. Is that all?'

'One more thing.'

'Make it quick.'

'Our victim slept through most of the evening,' Morton said. 'Why? And what would it have taken to wake her?'

'Booze and drugs. Nembies are barbiturates. It wasn't that long ago we used a similar formula for common sleeping tablets. They probably just wore off.'

'Thanks.'

The coroner clicked off without saying goodbye.

Chapter 44: Three Down, Two to Go?

Sunday had flown by for Morton in a whirlwind of chores. He barely stopped to put his feet up for more than five minutes before suddenly it was Monday morning and he found himself back at work once more.

They were two weeks into the investigation, and the pressure to solve the case was getting worse. Ellis' murder was still hot gossip on the Internet, and both Kallum Fielder and Aleksander Barchester were facing ridicule left, right and centre.

They had two suspects. Both could have been in the house at or around the time that Ellis died.

It was almost as if they had two halves of one prime suspect. Brianna had motive, but couldn't be definitively put in the house. Gabriella was definitely in the house, but had no reason to kill Ellis.

Mayberry's trip to the Hub had proved fruitful. Brianna left the district line service, as Morton predicted. She had alighted at Kew Gardens using a second Oyster, which was a pay-as-you-go card.

It seemed to Morton an absurd loophole. To buy an Oyster card, the traveller simply paid a small deposit. Transport for London offered a form to register a card, which was quite handy, as it meant it could be cancelled should it be lost, but registration was never required. It was entirely optional.

Morton supposed it came down to privacy, or the illusion thereof, not that Londoners really enjoyed much privacy. For a city where everyone lived in cramped shoeboxes, traveled on sardine-like public transport and flocked en masse to the few green spaces as soon as the sun comes out, Londoners seemed to love the illusion of being alone.

Even on the tube, with a carriage packed heel-to-toe, Londoners were notoriously staid. Heaven forgive the poor tourist that smiles at another human being on the Northern line. Morton rarely took the tube as his badge let him park pretty much wherever he wanted.

The worst part was that isolation makes for poor witnesses. With everyone so focussed on what they are doing at any given moment, they tend not to notice what others are doing.

Morton paced upon and down, pausing to stare at the exhibits photographed on the Incident Room wall. The crime was a contradiction. Nothing that could have been used as a weapon was left. But none of the suspects could easily have brought such a weapon with them.

'Unless…' Morton muttered to himself. He quickly flicked through the printouts of the crime scene photographs. She'd died on her birthday. What if the murder weapon had been a birthday gift?

Nothing jumped out at him. It was almost like it hadn't even been a birthday party. There was no evidence of gift wrap, though they had found a small assortment of greetings cards in Ellis' room.

The door creaked as it opened, and Ayala came in.

'You're late,' Morton said.

'Sorry, boss.'

'Why are you late?'

'I overslept. It won't happen again.'

'Damn right it won't.' Morton felt his temper rise suddenly.

'Whoa. What's up with you?'

'What's up with me? I've got a murder to solve, and my team can't make it in for nine o'clock. Where the hell is everyone?'

'I saw Mayberry on the way in. He's gone down to Computer Crimes. He said he'd found something interesting in our victim's emails.'

'What did he find?'

'She'd booked herself into rehab. She was planning on going the moment she finished her New York trip.'

'Nobody mentioned that,' Morton said. 'Perhaps they didn't know.'

'If she was getting clean… then why throw a party with so many temptations?' Ayala asked.

'One last blowout? Or perhaps she was intending to tell them that night? The fight. Did you ever believe it was over money? That she'd stolen two hundred pounds?'

'No, boss.'

'Now it seems even more ridiculous. If she was getting clean, she wouldn't be stealing money for drugs.'

'She had nembies in her system,' Ayala said.

'She did… I guess it doesn't prove much. She wanted to give up. So what? Don't most druggies want to? It's doing it that's the difficult part. This doesn't add up.'

'Boss. What if she split up with Kal? He's an addict too. If she really wanted to quit, maybe she wanted him gone.'

'Or she wanted him to quit with her. Plausible. But we've ruled him out.'

'Could either Brianna or Paddy have been affected by the decision to quit?'

Morton stroked his chin thoughtfully. 'Absolutely. We know she had to get her drugs somewhere. Paddy says he didn't supply her.'

'And drug dealers never lie,' Ayala said sarcastically.

'Not when they're offered blanket immunity. He could have told me about it, and been off the hook. This way he doesn't get immunity because he didn't disclose. I think someone else was her dealer. Think for a second, where have we been that we could have found Pentobarbital?'

'The veterinary clinic! Brianna!'

'Exactly.'

'You think Brianna was her dealer, then?'

'I do, and I think the £2000 a month we saw Ellis transferring to her sister—'

'Was payment?' Ayala said.

'Yep, and if I were her then I wouldn't want that money to stop. Would you?'

'Nope. I wouldn't. I can't say I'd kill for it though.'

'But it isn't killing for the £2000. It's killing for the whole estate. People have killed for far less,' Morton said.

'But we already knew about the estate. What is Mayberry looking at down at Computer Crimes?'

'Let's go find him and find out.'

Chapter 45: The Dungeon

Computer Crimes had a different vibe to the rest of New Scotland Yard. Where Morton's floor was staid, practical and authoritative, the Computer Crimes guys had Red Bull and comfy chairs. Monitors ran the length of every available space, often two to a computer.

Mayberry was sat down at the back of the department. It looked like he'd resorted to writing down all of his conversation with the tech sitting next to him.

Mayberry waved Morton and Ayala over.

'Gentlemen,' Morton greeted them.

'Morning,' the tech said. 'I'm Zane Lightbody.'

'Poor you!' Ayala said with a grin.

'Now, now, Bertram. Play nice,' Morton said.

Ayala's grin dissipated.

'What exactly are we up to, gentlemen?'

'Your victim was trying to book herself into the Sparks Rehabilitation Clinic. It's a lock-down rehab overlooking Windsor Park,' Zane said.

'We knew she'd emailed. How far did she get?'

'She paid a deposit. The balance was to be paid on check-in. But get this: she contacted them about multi-person discounts.'

'She wanted to take Kal with her,' Ayala suggested.

'Unless Kal is a woman, I don't think so. Sparks is a women-only facility,' Zane said. He brought up their website, and right there in bold it advertised the clinic as *'The UK's #1 Clinic for Women to Rebuild Their*

Lives'.

'That's a bit of a mouthful. I'd be looking for a new marketing guy, or gal, if I were them,' Morton said. 'If not Kal then it's got to be her sister.'

'Or her best friend,' Ayala said.

'Right. We're stuck with two options again. A pattern seems to be emerging. Did she email either of them about it?' Morton asked.

Zane shook his head. 'No emails. No texts either. If they talked about it then they did it face to face.'

'No emails about rehab, or no emails at all?'

'Nothing. Her email looks like it was mostly for business use, and a bit of online shopping.'

'Stranger and stranger. There's got to be a second phone. What about her landline?'

Zane pulled up Ellis DeLange's laptop, and opened her e-billing account for Virgin Media.

'Hang on, are we supposed to be able to do that? Go into a victim's online billing account at will?' Ayala asked.

'Quieten down, Bertram. She's dead. I think, in the circumstances, she'd rather we know how much her phone bills were than let her killer off the hook. Get a bit of perspective,' Morton said. 'Go ahead, Zane.'

'Here we go. We've got calls to several numbers. One is a landline belonging to Kallum Fielder—'

'No surprises there,' Ayala said.

'One is the number of the Wiles switchboard.'

'That'll be Aleksander Barchester then.'

'And the rest are to mobiles. All pay-as-you-go. All unregistered.'

'Damn. This lot do seem to operate under the radar,' Ayala said.

'That's no surprise. We've got a model, a television presenter and a drug dealer. They've every reason to jealously guard their privacy. Do me a favour. Call the numbers, see if you can match up the voices to our suspects.'

'W-we already d-did, boss,' Mayberry stuttered.

'And?'

'V-voicemail answers get us nowhere. No custom r-recordings.'

'Find a way then. Look up where the phones have been active, and see if the locations can be matched to our suspects. Ayala, I need you to call the management team at Sparks. They might well throw up doctor-patient confidentiality, but if you can I want to know who she was trying to book for. And find out what their standard rates are too. The place looks pricey, but Ellis wasn't cash rich.'

'You think she had funding elsewhere?'
'She had to pay for it somehow.'

Chapter 46: Rehab

Sparks Rehabilitation Clinic was a little over twenty miles from Richmond. It was situated on the eastern perimeter of King George VI Coronation Grove, and was technically within the parish of Englefield Green.

Its nearest neighbours were a golf course, a spa hotel and a tiny pub that served the locals. Morton wondered if it were wise to situate a rehabilitation clinic so near to a pub, but he suspected it was the kind which would fall deathly quiet should a stranger venture inside.

He needn't have worried. Sparks was far enough from its neighbours to qualify as out in the sticks. Proper road gave way to gravel driveway and the crunch of stones under tyres as Morton approached.

The building was beautiful. It wasn't as homely as Culloden Manor, but it was much bigger, with a front façade stretching many hundreds of feet wide.

The west wing appeared a little more modern than might be expected. A giant glass frontage had been added, as if part of the old building had been chopped away and rebuilt.

Morton clicked his car's immobiliser with a press of his key fob, and headed for the reception. Above him, dozens of pairs of eyes appeared in the windows on the second and third floor, watching him as he approached. Morton felt a shiver run down his spine, and was immediately thankful that he was visiting on a sunny Monday afternoon in April rather than a dark wintery night.

At the reception, he was greeted by a burly young man in a corporate polo shirt and khaki slacks.

'Can I help you?' the man asked.

'Detective Chief Inspector Morton. I rang earlier.'

'I'm Matt. Welcome to Sparks.'

'One of your would-be patients, Miss Ellis DeLange, was murdered two weeks ago.'

'We're aware of that. How can we assist you?'

'When was Miss DeLange due to come to you?' Morton asked.

'I'm afraid that's privileged information, Detective.'

'She's dead. There's no one left to fight for her privacy. We know she booked in.'

'Detective, I'd love to help you, but I have rounds to do. Walk with me,' Matt said.

Morton followed Matt through reception up to a locked door marked 'Staff Only' and averted his eyes as Matt punched in a security code.

'Tell me about Sparks in general then.'

'Sparks is a complete lockdown facility. All of our guests are self-committed–'

'They choose to be locked up?'

'Yes, they do.' Matt led Morton down a short hallway which ended in another security door. 'This is our airlock system. It's the only way in or out of the facility. This door only opens when the door behind us,' Matt waved a hand over his shoulder, 'is closed.'

'What about fires?'

'We've got fire doors installed as required. This is a listed building so they're interspersed throughout the wings a little haphazardly, but we can clear the building in three minutes if we have to. Patients do occasionally hit the fire alarm to break out for the night, but it's not common. Our guests choose us because we get results. They're free to leave at any time, as long as they accept that we do not allow guests to return within six months of a walkout.'

Once they were past the security door, they came into what could have been mistaken for a plush country hotel – if not for the patients milling about in grey shirts and sweatpants.

'Do they have to wear those?'

'The uniform? Yes. They're not fashionable, but they are comfortable – and we provide them, which reduces the need for searches on arrival. We're going through here next,' Matt said. He indicated a double door to their left.

They entered a grand hall which had wood panelling along every wall, and a grand piano in the centre. A dozen or so sofas had been laid out in a zigzag bisecting the room.

'This is our lounge. The bar at the back serves tea, coffee and any medicine that our patients need. This is a totally dry establishment so we have no booze anywhere on-site.' Matt walked over to a patient, leant in and asked her something quietly. She nodded, and Matt returned to Morton, who looked on with curiosity.

'What kinds of addiction do you treat?' Morton asked.

'Any kind of compulsion you can think of. Drugs, alcohol, sex, gambling. One of our patients is a compulsive texter.'

'A what?'

'Can't stop texting people. She's always attached to her phone, the poor lass. We're getting more and more enquiries like that. Just this morning, a lady called to ask if we could take her daughter. She's addicted to an online video game apparently.'

'Are you going to take her?'

'Heavens, no. We don't take minors here. Imagine locking up an impressionable teenage girl with nymphomaniacs and drug addicts.'

'Sounds like an experience some teenagers would pay a fortune for. How much do you charge?'

'Two thousand.'

'Per treatment?'

'Good lord, no. Per week. That buys you half a twin room and basic rations. We do occasionally cater to the rich and the famous, so there are upgrade packages available too. At any given time we've got roughly eighty of our ninety beds filled, so there's a bit of a waiting list.'

'And this is paid for by the taxpayer?'

'This is a wholly private facility. We do some insurance work. But it's mostly self-funded.'

'And was Ellis self-funding?'

'You know I can't tell you that. Mr Morton, I'm afraid I have to dash. Would you mind if Melissa took you back to reception? She's been here even longer than I have, so I'm sure she can answer any further questions you might have.' Matt pointed to the woman he'd spoken to the moment before.

'Sure. Thank you for your time, Matt.'

With that, Morton was left with Melissa.

'Hi,' she said shyly.

'Hello.'

'Are you the policeman? Matt said I have to take you back.'

'Lead on then,' Morton said. He followed her out of the dining room, looking up and down the halls as he went. 'What's it like in here?' he asked.

'It's OK,' Melissa said. 'I don't really like it.'

'I'm sorry to hear that. Does Matt ask you to escort guests often?'

'Sometimes. We get a lot of visitors, and I do get a little lonely in here.'

Morton looked at her, trying desperately not to ask what she was in for.

'Anorexia,' she said with a sad smile. 'You don't have to be bashful, Detective. Ask whatever you want to ask.'

'Did you meet Ellis DeLange when she visited?'

'I did. She was awful nice to me. We spoke for a few minutes.'

'Can I ask what about?' Morton said.

'What it's like here, why she wanted to come here, that sort of thing.'

'Why did she want to get clean?'

'She said she was having a birthday soon,' Melissa said. 'And that she couldn't keep going as she was. I didn't think she was going to come here though.'

'Why was that?'

'Her friend didn't seem very interested.'

'Her friend?' Morton asked as they approached the first security door. From this side, it had an intercom button only. Melissa pressed it, and they were buzzed through.

'Yes. She had another woman with her.'

'What did she look like?'

'I don't know. Sort of like her, I guess.'

Brianna, Morton thought immediately. 'Thank you very much for your time, Melissa.'

'Is there anything else you need to know?'

'Did she mention how she was paying for her stay?' Morton asked.

'No. She didn't,' Melissa said sadly, as if afraid to disappoint Morton with her answer. 'But we can check.'

'How?' Morton asked. They buzzed the intercom for the second door, and it again swung open, allowing them back into reception.

'It'll be on the computer. The one over there. Matt's password is "mustang". I help him in the office sometimes.'

Morton looked over at the desk. Matt's PC was on, and locked on the login screen. He knew he shouldn't look. It would make admitting the evidence difficult.

Melissa saw him looking. 'Oh, you're not allowed, are you?'

'No, I'm afraid not,' Morton said.

'Can I look?'

Morton bit his lip. If he said yes, he was procuring the illegal search. If he said no, he'd miss out.

Melissa saved him the trouble of answering. She unlocked the PC and opened up Sparks' patient files.

'How do you spell her name?'

'D-E-L-A-N-G-E,' Morton replied. He wondered if that small discretion was enough to put him on the wrong side of defence counsel.

'Here we are. Her deposit was paid for by A. Barchester. Do you know him?'

'I do. Can you print me that out?'

'OK.'

Morton's heart began thumping in his chest as a large industrial laser printer whirred to life. It was loud enough that he was sure Matt would hear and reappear to confront them. But he didn't.

Sixty seconds later, Morton walked out the door with Ellis' patient file in hand.

Chapter 47: Connections

Mayberry made swift progress tracking down the unknown PAYG numbers. He had made contact with all the major networks and asked them to ping the locations of those phones over the weekend.

From that, he had been able to discern who owned each phone. One number pinged most frequently near Birkbeck University where Gabriella was a student. Another had pinged off a tower near the Culloden Estate. Mayberry marked that one down as belonging to Aleksander Barchester.

A third had been in Portland Place during Kal's filming sessions for *Wake Up Britain!*, and the fourth number which the victim had frequently called belonged to someone who spent most of their time in Southwark. Mayberry wrote down Brianna next to that one. The fifth and final number had not been on for a while, but by process of elimination, Mayberry scribbled down Paddy Malone next to that one albeit with a question mark.

He pinged off a quick text to Morton telling him that the phone numbers had been identified, and then scanned through the call logs. The phone companies had supplied the recent calls made by each of the PAYG phone numbers.

Unsurprisingly, the number that Mayberry thought belonged to Paddy had a history of texting a large number of people. His logs alone ran to thirty thousand lines, most of them to different numbers, one or two texts at a time. They were almost certainly clients of his. Mayberry forwarded the lot on to a colleague in the drugs squad.

The most interesting thing wasn't the number of calls placed to each other, but the times of those calls. He pinged Morton another text: '*Boss, you're going to want to see this.*'

When Morton arrived, Mayberry had collated all the information he'd found, and was ready to explain the lot. He'd take the time to write out what he wanted to say to minimise stuttering too.

'B-boss. They all c-called each other. All the t-time. But l-look at wh-when they called,' Mayberry said. He pointed to the calls from Ellis to Aleksander Barchester and vice versa.

'Two o'clock in the morning, three o'clock in the morning,' Morton read. 'Nice spot. She's called him on the Wiles switchboard as well, so we can't rule out business solely on the timing.'

'In the m-middle of the night? Not l-l-likely.'

'Not likely, but not impossible. Both of them travel for work so they might not appreciate normal office hours as much as those of us who do nine-to-five jobs. I think the use of a PAYG burner phone for the calls is more interesting. Barchester wanted to keep it quiet.'

'And E-E-Ellis didn't?'

'Ellis lived alone. She didn't have to hide who she called early in the morning. We know she had an online account for her billing so she wouldn't have needed to even hide paper bills. Kal would have no reason to go looking through her Virgin Media account. I think they were sleeping together.'

'Wh-why?'

Morton thought Mayberry had a point. Barchester was much older, and he wasn't good-looking. 'Money I expect. Hang on. I've had a thought. Barchester was paying for Ellis to go to Sparks Rehabilitation Clinic. We know that costs £2,000 a week. What if the charge on Edgecombe Lodge in favour of Aleksander Barchester was security for that? I can't see how she was going to pay him back otherwise.'

'M-makes sense to m-me. How do we convince it?'

'We don't need to prove it. He isn't a suspect. We can just ask. He has no reason to lie. But if he was having an affair then it does give someone else motive, doesn't it?'

'Wh-who, boss?' Mayberry said.

'Gabriella, of course. We already know she's pregnant with his child. We know they fought on the night of the murder. What if, instead of fighting about her drinking as Barchester claimed, they fought about Ellis? I can't see a woman like Gabriella being too happy about a man like Barchester sleeping with her best friend.'

Morton's phone rang. 'One minute,' he said to Mayberry. 'DCI Morton.'

'David, it's Stuart. I need you down here.'

'Ah, I was going to call you. Is there any male DNA on the sheets in the master bedroom that doesn't belong to Kallum Fielder?'

'Forget about the sheets. There's something much more interesting in the DNA evidence.'

'Then spit it out, man.'

'Two of the guests were related to the victim.'

Two? 'Who?'

'No idea. We don't have samples for Brianna Jackson or Gabriella Curzon yet. Both declined to volunteer a sample.'

'Brianna is her sister. We know that. Let's take it as read there's nothing unusual going on there, and that they really are siblings. Is the other match male or female?'

'Female. It's a half-sibling match. No shared mitochondrial DNA but thirteen chromosomes in common.'

'A half-sister then. That's got to be Gabriella Curzon.'

'That's what I thought too.'

'I'll go pick her up. Let's compel DNA evidence and prove it.'

Chapter 48: The Queen Did It

Morton quickly obtained a search warrant for the home of Gabriella Curzon. It was impossible to compel Gabriella to volunteer a DNA sample, but if they could find a reason to arrest her then her DNA could be taken without consent. They had the testimony of Aleksander Barchester that Gabriella was taking drugs, which was enough to satisfy a magistrate to let them go fishing in Fitzrovia.

Morton stood outside Gabriella's apartment, bashed three times on the door and yelled 'Police, open up!'

When no reply was given, he motioned for Ayala to break down the door down.

The junior officers went in first.

'Clear!' one shouted. The call was echoed as officers checked the bathroom and kitchen. Then Morton, Ayala and Mayberry began their search.

Morton headed for the bathroom. There was a small glass shelf above the sink upon which sat an electric toothbrush. Morton reached inside his jacket and surreptitiously swabbed the brush while no one was looking. It wouldn't be usable in court, but he'd be able to confirm the relationship anonymously if push came to shove.

'Boss! You've got to see this,' Ayala called out from the bedroom. Morton found Ayala stooped over a desk in the corner of the bedroom. A shelf about the desk had a strip light mounted along the bottom and a row of thick heavy textbooks on top of it.

'She's got legal textbooks. So what?' Morton asked.

'Look at the one that's open.'

Morton closed it over, keeping his finger on the page, and read the spine: *Llewellyn and Dean on Probate*.

'Look at the page she was reading,' Ayala said. It was headed *Intestacy Rules*, and a section had been highlighted.

Where a person has died intestate, his or her estate shall pass as follows:

To the parents, in equal share.

If none exist, to brothers and sister of full blood.

If neither parents nor siblings of full blood survive, then the estate shall pass to half-brothers and half-sisters in equal share.

The phrase "Half-sisters" had been underlined and highlighted. Morton swore.

'She knows.'

'How?'

'Does it matter?' Morton said. 'She could have known for years.'

'But boss, it doesn't matter. Brianna is a full sister, so she'll get the whole estate. It doesn't matter if Gabriella is a half-sister or not.'

'Read the paragraph towards the bottom of the page,' Morton said.

Ayala leant in to close to read the tiny text. He read aloud: '*Bona Vacantia*. Where no parties entitled to inherit under the Intestacy Rules exist the estate shall be deemed to be *Bona Vacantia*, and shall pass to the Crown.'

'Not that bit, you idiot. As if the Queen is a bleeding suspect.' Morton pointed slightly lower down the page.

Survivorship Period: Pursuant to the Administration of Estates Act 1925, a person of a class entitled to inherit under the Intestacy Rules must survive the deceased by a period of 28 days. If they do not do so, then they shall be disregarded and the estate shall be divided amongst other members of that class. Where none exist, it shall be distributed to the next class in the hierarchy.

'What does that mean, boss?'

'We need to find her – and fast,' Morton said.

Ayala scrunched up his forehead, and scratched his temple. Morton watched him. It was as if cogs were whirring ever so slowly.

"Oh my god. Ellis died on the 30th of March. That means Gabriella gets everything if...'

'If Brianna dies before the 27th of April.'

'But that's less than a week from now!'

'Then we'd best get moving,' Morton said. 'You take Mayberry and find Gabriella. I'll go warn Brianna.'

Chapter 49: Lost

Speed cameras flashed repeatedly as Morton slammed his foot down driving from Fitzrovia. He'd probably tripped three or four cameras on the A301 alone. It was a minor miracle that the streets weren't too clogged at the back end of rush hour.

Morton felt the hairs on his arms stand on end, and his heart thundered in his chest. He knew it had to be about the money, but he'd never thought that it could be Gabriella behind the death of Ellis DeLange. And who would have guessed that they were half-sisters? They looked a little alike, but Morton had put that down to both being in fashion, and hanging around together. Gabriella was so much younger that she didn't have the weather-worn look of her half-sister.

He came to a screeching halt outside the Walworth Veterinary Clinic and Pet Hospital. A mere three miles had taken him nearly fifteen minutes despite his speeding.

Morton leapt out of the car, and dashed inside. The same receptionist from his earliest visit was behind the counter, and Morton could see from the reflection in her glasses that she was surfing the net rather than working.

'Brianna Jackson. Where is she?' Morton barked.

'She's not here. And quieten down. You'll disturb the animals.'

It was true. Morton's arrival seemed to have caught the attention of a number of dogs in the waiting room. A Doberman stood to attention, its hackles raised, and stared intently at Morton.

'Where is she?' Morton said, more quietly but just as quickly.

'Home, probably. She's not working today.'

'Is that normal?'

'Nope. Tuesdays she's usually on. But she called the boss, and I got the message not to expect her.'

'Did she say why she wasn't coming in?'

'Not to me. Nobody tells me nothing. I'm just the daft temp on reception. But if you see her, tell her she owes me one. I'm not supposed to be cleaning out the housing. The agency don't pay me enough for that.'

'Right,' Morton said. He was barely listening as the receptionist spoke. He was halfway out the door before she could finish what she was saying.

'Ayala. Tell me you've found her,' Morton spoke to the empty cabin of his BMW. He was on hands-free on his mobile as he drove the half mile to Brianna's bedsit.

'I'm on my way, boss. I'll text you the moment I've got her.'

'Good. Brianna wasn't at work. I'm heading to her apartment now.'

Morton clicked off, and rocked back and forth. Traffic seemed to be getting busier. Halfway to her apartment, Morton got stuck in a queue behind a great column of cars on the A215. There'd been an accident up ahead.

'Sod it,' Morton said, and yanked the steering wheel abruptly to the right. He slammed his foot down and shot across the road, cutting off traffic coming the other way. He narrowly missed causing a second accident, and shot onto a garage forecourt. He switched off the motor. Another quarter of a mile to go.

Morton ran. He sprinted past the scene of the accident that had caused the tailback, and turned right onto Amelie Road. Thirty seconds later, he came to a halt outside Brianna's building.

He glanced at his watch. Just over a minute. Not bad for an old feller, though it was far from his quickest ever run. He took a few short, sharp breaths and then tackled the stairs. After what felt like a marathon running up the stairs, Morton screeched to a halt outside Brianna's front door. He slammed his fist against the door, causing it to reverberate in its frame.

'Brianna! It's Detective Morton! You need to open up, right now!'

No answer. 'Brianna!' Morton yelled again. He pressed an ear to the door for any signs of life within. 'This isn't an arrest. Open up!'

A door opened, but it wasn't Brianna's. A neighbour shuffled out into the hallway.

'Can you keep it down? My baby is tryin' ta sleep here, man.'

'Have you seen Brianna Jackson?'

'Yeah. She gone. That girl left hours ago. I heard her door bang shut.'

'Where'd she go?'

'Do I look like her keeper?' The neighbour slammed the door, making as much noise as Morton had if not more.

Strike two. *I hope Ayala is having better luck.*

Chapter 50: In the Wind

Ayala gave a sigh of relief. The boss had sent him off to find Gabriella Curzon, which was much easier than traipsing across London in search of Brianna. He already knew where Gabriella was.

Her university timetable was pinned to the wall above her desk. Ayala scanned down the day's schedule:

09:00 – 10:00: Criminal Evidence (Seminar Group A), TS305
10:00 – 11:00: Family Law (Seminar Group B), TS206
11:00 – 13:00: Equity and Trusts (Lecture), B35

'Anyone know where Birkbeck School of Law is?' Ayala had asked of the search term rifling through Gabriella Curzon's flat. He'd been pointed in the right general direction easily enough, which led him almost half a mile due east until he hit Gower Street. But once he got that far, there was no sign of any lecture hall.

Gower Street was a major north-south artery running all the way up to Euston Road, and he was about halfway down it. Ayala whipped out his mobile and searched for an address for the Law School, which told him to head up to number four.

But number four was obviously an office. It wasn't a lecture theatre. He rang the doorbell. No answer.

Ayala spun around on the spot, looking up and down the street. Nothing looked vaguely like a law school. The entire street seemed to consist of townhouse after townhouse as far as he could see.

People milled by as Ayala searched. Ayala spotted a group clutching textbooks in their hands heading down a side road to the east. *Students!*

'Hey!' he called after them. 'Where's the law school?'

They shook their heads, and the nearest one held up a textbook that read '*Human Psychology: The Truth in Emotion*'.

Ayala followed them anyway, hoping to find students who did know where to look. He walked along Keppel Street, and a grand building with a sign that read Senate House Library came into view. He was close. When he turned onto Mallet Street the throngs of students seemed to grow larger. Ayala could hear voices yammering away in a dozen languages, none of which he spoke.

The throng were all headed in one direction. Ayala jogged through the crowds until he reached Torrington Square, where a security fence separated the hallowed halls of academia from tourists who had taken a wrong turning while looking for the British Museum.

Ayala almost went too far to the east, but a quick double-check of the map on his phone stopped him from straying onto the adjacent campus belonging to the School of Oriental and African Studies. The big building in the centre of Torrington Square, which seemed to be a hive of student activity, seemed like the logical place to start. He entered, and saw a security guard just inside.

'Detective Inspector Ayala, Metropolitan Police. Where's B35?' Ayala showed the man a photo of the timetable from Gabriella's apartment. He held out his ID for inspection.

The guard took his time checking that Ayala was who he said he was, and then beckoned. 'Follow me.'

He followed the guard downstairs, and along a corridor until a door marked B35 came into view. The door opened into the back of the lecture theatre, and creaked loudly as Ayala made his way inside. A middle-aged man at the front of the room looked up quizzically, then to the clock on the wall.

'You're late,' he said.

Ayala smiled, and walked down to the lectern behind which the lecturer stood. A giant projector screen showed a slide entitled 'Secret Trusts'.

The lecturer paused mid-sentence as Ayala approached, trailing off before finishing his explanation of how secret trusts allowed gifts to be made outside of a formal will.

'Detective Inspector Ayala, Metropolitan Police. I'm looking for Gabriella Curzon,' Ayala said. He looked around the lecture theatre, then recoiled as bright light from the projector almost blinded him. He cupped his hands like a visor and tried again. Students looked at him curiously. But there was no sign of Gabriella.

'Gabriella Curzon! Has anyone seen Gabriella Curzon?' he yelled.

A muffled voice replied from the back: 'She's not here.'

'Who said that?' Ayala demanded.

A hand rose in the third row from the back. Ayala moved as if to talk to her where she sat, but then the lecturer coughed politely. 'Outside,' the lecturer said. 'Please.'

'Ah. Sure. Miss, could you join me outside please?' Ayala asked of the student who had raised her hand.

She followed him out into the hallway, dragging her backpack and notes along with her.

'You didn't need to bring your things with you.'

'Oh yes, I did. You've just saved me from another hour of boredom.'

'You're friends with Gabriella?'

'Friends? No. Not really. We swap notes sometimes. And we cover for each other.'

'Cover for each other?'

'On the register. We have to sign in to each class, and they check out attendance percentages to make sure we've been showing up. Totally pointless, 'cause we just sign each other's name. It's not like they run handwriting analysis on the lists. I mean, they caught a guy red-handed once, but that was just bad luck. Pretty much everyone does it. You saw all the empty seats in there. How many of us would you say there were?'

'Fifty people,' Ayala guessed.

'Two hundred signed in today. It's obvious what's going on, but the staff turn a blind eye.'

'Right. You sign in for Gabby. She signs in for you. Did you sign her in today?'

'Yes.'

'But she's not here,' Ayala said. 'So where is she?'

The girl shrugged. 'No idea, sorry. We sit next to each other, and our row signs off our whole group so we don't get dinged on the percentages. I imagine she's hung over or something.'

'She's not at home. Do you have any idea where she might go if not to class?'

'The library maybe, if she's got a paper to finish. Otherwise, shopping. That girl loves Oxford Street more than anything.'

'Thanks for your time, Miss...?'

'Tate. Katrina Tate.'

'If you see her, call me please.' Ayala handed over one of his cards.

Chapter 51: Against Time

Morton answered his phone on the first ring. He barely had time to read the caller's name on the screen and register that the call was from Ayala before picking up.

'Morton. Tell me you've got her.' Morton tapped his fingers against his steering wheel impatiently, and gazed out at the main road. The backlog from the accident hadn't been cleared but those involved had been rushed off in stretchers. The garage owner had demanded Morton move or risk his car being clamped. Morton had fended him off with an explanation that he was a policeman, but Morton could still see the man working twenty feet away, glancing up at him occasionally as if to suggest Morton needed to get a move on.

'No dice. She's supposed to be in class today, and didn't show up. Her classmates have no idea where she is.'

'You and Mayberry get back to office, and I'll go check neither of them are at Edgecombe Lodge. I wouldn't put it past either of them to start stripping anything of value to pawn.'

'Err, I already sent Mayberry back. He's a liability.'

'Ayala, now isn't the time, but we're going to have words about this later. I asked you to take Mayberry with you and you disobeyed me. Go get me something, now. I've got another call coming in.' Morton hung up, and took the waiting call.

'Morton.'

'It's Stuart Purcell. I've got DS Mayberry with me. He said you're trying to get hold of Brianna Jackson and Gabriella Curzon.'

'Where are they?'

'Hold your horses. I've not got a location, yet. We checked their phones. Both off. We checked Facebook for any updates; all profiles are private, if they even have profiles. I've got one lead–'

'Damn it, Stuart. Just tell me what the lead is!"

'Brianna has charges on her primary credit card, the one we flagged, from Buds 'N' Blooms. It's a florist in–'

'Southwark. I walked past it ten minutes ago. When was the charge?'

'An hour ago.'

'Right.' Morton hung up, jumped out of his car and slammed the door shut, then ran back towards the high street. Moving the car would have to wait.

The florist was a small family-owned business with a peeling lilac façade, and buckets of cheap seasonal flowers out on the pavement. Dozens of cheerful yellow daffodils were advertised at ten for a pound. Morton burst through the door, and a bell announced his arrival.

'Hello! Welcome to Buds 'N' Bloom–'

'DCI Morton. You served a customer this morning, Brianna Jackson. Brunette, twenty-eight, a little on the short side.'

'Oh no, dear,' the florist said. 'I've not seen Miss Jackson since last week.'

'You charged her this morning.'

'Well, yes, after I delivered the flowers.'

'Where to?'

'Adelaide Church.'

Morton's eyes narrowed. 'Funeral flowers?'

'Yes, dear.'

'Thanks.'

Morton dashed back out of the florists' and towards his car, where an unwelcome sight awaited him. The garage owner had made good on his promise and immobilised Morton's beloved BMW.

'What the hell have you done?' Morton roared. 'Take it off, now!'

'After you pay me my seventy-five pounds,' the garage owner said. He pointed at a sign on the wall warning against parking on his forecourt.

Morton stomped towards the garage owner. 'Take it off, or you're under arrest for obstruction of justice,' he said in a much-too-calm voice.

The garage owner sized Morton up, and then caved. 'It'll take ten minutes.'

'Damn it, I don't have ten minutes. Is that thing road legal?' Morton pointed to an Aston Martin. It was an older-model V8 Vantage in navy blue, which an apprentice was polishing up. The keys were in the ignition.

'Detective, don't even think–'

It was too late. Morton had already run towards the Aston Martin. He jumped in, revved up the engine, shouted 'I'll bring it back!', and slammed his foot down. Before the garage owner could stop him, Morton was gone.

Morton grinned like a schoolboy as he tore away. *So this is what being a criminal feels like.* He pulled his phone from his pocket, tapped the speakerphone button and chucked it onto the passenger-side seat.

'Call Ayala,' he said clearly.

'Calling Malala,' his phone replied.

'God damn it.' He snatched the phone back up, used his left thumb to hang up and voice-dialled again. On the second try, it worked and Ayala's phone began to ring.

'Boss, you got her?'

'Ayala. Today's the funeral. Call ahead, see if they're both there. Adelaide Church. Meet me there.' Morton hung up, and floored it through a red light. *In for a penny, in for a pound.*

Chapter 52: Burning

Adelaide Church in Richmond was a hair shy of twelve miles from where Morton commandeered the Aston Martin. It was one of the best drives of his life. The road seemed to glide by underneath him, and the engine purred contentedly as it ate up the asphalt. *It's a shame Sarah would kill me if I bought one.*

The miles flew by, and forty minutes later Morton parked outside Adelaide Church. It was a beautiful old church, Lutheran by denomination, with stained glass windows that seemed to radiate in the sunlight.

Morton walked into the foyer, where an elderly lady was shuffling about singing to herself cheerfully. The door into the main church was closed.

'Excuse me, ma'am. Is the DeLange funeral in progress?' Morton asked. He hadn't spotted many cars outside.

'Oh no, dearie, that finished a good fifteen, twenty minutes ago.'

'Damn!'

'Watch your language, young man.'

Young man? 'I'm sorry. Do you know if they were headed to a wake or a burial?'

'The crematorium, I think.'

Morton sighed. 'Where is it?' he asked, expecting to have to zig-zag back across London. *At least I'll get to drive the Aston Martin a little further.*

'The other side of the road.' She pointed out the door towards a hedgerow beyond which Morton could just about make out the outline of a low, squat building.

For the third time that day, Morton ran.

The committal ceremony was well underway by the time that Morton arrived at the crematorium. He paused to text Ayala a quick update, and then headed inside. The second he stepped through the front door, he could hear sobbing coming from the main hall. At first, he thought nothing of it.

Then he heard screaming.

Morton sprinted across the foyer, through the double doors leading towards the source of the scream, and stopped dead in his tracks just inside the main hall.

The scene before Morton was surreal. Ellis' coffin lay atop a metal retort in the far left corner, waiting to be loaded into the incinerator.

In the opposite corner, a pastor, presumably from Adelaide Church, cowered in the corner with his knees tucked up under his chin, and his eyes cast downwards. Halfway down the hall, which was filled with a hundred chairs either side of a central aisle, Kallum Fielder sat frozen in a chair, bewitched by the scene unfolding in front of him.

Gabriella and Brianna were at the front of the room. Gabriella, the taller of the two half-sisters, held her left arm around Brianna's chest, with her fist clenched. In her right hand, she held a knife to Brianna's throat.

'Stop right there. Don't move any closer,' Gabriella said.

Morton held up his hands, and paused a few feet along the aisle. Behind him the double doors swung on their hinges, making a slight swooshing sound until they too came to a complete stop.

'Gabriella, don't do this,' Morton said. He kept his voice calm and quiet.

'Don't do this? It's not what I've done. It's what she's done,' Gabriella said. She held the knife closer still to Brianna's throat. The slightest slip and it would be over.

'What did she do?' Morton asked.

'Tell him. Tell him what you did, Brianna. Tell him!'

Brianna gulped, and a tear ran down her face. 'She's crazy. Help me!'

Morton looked between them. 'Why don't we sit down and talk about this?'

'You wish. I'm not leaving until this wretch admits what she did. She killed Ellis!' Gabriella yelled. Her hand trembled with rage as she spoke, and the knife, already dangerously close to Brianna's jugular vein, quivered.

'She killed Ellis,' Morton repeated, in an even tone. 'How do you know that?'

'I know I didn't kill her. And I know you're after me. Katrina called the church to say you were looking for me. The silly mare thought you wanted me for drugs. But I know better. You think that I killed Eli. Don't deny it. I know you barged into my lecture hall.'

Morton silently cursed Ayala. He had taken a sledgehammer to crack a nut, and made clear their intentions.

'That doesn't answer the question. Why Brianna?'

'It wasn't me. Kal was gone. Paddy was with me. Alex was running around Richmond naked. That only leaves one person, doesn't it? And you said it yourself, that house is three million reasons to kill.'

'Where is Paddy?' Morton asked. He edged forward ever so slightly.

'Jail, as you well know. The Governor wouldn't let him come today even though he's getting out this week,' Gabriella said. She eyed Morton warily as he shuffled forwards. 'Stop moving! Sit down. That seat to your left.'

Morton sat down slowly. As he did so, he pressed his hand against his jacket, feeling for the button that would activate voice dialling. 'Call Ayala,' he whispered, and hoped that his phone would, for once, obey him.

Thankfully, Gabriella didn't hear him whispering, and continued to rant. 'My sister's funeral, and you – you denied her friend the chance to attend!'

'I'm sorry Paddy couldn't make it. I didn't stop him. It was me that brokered his deal for immunity. I'm sorry the paperwork took so long. At least Kal is out on bail.' Morton looked over to the former footballer. Kal faced forward, but he wasn't paying attention to what was going on. Instead he stared off into space, glassy-eyed and dissociative.

Gabriella saw Morton looking. 'Don't mind him. He's been like that for a while now.'

'He needs medical attention.'

'Nonsense. There's nothing wrong with him. God knows why men always fall to pieces in a crisis.' Gabriella looked over at the pastor, who rocked back and forth with his knees tucked up beneath his chin.

'Gabriella, you don't want to do this. You haven't hurt anyone yet. If you didn't kill Ellis then let everyone go, and I'll ask the prosecutor to be lenient.'

Gabriella looked uncertain for a moment. She glanced over towards Kal, and then towards the pastor, but when she turned back to Morton, her face had hardened into an impassive mask. 'Do you think I'm stupid?' she sneered. 'If I let them go, you'll arrest me and then it's over. I want you to listen to the truth.'

'You're an intelligent woman so I won't lie to you. You had to know that being arrested was a forgone conclusion the moment you took a hostage. You know this isn't going to end with you walking out of here a free woman. Let everyone go, and I promise I'll listen to what you have to say.'

'No. She's going nowhere.' Gabriella jerked her head towards her hostage.

'Then let the others go.'

'I need them. I need witnesses.'

'You've got the best witness in London right here. I'm going nowhere. Show some good faith. Let Kal and the pastor go, please,' Morton said.

Gabriella looked between them for a moment. 'One. I'll let one go now. If I let Pastor Roberts go then you'll hear me out, won't you?'

It's a start, Morton thought. He nodded, and Gabriella called over to Pastor Roberts. 'You can go, Pastor.' The pastor looked up, then over to Morton for reassurance. When Morton nodded, the pastor leapt to his feet and then bolted from the room.

'Thank you,' Morton said. 'Tell me what happened.'

'She set me up.'

'Brianna set you up? How?' Morton wanted to check to see if his phone call had gone through, but dared not be seen looking.

'The money,' Gabriella said.

'That wasn't a set-up. That was a test,' Brianna said. Her eyes were closed, and she took short sharp breaths.

'Oh, yes, it was. It was a set-up. You made me take it.'

Morton realised what they meant. 'You two took the money from Kal's wallet.'

'Damn right we did. She told me it was to test if they would argue. We knew what he was planning. We had to know if he trusted her. He didn't,' Gabriella said.

Morton leant forward, and glanced inside his jacket. He could see a faint glow emanating from his breast pocket. *Yes! The call went through.* 'That's what Kal and Ellis argued about on the night she was murdered.'

'Yes, and that's why this bitch wanted me to take it. To make it look like that great oaf killed her.'

'But you said Kal was planning something. What was it?' Morton said.

'He was going to propose. Brianna found a diamond ring in his pocket. He left his jacket on the back of a chair in the kitchen. She looked through it for coke, and found the box, didn't you Brianna?' The knife trembled dangerously again, and Brianna whimpered.

'Then what happened?'

'He caught us looking at it, got angry. Then he begged us not to spoil the surprise. He was going to propose that night.'

Everything clicked into place for Morton. If Kal had married Ellis then he would have become her next of kin. Brianna would never have been able to inherit at all. *It wasn't planned. The murder weapon must have already been in the house that night.*

'It's not true! None of it is.' Brianna cried. 'Can't you see, she's manipulating you? She wants you to think I did it so you won't arrest her. She killed Ellis, and now she's going to kill me.'

'Quiet!' Gabriella hissed. 'One more lie, and I'll slit your throat. It's no less than you deserve. Ask him. Ask Kal if he was going to propose.'

'OK,' Morton said. 'I'm going to get up now. I'm going to go over to Kal. That's OK, right? He's still fifteen feet from you. I promise I won't do anything else.'

Gabriella nodded her assent, and Morton stood, then edged slowly down the aisle. He sat down opposite Kal.

'Kallum. Kallum. Mr Fielder, are you OK?' Morton asked.

Kal turned slowly at the sound of his name. His cheeks were stained with tears, and his eyes were bloodshot. He clenched an order of service in his left hand, and a tissue in his right.

'Are you OK?' Morton repeated. He wanted to reach out, to assure Kal that everything was going to be OK. But it would have been a lie.

Kal nodded, and released his grip on the tissue. It fell to the floor almost in slow motion before landing at his feet. Morton watched as Kal slowly reached into his pocket.

'Hey! What are you doing?' Gabriella demanded.

Kal ignored her and produced a velvet ring box from his pocket. He held it out, palm up, to let Morton see. Morton leant across the aisle, and opened the lid without taking it from Kal.

Inside was a platinum ring set with a blue diamond solitaire almost a quarter the size of Morton's thumbnail. Morton gazed at it in awe, then snapped the box closed.

Kal clutched at it, his fingers tightening around it as if afraid to let it go. He began to sob. Gone was the brash arrogant suspect Morton had first met on the set of *Wake Up Britain!* Kal had become a broken man, a shadow of his former self. There was no doubt in Morton's mind that Kal would never have hurt Ellis.

Morton heard the sound of an engine outside. His heart rose in his chest. He had to act fast.

'Gabriella. I know you heard those engines. That will be the police. Let me help you. Put the knife down.'

'No! Not until she admits what she did.' Gabriella's arm wavered as if her muscles were beginning to cramp from holding the knife for so long.

'Brianna,' Morton said. 'Tell me why you went back that night.'

'I... I went to apologise. For stealing the money. I felt bad about leaving them to argue over a set-up. I wanted to make things right.'

'Liar!' Gabby screamed. She pressed the knife in closer against Brianna's jugular, breaking the epidermis but not yet drawing blood. A few millimetres further, and Brianna would bleed out before Morton could do anything.

Brianna fell silent. Morton could see the terror in her eyes.

Then they heard the megaphone.

Chapter 53: Ayala in Charge

Ayala arrived on site not long after Morton. He had his phone on loudspeaker so that Detective Mayberry and the six constables crowded around him in the car park could listen in to Morton's one-sided phone call.

Obviously something major was going down, but without video it took a while to realise what.

'We need to secure the perimeter,' Ayala said. He turned to the nearest two uniformed officers. 'I need you to recon the outside of the building. Look for points of entry and egress. If there is a back or side door, one of you stay there while the other loops back around to me.'

The officers nodded and made their way towards the building.

'Mayberry, make sure the rest of the building is evacuated. Go inside quietly, and don't disturb the main hall,' Ayala ordered. He watched Mayberry head off towards the entrance. Mayberry kept his body low and shuffled through the doors, making as little noise as possible. Ayala turned to the other four constables.

'Gents, I want two of you to watch the road at the front, and two the road at the back. The boys from hostage negotiation will be here soon, but until then, we're responsible for what happens. If you hear anything going down, wait until my say-so before you storm the building. Hopefully, the hostage negotiation team will be on site before we have to face that possibility. We have a man inside, and an open phone line. But we need to get communications open, and figure out what demands are going to be made.'

'What about the media?' one of the constables asked.

'What about them?'

'They're here.'

'Shit.'

Mayberry half-crouched and half walked as he approached the crematorium. His heart thundered in his chest as the front door creaked. He paused, sure that Gabriella must have heard him enter the building.

The foyer was smaller than his lounge at home. The double doors obviously opened onto the main hall, to be avoided at all costs. That left two doors remaining, one on either side. Both appeared to open onto corridors. The door on the right had a sign labelled 'Toilets'. Mayberry headed there first. He followed the passageway around to the right, away from the main hall, where he found the men's, women's and disabled bathrooms.

He gingerly knocked on the door marked ladies. When he was certain no response was forthcoming, he walked in. Mayberry breathed a sigh of relief. All the cubicles were empty. He headed next door to check the men's room: also empty.

He thumbed his radio. 'B-bathrooms c-clear. Over.'

As Mayberry returned to the entrance foyer, the doors to the main hall swung open and a man dressed in religious garb burst through the door at a rate of knots. Before Mayberry could stop the man, he was gone. Mayberry thumbed his radio again.

'P-p-priest! I-incoming!'

Ayala's team had just enough time to set up a barricade by parking their vehicles across the entrance to the crematorium car park before Pastor Roberts came flying out of the building at top speed.

A multitude of white lights flashed. The journalists had set up camp across the road outside Adelaide Church, and were using telephoto lenses to record the proceedings.

Ayala ran forward to intercept the pastor. He seized the pastor's arm, and immediately noticed how the pastor shook with fear. He steered him away from the media and into the nearest squad car.

Ayala crouched by the car. 'Pastor, are you all right?'

The pastor looked upwards, his eyes hollow. He clasped his hands together in prayer; his lips moved, but he said nothing.

One of the constables appeared at Ayala's elbow with a blanket. 'To help with the shock, sir. Until paramedics are on-scene. I'll go fetch him a cup of tea.'

Ayala nodded his thanks, and draped the blanket over the pastor.

'Who's in charge here?' A deep voice called from behind him.

Ayala turned to see a suited gentleman slide over the bonnet of a squad car. 'Hey, you can't be back here. No press.'

'Do I look like a journo?' He held out a hand. 'DS Harper Lawson, Hostage and Crisis Negotiation. And you are?'

'Detective Inspector Ayala. We've got two men inside. DCI Morton is in the main hall where Gabriella Curzon has two hostages remaining. She has released one already.'

'And the other man you have inside?'

'DS Mayberry is evacuating civilians from the rest of the building.'

'Good. I'll take it from here.'

Chapter 54: Crisis

'Gabriella Curzon! This is the police. We want to know what your demands are. Do you have a phone?'

Morton watched Gabriella jump as soon as she heard the megaphone. It wasn't Ayala's voice, which meant the Hostage and Crisis Negotiation Team had been called in.

'Gabby. Listen to me. They'll have the whole building surrounded. Let me call out to my team, and let them know everyone is all right. Can I do that?'

'Tell them to leave. I want to get out of here. I don't want anyone to die. I just want the truth!' Gabriella said.

She's losing it, Morton thought. *But at least she's said she wants this to end peacefully.*

'OK. I'm going to reach into my pocket, and call my second-in-command. I'll put it on speakerphone so you can hear.'

Morton made a show of putting his hand into his pocket very slowly. As he did so, he turned the phone off. 'See, it's off. Now, I'm going to turn it on and call Detective Ayala.'

The phone took a moment to boot up, and then Morton punched in his security code. He dialled Ayala.

'Ayala, it's me. We're all OK in here. Pass your phone over to whoever is on the megaphone.'

'I'll do that now, boss. Hold on.'

Morton heard the phone crackle as Ayala handed it over.

'Harper Lawson. Crisis Management Negotiator. To whom am I speaking?'

'This is DCI Morton. I've got you on speakerphone. With me are Kallum Fielder, Brianna Jackson and Gabriella Curzon.'

'What does Miss Curzon want?' Lawson asked.

Gabriella called out across the room. 'I want Brianna to admit the truth. I want her to tell you she killed Eli.'

'Sorry. We didn't quite catch that. Can you move the phone closer to Miss Curzon please?'

Morton looked over at Gabriella, dying for an excuse to get close so he could disarm her.

'Kick it over,' she said.

'Can't I just—'

'No. Slide it along the floor.'

Morton did so. Gabriella repeated her request.

'I can't give you that, Miss Curzon.' The doubt and confusion in Lawson's voice was obvious. He was used to hostages making much more tangible demands – money, escape, food. Before he could suggest any of those things, Gabriella spoke again. 'I want you to hear her tell the truth. I want you to record her confessing to Eli's murder.'

'I can record everything. But I need a show of good faith.'

'I already released a hostage!'

'That was a start, but you want something and I want something. Can we do a deal?' Lawson asked.

Gabriella fell silent, and looked over to Kal, who was still nearly catatonic.

'I don't think he's going anywhere anytime soon,' she said. 'He's not up to moving anywhere.'

Lawson's voice came back immediately. 'Who isn't moving? Is he injured?'

Morton held up a hand to forestall any reply from Gabriella. 'Mr Fielder appears to be suffering from some shock, but is physically unharmed. I believe Miss Curzon was suggesting that Kallum might need assistance to get to the door. Am I right about that, Gabriella?'

She nodded. 'Yes. He isn't fit to move.'

'Let me help him to the door,' Morton said. Gabriella scowled at the thought of losing her last witness. 'I'll come straight back – not that you need me now that you've got a live recording for testimony. Is that OK?'

Gabriella bit her lip, obviously wavering. Then she nodded. 'But no sudden moves. If anyone other than you comes back through the door,

Brianna dies.'

'Mr Lawson, I will be bringing Mr Fielder to the door. Can you have someone waiting to receive him?'

'Absolutely.'

⚖

In a back room to the left of the main hall, Mayberry found two men, both dressed in overalls, apparently waiting to turn on the incinerator. Both held mobile phones to the paper-thin walls, to record the goings-on of the hall on the other side.

'G-give m-me those r-radios,' Mayberry whispered. 'You've g-got to leave.'

The nearest man looked at Mayberry, then shook his head. 'No chance, mate. I've been here ten years, and this is the first time anything exciting has happened.'

'Keep y-your voice d-down! They'll h-hear.'

The other man, no more than a teenager, looked worried. 'Maybe we should go with him, Dave. But keep the phones, yeah?'

'Is th-there anyone else h-here?'

The younger man shook his head. 'Alright. Lead on, Mister Copper.'

Mayberry held out his hand palm up. 'F-first, g-give me your ph-phones or y-you're under a-arrest.'

Dave threw his mobile towards Mayberry, who barely caught it in time. 'Have it your way. The recordings are already in the cloud anyway.'

⚖

Two hostages had been released, but Gabriella kept the knife pressed against Brianna's throat. Her hand continued to quiver. She wouldn't be able to hold it there much longer.

'Gabriella, if Brianna killed your sister then how did she do it without you seeing her? You were there too,' Morton said.

'I don't know how, or why I didn't see her. But you tell me who else could have killed Eli? I know I didn't.'

She's got a point, Morton thought. *Unless she's lying.* 'Let's go through the night again. Paddy left you at the house, and then what?'

'Then I used the bathroom, went outside for a smoke and we left.'

'But you didn't see Brianna at all?'

'No. But she did it. I know she must have. No one else could have,' Gabriella repeated stubbornly. 'I know she came back. As if she'd go all that way to apologise.'

'But you've got no proof,' Morton reasoned. 'Everything is circumstantial.'

'You've got no proof I did it either. That didn't stop you barging into my lecture.' Gabriella furrowed her brow. Her hand shook more violently. 'I'll get you your proof. Tell him, Brianna. Tell him what you did.'

Brianna looked over to Morton, her eyes wide with terror. 'I didn't,' she whispered.

'Liar!'

Morton took another step down the aisle. 'Gabriella, stop. Put the knife down. Ellis wouldn't want you in jail. The only person that is committing a crime here is you.'

'If you can't get justice for my sister, I will.' Gabriella angled her hand as if preparing to draw the knife across Brianna's throat.

Morton wanted to spin around to look at the door. He knew Gabriella would have only a moment before the Hostage and Crisis Team burst in. The threat of imminent harm took all other options off the table. They had to risk an arrest.

'Last chance,' Gabriella whispered in Brianna's ear.

Brianna sobbed in terror. 'OK! I did it. I killed Eli.'

'Why?' Gabriella demanded.

'The money. I wanted the money.'

Gabriella dropped the knife, which clattered to the hardwood floor noisily. Just as she did so, the police burst in through the door.

Morton yelled out for them to stay back, and dashed forward, but Brianna was too quick for him. She snatched up the knife, and turned it on Gabriella. Morton was three feet away. Time slowed as he approached.

He swung his right fist at Brianna, connecting with her left shoulder blade from behind. She spun around, the knife glinting wickedly in her hand.

As Brianna flailed, Morton threw his leg out to counteract the momentum of the punch. He steadied himself in time to see Brianna still holding the knife, closing in on her would-be captor. He lashed out with his foot, connecting with the back of her knee. Brianna dropped to the floor; the knife tumbled from her grasp and clanged to the floor.

Morton flicked the knife away with his foot, and stepped over Brianna to where Gabriella cowered. She seemed shocked to have gone from captor to victim in less than a minute. Morton slapped a pair of cuffs on her. A similar click came from behind, and he knew someone had cuffed Brianna.

The slow motion ended in a whir and a din of shouting. Officers flooded the room. With the hostages now safe, all that remained was to drag the half-sisters outside. Then Morton's team rushed in.

'Boss, you all right? You're bleeding.' Ayala pointed down at Morton's leg.

Morton rolled up his trouser leg to take a look. The knife must have nicked him as he disarmed Brianna. The cut wasn't long, but it bled profusely.

'You're going to have to get that checked out. It looks pretty serious.'

'It's miles from the femoral artery. I'm in no danger,' Morton said. 'I have been cut before, you know. She barely grazed my leg.'

'Go get it checked out. Or I'm calling Sarah.'

The ultimate threat. 'Ayala, you'll pay for that. Escort the two women back to New Scotland Yard. They'll undoubtedly both want lawyers.'

'Got it. There's an ambulance waiting outside. They'll fix you up.'

Morton's eyes narrowed. If there were an ambulance and a negotiation squad out there, then the media wouldn't be far behind. 'Journalists?'

'A few,' Ayala admitted.

'Then we'll distract them. Take me out first – and while their cameras are pointed my way, Mayberry can take our detainees around the side.'

'You got it.'

'And Ayala?'

'Yes, boss?' Ayala's tone was hopeful, as if he might finally get complimented on a job well done.

Instead, Morton tossed him a key ring. 'There's an Aston Martin parked across the street that I, ah, borrowed. Could you see it gets back to its rightful owner please?'

Chapter 55: Means

TUESDAY APRIL 21ST – 15:15

The leg wound wasn't as serious as it looked. The blood certainly made for a bit of a scene, and it almost worked as a lure for the journalists – until one of them spotted Mayberry taking Brianna out a side door, with Ayala and Gabriella trailing behind. They'd both been bundled into squad cars, and were now waiting down at the station for Morton to interview them.

If only he could get past all of the well-wishers first. Morton waited half an hour in his office, then headed down towards the interview suites that Ayala had hastily set up. On the way, he spotted Purcell ambling along the corridor in the direction of his office.

He turned around quickly. Purcell might not have seen him.

'David, wait up!'

Morton continued to limp away.

'Hey, Morton!' The tech waddled towards Morton as they ran out of corridor. 'Where you going?'

'Erm... To find Ayala.'

'He's downstairs. Walk with me. I've got something for you.'

Morton led on towards the main lifts, and Purcell nattered on as they made their way down.

'I've been going through pictures of Edgecombe Lodge from *The Impartial*. You know they've got their annual design awards? Guess what? Edgecombe Lodge–'

'Won last year. Yes, yes. Ayala told me. What's the big deal?'

'Look at this,' Purcell said, and then handed Morton a copy of the article.

'Stu, I'm in pain. What am I looking at?'

'Look at the swimming pool pic. Sorry about your leg, by the way. What do you see?'

'A clean, tidy pool area.'

'OK. Now the crime scene photos. What's missing?' Purcell put another photo into Morton's hands. 'You see it, right?'

The chubby man bounced up and down excitedly as they reached the lift. Morton looked, but saw nothing amiss.

'Pool bricks.' Purcell pointed.

Morton squinted at the photo. Sure enough, there were three pool bricks, the rubber kind used for diving games, stacked neatly under a table.

'That's what she was hit with. It's large, heavy and has a big surface area. I've done some testing–'

'By testing, do you mean you bought a pool brick and started hitting watermelons with it?' Morton asked. He hit the button for his floor.

'Well, yeah. But it works. I think Ellis was hit from the right-hand side with the long flat end of a pool brick. They're gone from the crime scene.'

'They've probably been tossed into the Thames, but I'll get Ayala to search Brianna and Gabriella's homes for any sign of them. And all of our suspects are right-handed, so that doesn't narrow things down a jot.'

The lift doors pinged open, and Morton stepped out. 'It's good work, but it doesn't help. Get me something that can actually prove which sister is the killer.'

Chapter 56 Motive and Opportunity #1

Brianna and Gabriella had been checked over, offered counsel and placed into two separate interview suites. Morton found Ayala waiting for him in the corridor.

'They both accept lawyers?'

'Yep. Your lucky day too. Guess who.'

Morton resisted the urge to go and peek into the interview suites. 'Who?'

'Elliot Morgan-Bryant.'

'You're kidding. He's representing three of my five suspects? That's no coincidence. Which one of them is he representing now?'

'Brianna.'

'Paid for using her inheritance, I presume. A year of working as a veterinary assistant doesn't pay for a week of his time, after all. Who has Gabriella got?'

'Duty solicitor. Miss Genevieve Hollis.'

'Brilliant. London is such a small city sometimes. I swear there are eight million people in this miserable hellhole, but I have to run into those two twice in a week.'

'Maybe it's like the birthday paradox?'

'Don't start quoting statistics at me. Let's go after Brianna first. She's just confessed after all.'

'Three times in one month. Business must be booming, Mr Morgan-Bryant,' Morton said.

'Isn't it always?' Morgan-Bryant said. 'What are you planning on charging my client with today? Probate fraud, again? Or a little public indecency?'

'Just murder.'

'Murder? What evidence do you have?'

'Your client returned to her sister's home after leaving her birthday party.'

'To apologise. She has already explained that to you.'

'And she concealed her journey with a spare Oyster card,' Morton said.

'That one's easy to explain. She bought that for a friend who visited London, and it's been in her purse ever since. All Oyster cards look identical, so Brianna must have mixed them up.'

'You've got an answer for everything, don't you? Brianna confessed to killing Ellis less than an hour ago, in my presence.'

'My client had a knife held to her throat! If that isn't a classic example of duress, I don't know what is.'

'And then there's the fact that your client is inheriting three million pounds' worth of prime real estate.'

'I don't see how that's a crime.'

'It goes to motive,' Morton said. 'Miss Jackson, did you visit Sparks Rehabilitation Clinic with your late sister?'

'Well, yes, but–'

'And is it not true that she wanted to get clean?'

'Yes, but–'

'And you're the one that's been selling her pentobarbital, aren't you?' Morton bluffed. He didn't have any proof yet.

'No comment,' Brianna muttered.

'You don't need to comment. I've got a team searching your home now. If we find nembies, I'm sure that'll more than enough for magistrates.'

'She said no comment, Mr Morton.'

'Right. Then we'll park that until my team gets back. You were receiving money from your sister each month.'

Brianna nodded. 'Yes.'

'Two thousand pounds?'

'About that much.'

'Why?' Morton asked.

'She was helping me out,' Brianna said. 'London is expensive, and I don't earn much.'

'You can't spend much either. Your flat can't be much more than a hundred and fifty square feet. I assume, by the way, that you'll be declaring the last seven years of gifts for inheritance tax? By my calculations, that's, let's see, a hundred and sixty-eight grand at forty percent – about £67,200 or so you owe HMRC. Plus interest.'

Brianna paled, and looked over at her lawyer in dismay.

Morgan-Bryant turned towards Morton with a cold stare. 'Mr Morton, I wasn't aware that you were a tax accountant. Do you fancy doing my VAT returns for me? No? Then perhaps you could ask a relevant question next.'

Morton bristled. 'Miss Jackson, did you kill Ellis?'

'No!'

'So you didn't bash her head in with a rubber pool brick?'

Brianna's jaw dropped. She sat there, stunned.

'Miss Jackson,' Morton prompted again. 'Did you or did you not bash your sister in the back of the head with a rubber pool brick?'

'My client won't be commenting on that.'

'Did you ditch the body in the pool to make it look like drowning?'

'No comment,' Brianna said tersely.

'And did you set up Kallum Fielder by asking Gabriella Curzon to steal money from his wallet?'

'It was a prank! We wanted to see if he'd argue with Gabby. It was a test–'

'Because he was going to propose to her?'

'Yes.'

'Glad you brought that up,' Morton said. 'Isn't it true that if Ellis married Kal, you'd never inherit the house?'

'She isn't a lawyer, Mr Morton. She wouldn't have the expertise to answer that question.'

'Perhaps you can answer that one then.'

'I could, if you'd like to give me eight hundred pounds an hour for my services. I may be a lawyer, but I'm not your lawyer,' Morgan-Bryant said.

'Eight hundred an hour? Blimey. How are you affording that, Miss Jackson?'

'Our funding arrangement is none of your business, Mr Morton. Stop going off on tangents and present your evidence. Then either charge her or let us go.'

'Miss Jackson, what time did you return to the house?'

'I don't know. Half twelve maybe?'

'After you exited the District Line service at Kew Gardens?'

'Yes.'

'Did you go straight back to Edgecombe Lodge?'

'No. I walked for a bit, thinking. I wanted to word my apology just so.'

'But you think you got back about half twelve. Who was in the house when you got there?'

'Nobody, as far as I could tell. I went in, the lights were off. All was quiet. I assumed Ellis had gone to bed, and I left.'

'That's interesting. If you arrived at half twelve then you'd have arrived when Gabriella was still there.'

'Maybe it was a little after that, I don't know.'

'How did you get in?'

'Through the front door...' Brianna gave Morton a quizzical look as if to ask 'How else would I get back in?'.

'Was it unlocked?'

'No. I've got a key,' Brianna said. 'We all do.'

'You all do?'

'Kal, Gabby, Paddy and I.'

Everyone except Culloden. 'Is it true you hated your sister?'

'Absolutely not. We had our ups and downs, but don't all siblings argue?'

'Speaking of siblings, did you know Gabriella is your half-sister?'

'I only found out today when that lunatic took me hostage. She's the one that killed Ellis. Can't you see that she's using me to distract you?'

'You picked up the knife afterwards.'

'I was defending myself!'

'From a police officer?' Morton gestured down at his bandaged leg.

'Sorry about that.'

'Two inches higher, and you'd have nicked my femoral artery and you'd be having this conversation with one of my colleagues. You clearly don't have much compunction against wounding other human beings. I think you killed your sister. Your timeline doesn't add up. You returned after midnight for a spurious reason–'

'To apologise!'

'Why not wait until morning? Why not call or text?'

'I felt bad. I doubled back. And unless you can prove otherwise, I'll be leaving.'

'Not yet you won't. I've got detectives searching your home right now.

Want to tell me what they're going to find? A pool brick perhaps?'

'Morton, you're badgering my client. This interview is over.'

It took Ayala just ten minutes to find what he was looking for in Brianna Jackson's flat. The nembies were hidden inside a Ziploc bag in the toilet cistern.

He called Morton with the news.

'Good work. Get the sample to the lab, and check for consistency with the sample we found in Ellis' blood. Any sign of pool bricks?'

'Nothing, boss. We've searched every inch of this place, not that that's saying much. How's it going with our suspects?'

'I've got Gabriella to go, but Brianna wasn't giving anything up. She admitted returning, so we've got her in the right place at the right time, which she claims was half twelve–'

'When Gabriella was there alone,' Ayala said sharply.

'That's the thing. Brianna claims not to have seen Gabriella, which either means she's lying or her timing is off. A few minutes could make all the difference here.'

'Do you think she did it?'

'I honestly don't know. One of the two sisters did it. If Brianna didn't then Gabriella did, and vice versa. I'm reserving judgement until after I've had the chance to interview Gabriella. If you're going to be quick getting back, I'll wait for you to join us.'

'Sounds like fun. I'll be half an hour if I swing by the lab. Can you spare Mayberry for a bit?'

'What do you want from him?'

'I need him to fetch the victim's toxicology report, and the chemical analysis of the pento sample we collected from Walworth Veterinary Clinic. I want to compare those with the sample I just collected.'

'Done. Good work, Ayala. Keep it up.'

Chapter 57: Motive and Opportunity #2

Gabriella refused to make eye contact with DCI Morton as he prepared the tapes and introduced the attendees. Instead, she simply stared at the table, her eyes fixed upon the knife she had used to hold Brianna Jackson hostage. Her lawyer, Genevieve Hollis, started talking the moment Morton began the tape.

'My client would prefer to make a brief statement before any questions begin, if that is permissible, Mr Morton?'

'By all means, go ahead. I may still have to ask questions of her, though.'

'My client would like to put it on the record that she feels a great deal of remorse for her actions today. She would like to make it clear that she had no intention of threatening Brianna when she attended the funeral, but went into a state of agitation when she heard Brianna discussing her home renovation plans for Edgecombe Lodge. After the funeral, the party travelled to the crematorium, where Brianna denied my client the chance to speak at the Committal Ceremony. Brianna told my client that "only family get to speak" and that "she was no sister of hers". Brianna went so far as to call my client a "mongrel half-blood". It was at this point that my client snapped. She has no memory of anything that happened after that point.'

Here we go. Time to set up a dodgy defence. 'She doesn't remember anything? Then let me refresh her memory. She held a knife to Brianna Jackson's throat, and had an entire room subject to her whim, including me. We have an audio recording if you'd care to listen to it.'

'That won't be necessary. My client admits what she did, knows it was wrong and is truly very sorry for what she did. This was not a planned act–'

'Not planned? Why did she have a knife then?'

'If you'll allow me to finish please, Mr Morton. I will ensure my client answers your questions but you have to allow me to explain her position before then. The knife was brought to the scene by Brianna Jackson. It was a craft knife made of Damascus steel that Ellis received from her father on her eighteenth birthday, and Miss Jackson wished to see Ellis buried with it. It was set aside with all of Ellis' personal effects prior to the cremation.'

Morton nodded. It made sense. Only the body and the coffin could be loaded into the chamber.

'We would therefore like to offer a guilty plea in consideration of your prosecutor making a sentencing recommendation. Pursuant to the B3-4.3A guidelines, this was a minor kidnapping committed without planning, and by a person suffering from severe grief. She had just lost half of her known family.'

Morton waited, in case Hollis was going to carry on. 'Very well. I'll speak to the prosecutor about that, but it is out of my hands. I still have a few questions, Miss Curzon.'

Gabriella looked up from the knife at the sound of her name, but seemed dazed, confused even.

'How long have you known that you were related to Ellis and Brianna?' Morton asked.

Gabriella shrugged. 'Forever. Ever since she came to my school. We've got the same birthmark. Our father had it too.'

'What birthmark?'

'A half moon and stars,' Gabriella said. She stood and lifted her shirt to expose her navel. 'See?'

Morton looked at it carefully. Gabriella did have a darkened area that looked like a crescent moon surrounded by splotches that could generously be interpreted to be stars.

'Ellis saw this mark?'

'Yes. When she photographed me. We got to talking afterwards, and the truth came out. That was the summer I moved down to London to become a model, and I stayed on her couch.'

'You assumed from a birthmark that you were related?'

'Not just that. Ellis spoke to her father. They argued about it, but a

DNA test eventually proved that I was his. Her mother never found out, but I was just glad to have a family.'

'You grew up in the system?'

Gabriella nodded.

'How was your relationship with Brianna before Ellis' death?' Morton asked.

'Cordial. She never accepted me as her sister, and we had little in common. To tell you the truth, I always thought she was jealous of my relationship with Ellis.'

'If you two weren't close, why did you conspire to steal from Kal?'

'We didn't steal. I always intended to give him the money back. He wanted to marry our sister, and we needed to know that he trusted her. He didn't.'

'When was this little charade planned?'

'At the party. It was pretty impromptu. Brianna said we should do it.'

'You set up an argument on Ellis's birthday. Your timing is impeccable,' Morton said with only a trace of sarcasm.

'We had to. He was planning on proposing that night.'

'Kal was going to propose on her birthday?' Morton said.

'Yes.'

'Interesting. Miss Curzon, I have a few delicate questions I need to ask. If at any point you'd like to pause to consult with your lawyer please say so and I will vacate the room. Is that OK?' Morton asked. It was a little late to really build rapport, but he needed Gabriella to be amenable to answering his questions as fully as possible.

She nodded.

'I understand Ellis was intending to go into rehab.'

'Yes, she was. We visited a rehab clinic a couple of weeks back.'

Morton bolted upright. 'You visited Sparks Rehabilitation Clinic with Ellis? When?'

'A few Saturdays back.'

Interesting. Brianna claimed she was the one who visited Sparks with Ellis. 'When was she intending to go into rehab?'

'When she got back from New York. I was going to…' Gabriella's voice trailed off.

'You were going to what, Miss Curzon? Go with her? I'm not interested in any drugs offences you may have committed.'

'Yes. I wanted to do it with her, but I couldn't afford it.'

At two grand a week nor could I.

'I haven't taken anything lately,' Gabriella continued. 'Not since…'

She rubbed her hands over her stomach.

'How far along are you?'

'Fifteen weeks.'

'Congratulations,' Morton said. 'Aleksander Barchester is the father, isn't he?'

'Yes. We're going to be so happy together. I can't wait for baby Victoria to be born.'

'It's a girl then?'

'I haven't had the test, but I hope so. I shouldn't say that, should I? I'm supposed to say I'm fine either way as long as it's healthy.'

'Yes, you are,' Morton said. 'But Aleksander was sleeping around, wasn't he? With Ellis?'

'No! No, he wasn't!' Gabriella thumped her fists on the table.

'I'm afraid he was. We found his DNA on her bed sheets.'

'That bastard!'

'That must have made you mad.'

'It would have if I'd known. You think I killed her. You're wrong. I'm sorry I took Brianna hostage. I shouldn't have snapped like that, but I'm not a bad person. I own up when I do things wrong.'

'You only own up when there's irrefutable proof of it in the form of a policeman who witnessed the entire ordeal and taped it. That isn't courage. It's trying to salvage a deal from the prosecutor in light of overwhelming evidence. Don't pretend to be some sort of saint, Miss Curzon.'

Gabriella sat there, stony faced and open mouthed, at a loss for words.

'After Kallum and Aleksander left the party, did you see Brianna at all?'

'No. Not once. I had a drink with Paddy, then we left.'

'But he left you alone for a while, didn't he?'

'Yes. I finished my drink, and went outside for a cigarette. I didn't see Brianna, honest.'

'That just doesn't line up with what others are saying. We know you were alone about half twelve. That's the same time Brianna came back.'

'Maybe I missed her. It's a big house.'

'But if you were smoking outside then she'd have had to walk right past you.'

'I did go to the bathroom, come to think of it.'

'At exactly the moment Brianna came in?'

'I guess so. Stranger things have happened. I'm not lying, Mr Morton. I didn't kill my sister. Why would I lie to you?'

Chapter 58: Beyond Reasonable Doubt

As Morton waited for Kieran O'Connor to arrive, he couldn't help but admire Kieran's office. Kieran's latest secretary had the place looking much tidier than on Morton's last visit. The piles and piles of papers were gone, and the ratty old desktop had been replaced with a sleek new iMac and a digital photo frame which scrolled through various pictures of Kieran and his fiancée Miranda, whom Morton had never met.

Morton fiddled absent-mindedly with a Newton's Cradle that he found on a side shelf, watching the toy click-clack back and forth. When he heard footsteps, he hastily hid it out of sight underneath the desk.

'Sorry I'm late. Judge Milner kept us behind. Did Beatrice offer you a coffee?' Kieran asked.

'She did, thanks. Nice lass. How long has she been working for you?'

'Two weeks now. This,' Kieran swept his arm across the overly-neat office, 'will never last.'

'You never know. You might be a changed man.'

'She can digitise my files all she likes, but I'll still print 'em out before I read them.'

'Tree killer.'

'What can I say? I like it how I like it. And I get results.'

The lawyer had a point.

'Now then. Ellis DeLange. Where are you on this? I've been fielding calls on a daily basis. We need to be seen doing something.'

'We're down to two suspects,' Morton said. 'Both in the house at the time of the murder. Both with motive and opportunity. One of them took the other hostage yesterday.'

'I heard. Your leg all right?' Kieran's brow furrowed in concern.

'Fine.'

'Then give me a précis for each of your suspects,' Kieran said.

'Suspect number one is Gabriella Curzon. She's yesterday's hostage taker. She's the victim's half-sister, and best friend.'

'What does she do for a living?'

'She used to model,' Morton said. 'Now she's a law student.'

'So she knows the rules.'

'I'll get to that. First, means. Around the time Ellis was murdered, Gabriella was alone in the house for approximately half an hour. After Kallum Fielder and Aleksander Barchester left for the night, she was alone in the house with Francis Patrick Malone, a low-level–'

'I remember Paddy Malone. He's a regular.'

'Paddy left to deal drugs. He was gone for half an hour and got back at approximately five to one in the morning, right before the clocks went forward by an hour for British Summer Time.'

'He can't be sure?'

'Nope. The timings are all very loose other than those which we've taken from CCTV. Our suspects and witnesses were either drunk or high or both. Between that and the clock change, none of them can are sure what happened and when. We know that by 02:17, Gabriella was at Richmond Station. She caught a cab, and then went home with Paddy Malone.'

'Short window.'

'I agree,' Morton said. 'She was emotional that night. She had an argument with Aleksander Barchester. He said it was over her drug taking, but she claims she hasn't touched anything more than a glass of wine in over three months.'

'Do you believe her?'

'Yes. I think they argued over Ellis. We found seminal DNA belonging to Barchester on Ellis' bedroom sheets.'

'Bingo. There's motive.'

'If I'm right, yes,' Morton said. 'But Gabriella is no saint. She went home with Paddy after all.'

'This girl. She pretty? How would you rate her out of ten?'

'Seriously? You're going to letch on a suspect?'

Kieran shook his head. 'Don't be daft. Just answer the question.'

'Easily a nine. And if you tell Sarah that, you're a dead man.'

'Right. But Paddy, well, he's isn't the prettiest picture in the art gallery is he? It sounds like she was using him as an alibi,' Kieran said.

'But for that to work, she'd have needed to guarantee he left her at some point.'

'How drunk was he?'

'Very. He passed out in the taxi on the way home, and woke up without her the next morning.'

'Then she could easily have found enough time to commit murder.'

'Perhaps. But Brianna is the better suspect in terms of time. She could have slipped back into the house any time between half twelve and just before three. As long as Gabriella didn't see her, she'd be golden.'

Kieran stroked his chin thoughtfully. 'Brianna is set to inherit. She's got a much better motive.'

'What if both Ellis and Brianna died? Wouldn't Gabriella get Edgecombe Lodge then?'

'Normally, yes.' Kieran said. 'But you can't profit from committing a crime. If Gabriella had murdered Brianna, she'd have been disinherited automatically.'

'And if they're both dead, and no one else inherits, then it goes to the Crown, right? We're back to the Queen did it.'

'No, we're not. Gabriella is a half-sister. She can only inherit if Brianna doesn't.'

'Brianna's alive,' Morton said. 'Surely that means Gabriella doesn't get the house.'

The lawyer shook his head slowly. 'Not quite. Gabriella was never going to get the house by killing Brianna but–'

'Gabriella's notes on probate law said otherwise.'

'Well, there's why she's a law student and I'm a lawyer. The rule of survivorship applies to spouses, not siblings. There's only one way Gabriella can inherit.'

'Which is?'

'If Brianna is convicted for Ellis' murder then she will be disinherited. If Gabriella killed Ellis and then successfully sets up Brianna, she'll get everything,' Kieran said. 'All she's got to do is convince a jury to believe Brianna did it, and she'll get away with murder and inherit the lot in one stroke.'

'She was desperate for Brianna to admit she killed Ellis.'

'Did Brianna confess?'

'She did, but she had a knife to her throat at the time,' Morton said.

'You can't use that, can you?'

'No... But I'm dealing with this from a criminal lawyer's perspective. I don't know whether that admission would be admissible in probate court. I suspect not, and if it were then it wouldn't be particularly probative, but we can't assume Gabriella isn't working off some wonky student logic. Anything else against Gabriella?'

'She set Kallum Fielder up to argue with Ellis, but she did so at Brianna's request. They've both been open about this.'

'How did they cause the argument?'

'They stole two hundred pounds from his wallet, allegedly to see if he trusted Ellis or not. Kal was planning to propose. The missing money started the very public fight they had early on during the party.'

'If Kal and Ellis had married, he'd have become her heir. Neither sister would have inherited. It doesn't point to either of them alone.'

'True. It might explain why Ellis was murdered that night though.'

'I agree. But I'm more interested in who killed her than why she was murdered on that particular night. Tell me about Brianna.'

'Brianna Jackson is twenty-eight. She's divorced, no children, and she works as a veterinary assistant, which is why she access to pentobarbital. Ayala found a stash when he searched her flat, hidden inside the toilet cistern. The lab matched it to both the victim and Walworth Veterinary Clinic where she works.'

'Were she and Ellis close?' Kieran asked.

'Nope. Ellis encouraged her parents to leave their estate to good causes. Brianna inherited very little, and we believe this was a major source of contention. It doesn't help that Ellis was fabulously rich, which Brianna was clearly jealous of, and Brianna is scraping by, surviving on handouts from her big sister which I think was payment for pento rather than generosity.'

'And with your victim getting clean, that money was about to dry up,' Kieran concluded.

'Exactly. That and the window to inherit combined give her plenty of motive.'

'What about means?'

'She came back,' Morton said. 'We've got her leaving Richmond on the district line, disembarking at Kew Gardens and doubling back on foot. She claims she was doing so to apologise.'

'At gone midnight? That's flimsy.'

'I agree. She also set Kal up – via Gabriella. She had a key, and let herself in.'

'Sounds like means, motive and opportunity.'

'I agree. She was ostensibly the last person in the house. If she didn't do it, Gabriella did—'

'And vice versa. What time did Brianna return to the house?'

'Half twelve.'

'Wasn't Gabriella there then?' Kieran asked.

'Yes, she was. Both claim not to have seen each other. Gabriella said she had a drink in the kitchen, used the bathroom then went out front for a smoke. Brianna on the other hand claims she found the house dark and the party over. She says she only came in for a few minutes and then left – without seeing anyone or finding the body.'

'So the only way they could be telling the truth is if Brianna came in while Gabriella was in the bathroom, and left before Gabriella came outside for her cigarette – otherwise they would have seen each other. David, if that's a coincidence then buy me a lottery ticket, because the odds are insane.'

'What are you suggesting?' Morton asked.

'Two options. Either one of them committed an immensely complicated murder but left no conclusive evidence by sheer dumb luck.'

'Or?'

'Or they're working together. They've got neatly opposing stories. They've made you think they don't get on, and they've pointed the finger at each other without being prompted to do so. It's a classic cut-throat defence. If Gabriella says Brianna did it, and Brianna says Gabriella did it, then boom, reasonable doubt – and they both walk free. All they need to do after that is have Brianna issue a victim impact statement to minimise Gabriella's sentence for kidnapping and then split the money later. They're family so it wouldn't be illegal to help each other out. It wouldn't even be that suspicious.'

'Kieran, you've got a cynical mind. I just don't buy it.'

'Then what would you have me do? Pick one at random and hope for the best? You've got a virtually identical case against both.'

'Gabriella has proven bad character. She held a woman hostage!'

'And Brianna would have done the same in a heartbeat. She left a nick in your leg. And you think she's been dealing.'

'What do you want to do?'

'Charge them together as co-conspirators.'

'I don't think they both did it,' Morton said. 'Can't we charge them individually and let the jury decide?'

'I can't. If I charge both separately, they can point to the mere existence of two prosecutions as reasonable doubt. Neither case would make it as far as a jury. I have to make the case for them working together to murder Ellis.'

'I don't like it. If only one of them did it then you risk sending an innocent to prison.'

'Nobody in prison is innocent. Not legally. You're guilty if and when a jury says you are. It's up to a jury to decide the facts and base their decision on those facts.'

'This is wrong.'

'Is it? You said yourself you can only provide the facts as you find them. The facts support a prosecution of both of them as co-defendants. Then it's up the twelve members of the public to decide. They can find them both not guilty if they don't think my case is good enough, and they might well do. But we can't do nothing, and charging them individually isn't an option.'

'I'm not going to allow this.'

'Allow it? I'm the prosecutor. This is my case, Morton. You're overstepping your authority. I'm charging both of them with the murder of Ellis DeLange. Trust the jury. They'll make the right decision.'

Chapter 59: Richmond Magistrates' Court

It took a few weeks for the DeLange murder to wind up on the docket at Richmond-upon-Thames Magistrates' Court for the first stage of the trial, which was simply to transfer the case over to the Crown Court. It struck Kieran as a bit of an oddity but it was a formality which had to be adhered to, and so he had made an early trip up to Richmond.

The building itself was an unusual one. It was constructed out of whitewashed concrete and Plexiglas, and looked more like an art centre than a working criminal court. It sat at an odd juxtaposition to tree-lined streets filled with expensive apartments with balconies from which the residents could watch criminals being dragged into court.

And this morning there was quite a spectacle.

Camera crews were lined up outside the front entrance, clogging up the entire street, in the hope of hitting pay dirt when the defendants were hauled into court.

They were much too late. The defendants had been moved to the holding cells underneath the court the night before, so the only shots they were going to get were of the lawyers walking into court.

The morning's real winner was Oscar Bruehl, a civil parking enforcement officer for Richmond Borough Council. He was having a field day working his way along the street, dishing out enforcement notice after enforcement notice to waywardly parked cars. By the time he'd shuffled idly by the news crews, most of the street had been carpet-bombed with black-and-yellow parking tickets, and Oscar had fulfilled his quota for the month – not that he officially had one, of course.

⚖

Kieran always enjoyed the peace and quiet of the robing room before a court appearance. There was a certain ceremony to going into court, though today would not be a day to wear his wig and gown, as the plea before venue was a mere formality.

Kieran didn't mind. He was on the payroll. It didn't matter to him how often he had to appear in court. At the end of the day, he'd collect his salary and go home – unlike the defence counsel, who often had to work for legal aid rates, or wait on payment for months at a time.

He was happy with his lot in life. Being a prosecutor seemed to him the very best of both worlds. He got a salary and a pension, and there were none of the pesky ethical dilemmas of working defence. Every person that Kieran had put behind bars thoroughly deserved it. Morton might not have agreed with the decision, but it was his to make. He would put the case to the jury, and let them decide.

He looked in the mirror, straightened his immaculately pressed tie and Inns of Court cufflinks, and walked out into the hallway – and straight into opposing counsel.

'Miss Hollis.' He nodded.

'Mr O'Connor. Do you have a moment?'

An ambush. 'What do you want?'

'I'd like you to consider dropping the case.'

'You know I can't do that. The evidence merits a trial, and I have no intention of dropping anything. You make your case, and I'll make mine,' Kieran said and then began to walk away down the corridor.

'Then you should know that neither I nor Mr Morgan-Bryant intend to attempt severance.'

Kieran stopped dead in his tracks. He'd been expecting defence counsel to argue that being tried in the same courtroom was prejudicial. He'd have pretended to argue, but ultimately subtly lost that argument so that he could present two cases to two juries.

'You're not going for separate trials?'

'No. As we see it, no jury can convict both. The evidence of collusion is almost as flimsy as the circumstantial evidence you're trying to use.'

'There's an entire mountain of circumstantial evidence.'

'No jury is going to convict two women for the same murder. Your evidence is the same against both. That's more than enough for reasonable doubt.'

'I disagree but thank you for sharing your thoughts. I'll see you downstairs, Miss Hollis.'

'Mr O'Connor? One more thing. Watch your back. That Morgan-Bryant is out to get you.'

'I know.'

Court One had never been so full. Every seat in the public gallery was full, and a number of journalists waited in the hallway. Morton had to resort to flashing his ID to secure a seat.

The court rose as the district judge walked in, and then sank back into their seats as His Honour Judge Richards sat upon the bench.

'My, my, we do have a busy courtroom today. I'll warn you all at the outset to keep quiet during proceedings, and please don't forget to turn off any mobile phone you may be carrying. If I so much as hear a phone vibrate, I will hold those responsible in contempt.'

An usher stood, and read out the charges. Brianna and Gabriella stood in the dock with only a Perspex divider between them.

'Who do we have in court today?' Richards asked.

'Miss Hollis; I represent Gabriella Curzon. Mr Elliot Morgan-Bryant represents Brianna Jackson, and my learned friend Mr Kieran O'Connor appears for the Crown.'

'Then down to business. Do the defendants accept that there is a prima facie case to answer here?'

'We do, Your Honour,' Genevieve Hollis said. Morgan-Bryant stood for a moment to echo her.

'Bail?'

Kieran stood. 'We request remand, Your Honour. Both defendants are a flight risk. Miss Curzon is awaiting sentencing on another matter, and there are additional charges pending against Miss Jackson. We consider that neither defendant has substantial ties to the community and therefore represent a flight risk given that both of them have easy access to capital.'

'Mr Morgan-Bryant, Miss Hollis. What say you?'

Miss Hollis stood. 'My client is already on remand for the charge that the prosecution is alluding to. She has proven her willingness to appear when required by attending today. She has already surrendered her passport to the courts to secure bail on that charge pending sentencing. She has a home in London and is currently studying for her final exams, which are due to take place shortly. We would ask that you extend the same courtesy so that she can continue studying, which will minimise the disruption when my client is eventually proven innocent.'

'Proven innocent? You're very confident, Miss Hollis. Mr Morgan-Bryant?'

'I would ask for bail. My client has a home, a job, and is set to inherit a large estate. She has no reason to abscond.'

'Your Honour, the Crown would respectfully disagree. If Miss Jackson is found guilty, then she will not inherit and thus has every reason to flee.'

Richards nodded, looked down at his scribbled notes and then said: 'Brianna Jackson, you are remanded pending trial. Miss Curzon, I will release you on the usual bail conditions. You may not leave the jurisdiction. You may not contact any witnesses.'

Hollis rose. 'Thank you, Your Honour.'

'Are there any other pre-trial matters which I need to attend to?' Richards asked, and looked around the courtroom.

'None, Your Honour,' Kieran said. 'Both defendants have received advanced disclosure of the case against them, and the Crown stands ready for trial.'

'Then pursuant to section six subsection two of the Magistrates' Court Act 1980, I have no choice but to commit this case forthwith for trial in the Crown Court. All parties will be informed of the court date by post.'

Morton watched on. It was all routine stuff for Kieran, but it still fascinated Morton. In a mere three minutes, bail had been dealt with and the defendants sent off to be tried for murder.

Chapter 60: Three Sundays

The prosecution lawyer had been as good as his word, and once the agreement to testify was signed, Paddy was out of HMP Pentonville once more. Life was good.

He yawned, stretched languorously and looked around the hotel room. *This is so much better than prison.* Gabby had picked well. It was upmarket but discreet, with a large bed, soft pillows and all the anonymity of a big chain.

Nice view too. Paddy looked across the room towards Gabby. She was dressed in only a bathrobe, and sat next to the telephone. She twirled the cord of the phone around her fingers as she spoke: 'Three Sundays? I understand. And you can't do it any sooner?'

Paddy snatched up the complementary pen and paper by the nightstand. He wrote down a message and then held it up for her to read. *'When?'*

Gabriella waved him off, and continued to talk into the receiver. 'We can't. We'll only be able to make it up for the one day. Four weeks from tomorrow? The Tuesday morning? That's fine with us. No, no, no. We won't need any of that. Thank you. We'll see you then.'

Paddy smiled. 'Is it done?'

'It is. Now get out. Take the fire escape, and go. I can't have anyone know we were here. You know I'm not supposed to talk to you.'

Reluctantly, Paddy rose, pulled on his clothes then kissed her goodbye.

Chapter 61: The Old Bailey

It took the better part of thirteen weeks to make it as far as the Old Bailey. It was properly called the Central Criminal Court, but nobody ever used that name.

To Morton, it seemed a fitting place for the sorry saga of Ellis DeLange to end. It was a bright sunny day when Morton decided to sit in. Lady Justice, gilded in bronze, was on fire atop the roof. Something about the Old Bailey felt weighty, important and yet full of hope that justice would be served. Perhaps it was the inscriptions dotted around the Grand Hall. *Poise the cause in justice's equal scales* was Morton's favourite.

Yet in this case, justice really did hang in the balance. Morton didn't buy Kieran's theory that the two half-sisters had colluded. The animosity between them seemed far too ingrained to be an act. If Morton were right, and he usually was, then justice would be hard pressed to deal with two defendants, one guilty and one innocent, each accused on the same set of facts.

Attending court at the Old Bailey wasn't like going to just any old Crown Court. There were superficial differences, like dealing with the inevitable queues and heightened security amidst the tourists, but there were substantive differences too.

The aldermen of the City were entitled to attend court, though Morton had never seen one as far as he knew. More strangely still, the judges sat off centre. He had asked Kieran why this was, and had been told that it was so that, if he so chose, the Lord Mayor could sit in judgement in the centre chair.

Morton wasn't sure if Kieran was having him on or not, but chose to believe the story. He never could tell when the lawyer was telling the truth, and it appeared that the jury couldn't either. They were watching Kieran, transfixed, as he turned to give his opening statement.

'The defendants, Gabriella Curzon and Brianna Jackson, are charged with the murder of Ellis DeLange. Over the course of this trial, I will demonstrate that Miss Curzon and Miss Jackson conspired to ensure they were alone with the victim on the night of her thirtieth birthday. You will hear how they planted half-truths in order to conceal where they were, and who they were with. Miss Curzon and Miss Jackson attempted to use friends and acquaintances to muddy the waters, and paint the victim's boyfriend, Kallum Fielder, as the killer.' Kieran paused, and looked at each juror in turn.

'Three million pounds. That is how much Ellis DeLange was worth at the time of her death. Her full-blood sister, Brianna Jackson, is set to inherit that money. What you may not know is that both the women in the dock today are related to the victim. Gabriella Curzon is half-sister to both her co-defendant and the victim. All three of them have the same father.'

Kieran shot a nasty glance at the defence table where Elliot Morgan-Bryant and Genevieve Hollis sat.

'The defendants and their lawyers will be raising a simple defence. They will each argue that the other is responsible in the hope that you will be confused as to who is guilty and who is not. Make no mistake. This is a sham. The defendants conspired to set up Kallum Fielder. They were both in the house when Ellis was murdered, and they both stand to gain from Ellis' death. I would ask that you keep an open mind as you listen to witnesses, read the police reports and examine the evidence. Do so with a critical mind, and I am sure you will come to the same conclusion that I have: it is clear that the sisters worked together to plan the murder of Ellis DeLange. It matters not which sister struck Ellis the fateful blow. This is a joint enterprise, and both are responsible for her death. Do not allow them to profit from it.' Kieran sat back down. Game on.

Genevieve Hollis stood. Her style was nothing like Kieran's. Where he was loud, enigmatic and expressive, Hollis was much more reserved. When she spoke, it was soft, almost too quiet, and yet it carried throughout the courtroom and to the public gallery above.

'My client, Gabriella Curzon, is an innocent woman. The prosecution has asked that you consider all the evidence you will hear with a critical mind. Do so and you will see that none of the evidence that the prosecution intends to introduce proves my client did anything other than attend a party. She had the misfortune of being in the wrong place at the wrong time. There is no evidence. None. The prosecution can demonstrate that Gabriella was in the house on the night of the party. She doesn't deny that. They will assert that this opportunity to commit murder implies that Gabriella is guilty.'

Hollis turned to look at the dock where Gabriella and Brianna sat, separated by a screen.

'The prosecution have suggested that Gabriella worked with Brianna to plan Ellis' murder. They can't prove that either – because she didn't do it. The only thing you will hear is that they could have done it together. The only thing that matters is that they didn't. My client is related by blood to Miss Jackson. That is the only link they have. The prosecution will not be able to demonstrate any tangible proof that Miss Jackson and Miss Curzon conspired – because they didn't. The standard in this trial is beyond reasonable doubt. If you have any qualms then you must do justice by my client, and by the victim whose real killer would walk free if you convict an innocent woman. Do justice and vote to acquit.'

Morton squirmed in his seat. Hollis was an effective lawyer. The evidence was entirely circumstantial, and Kieran would have a hard time convincing the jury that he was right.

Chapter 62: Scapegoat

The jury's excitement was palpable in the courtroom. After days of police reports and forensic detail they were finally going to see the famous Kallum Fielder in court.

'The prosecution calls Kallum Fielder,' Kieran said.

The door to the court opened, and the usher led Kallum through to the witness box, where he stood to be sworn in.

Kal opted to affirm rather than swear on a bible. 'I do solemnly, sincerely and truly declare and affirm that the evidence I shall give shall be the truth, the whole truth and nothing but the truth.'

'Mr Fielder, tell us about what happened to your wallet on the night of the murder,' Kieran said.

'I left my wallet upstairs in Eli's bedroom on the bedside cabinet, and then I went downstairs to greet guests. A little later on, we decided to send someone out for pizza so I went upstairs to get my wallet, and it was empty.'

'How much was in it?'

'Two hundred pounds.'

'What did you think had happened to it?'

'I thought Eli had taken it. I asked another guest, Aleksander Barchester, to cover the cost of the pizza and then I asked Eli if I could have a word in private.'

'Then what happened?'

'We fought. I thought she'd taken the money. I mean, who else could have? It was in her bedroom.'

'Did she?'

Kal shook his head. 'No. It was a set-up. Brianna and Gabriella took the money to provoke an argument. I didn't know that at the time. They argued about it at the funeral.'

'How did that affect you?'

'I've been a wreck. The last night of Eli's life, and we argued over pizza money. And the police thought I'd killed her at first.' Kal turned to the jury. 'I loved her. I just wish I'd never left her alone that night.'

Kieran nodded. He barely resisted the urge to thank his witness. Kal was perfect. 'No further questions.'

Elliot Morgan-Bryant leapt to his feet. 'Mr Fielder, where do you currently reside?'

'HMP Wandsworth.'

'Is that a recent change?'

'You know it is. You were my lawyer.'

The jury laughed uncomfortably.

'You presented a fraudulent will in an attempt to steal Ellis' estate?'

Kal hung his head. 'Yes, but–'

'No further questions.'

The judge, an elderly white man (for weren't they all) by the name of Heenan turned to the defence table. 'Miss Hollis?'

'Nothing for this witness, My Lord.'

Chapter 63: Betrayal

'The prosecution calls Francis Patrick Malone.'

Paddy was led in by the usher. This time, the jury weren't so star-struck and paid him little attention as the usher produced a bible. He handed it to Paddy, who immediately handed it back.

'Would you prefer to affirm rather than swear in?' the usher asked.

Paddy grinned, revealing a crooked smile full of discoloured teeth. 'I'd prefer to be in the pub.'

The usher spun towards the judge, unsure how to respond.

'Mr Malone, is there a problem?' Heenan asked.

'No problem, My Lord, but I ain't testifying today.'

Kieran glanced towards the public gallery, searching for Morton. He tried desperately not to look at the jury lest they see him panic. *What the hell is going on?*

'Mr Malone, you've been summoned as a witness for the prosecution. If you don't testify, I will hold you in contempt of court.'

Before Kieran could remind Paddy that they had a deal, and that breaking it would send him back to prison too, Morgan-Bryant stood and cleared his throat.

'My Lord, Mr Malone cannot be compelled to testify today,' Morgan-Bryant said.

'Why the hell not?' Kieran demanded.

'Mr O'Connor, watch your language in my courtroom. Lawyers aren't immune from being held in contempt,' Heenan said. He turned towards

Morgan-Bryant. 'And why can't Mr Malone be compelled to testify?'

'Because–'

'My Lord,' Kieran interrupted. 'Perhaps we should do this without the jury present?' *This has to be an ambush.*

'Agreed. Bailiff, escort the jury back to the jury room please,' Heenan ordered. The jury stood and filed out slowly. Each juror bore a look of confusion, and stared at Kieran as they traipsed out. Kieran ignored them, and kept his eyes forward in the hope they wouldn't recognise his panic.

'And then on your return, could you empty the public gallery too please?' Heenan called after the bailiff, who turned to nod in acknowledgement.

Once they were alone in the courtroom, Heenan took off his wig and scratched his head. 'What is going on here? Patrick Malone has been on the witness list since the beginning of the trial. Mr O'Connor, is he or is he not your witness?'

'He was, My Lord.'

'Then what's going on?' Heenan looked towards the defence table.

'Mr Malone cannot be compelled to testify against Gabriella Curzon,' Morgan-Bryant said.

'Because?'

Morgan-Bryant grinned. 'Because they're man and wife.'

'What?' Kieran bellowed. 'This is outrageous!'

'I quite agree,' Heenan said. 'When did this occur?'

'Six weeks ago, My Lord,' Morgan-Bryant said.

'While she was on bail! Why weren't we notified?' Kieran asked.

'Her private life is no concern of yours.'

'Like hell it's not!' Kieran yelled. 'She was ordered by this court not to contact any witnesses. I think marrying one counts as contact!'

'I agree,' Heenan said. 'Your client will be remanded into custody for breach of her bail conditions. Mr O'Connor, do you have any submissions regarding Mr Malone's compellability?'

Kieran paused. *I haven't had a chance to research that. I bet Morgan-Bryant has though.* 'Yes, My Lord,' he said. 'This is clearly a sham marriage–'

'It's not,' Morgan-Bryant said bluntly.

'Of course it is! She doesn't love him.'

'What does love have to do with it? You said it was a sham marriage. My Lord, a sham marriage is an immigration law term pursuant to section twenty-four subsection five of the Immigration Act 1990 which says that a sham marriage is a marriage entered into to avoid immigration rules. Both Francis Malone and Gabriella Curzon are British nationals, therefore it can't legally be a sham marriage. And even if it were a sham marriage, a sham marriage is still a marriage. Mr Malone is not compellable.'

'Bollocks!' Kieran said, before he could help himself.

'Mr O'Connor, you were warned. That's three times. I'm finding you in contempt.'

'You should find opposing council in contempt,' Kieran spat. 'Mr Malone and Miss Curzon didn't come up with this charade on their own.'

Morgan-Bryant pointed a finger at him. 'Careful. You don't want a slander lawsuit as well.'

'My Lord, this is a flagrant abuse of the protection married couples enjoy. They're not in love!'

'That doesn't matter, My Lord,' Morgan-Bryant said. 'The protection extends to those who are separated and those about to divorce as well as every other married couple. They are legally man and wife. Mr Malone cannot be compelled to testify.'

'I agree. It is not for the courts to determine the strength of a romantic relationship, but merely to ascertain whether or not the parties are married. Plenty of married couples no longer love each other.' Heenan unconsciously rubbed at his own wedding ring.

'My Lord, Francis Patrick Malone agreed to testify. He was granted immunity in return for his testimony today–'

'Then you'll have to revoke it, won't you?' Heenan said. 'Mr Malone will not be compelled to testify today. Call your next witness.'

Kieran fumed. 'I don't have one.'

'Then rest your case.'

Genevieve Hollis leapt to her feet, and took the opportunity to stick the knife in by making a half-time submission of 'no case to answer'. 'My Lord, if it may please the court, the defence would assert that there is no case to answer here. The evidence laid out by the prosecution is insufficient for any jury, properly directed, to find a guilty verdict.'

It was a good try, and Hollis had little to lose by making it. If Heenan agreed, then the case would end before she had to present the defence case.

It didn't work.

'Nice try Miss Hollis, and a clever piece of sharp practice, but I cannot grant your request. There's more than enough evidence to proceed, with or without Mr Malone. You'll have to make your case to the jury. Motion denied.'

I've lost the battle, but the war isn't over yet. Kieran nodded his thanks to the judge.

Chapter 64: The Reason Why

Mitch Palmer sat at one end of the large table in the jury room. Seconds after they had been dismissed, the jurors had broken off into three smaller social groups. The older women were leaning against the far window discussing God-knows-what, while 'his' group occupied the main table.

They were an eclectic bunch. Six men, six women. Seven white, three black and two Asian. Housewives and students, stockbrokers and janitors. All of them stuffed into a tiny jury box for weeks on end.

He could still smell the janitor's body odour now. The man had been sat behind him the entire time, but it seemed he had yet to discover aftershave.

Across the table from Mitch, a motherly-looking teacher by the name of Beebie, who was also the forewoman, nursed a cup of tea with one flabby arm cradled around the plate of biscuits provided for the whole jury.

'Hey, Beebie, quit hogging the biscuits.'

'You shut your face. Always moaning, you are. Let Beebie have her custard creams. You know she's got diabetes. She needs the sugar,' Beebie referred to herself in the third person. A peculiar habit, affected, he thought to make herself appear grander, or maybe to make her fellow jurors feel like children.

'They're not your biscuits, Beebie. They're for all of us. Don't make me go get the bailiff again.'

'Fine. But first, you tell me what you think. You been sitting there listening to the rest of us. Why did they send that Paddy home?'

Mitch leant back in his chair. He had no idea. But the jurors had come to regard him as something of the leader, and he didn't want to show his ignorance. 'I'm not horse-trading just to get my own biscuits.'

'You just don't know.'

Mitch was saved from answering by the creak of the jury room door. Beebie jumped to her feet, and Mitch took the opportunity to lean forward to snatch a biscuit, but Beebie swatted away his hand.

The bailiff stepped through. 'You're done for the day. But His Lordship wants a word first. Follow me please.'

⚖

Later that night, in his apartment near the Silicon Roundabout, Mitch searched for news about the case online. An article popped up immediately.

'NOTHING SACRED: HOW GABRIELLA CURZON MARRIED FOR MONEY – BUT NOT IN THE WAY YOU THINK'

Mitch clicked through to the article. '*The case of Ellis DeLange's murder took an unexpected turn today when one of the defendants announced that she had married the prosecution's chief witness, which prevented him from having to testify against her...*'

Chapter 65: Cut-Throat

Hollis stood stock-still. She had a folder full of notes nestled in her left arm, and faced the witness box where a very nervous Alex Culloden alternated between watching the press in the public gallery and biting his nails.

Kieran wondered why he was nervous. Culloden was a defence witness, so Hollis was hardly going to tear him apart on the stand. That would come when it was Kieran's turn to cross-examine him.

'Mr Barchester, tell me who you spent the night of the party with,' Hollis said.

Culloden stop biting his nails, and his hands fell to his side. 'Gabriella Curzon.'

'The whole evening?'

'Most of it. We were with other people for the early evening.'

'Who?'

'Gabby went off with Brianna,' Culloden said. 'I chatted with Vladivoben and his partner.'

'What happened next?'

'Gabby and I had a few drinks, and we retired to the guest bedroom at around eleven.'

'Where was the host at this time?'

'Upstairs sleeping.'

'When did you leave?'

'About midnight.'

'Tell us what happened when you left.'

'Gabby and I fought–'

'What about?'

'Her baby. Our baby. She's pregnant,' Culloden said.

Kieran rolled his eyes. They were going for the sympathy vote.

'Congratulations. No further questions, My Lord.'

Kieran stood. 'Mr Culloden, you testified that Gabby went off with Brianna early on during the party. What did Gabby and Brianna discuss?'

Hollis jumped up. 'Objection! Hearsay.'

Too late. Now the jury know they were conspiring anyway. 'Withdrawn. Mr Culloden, how long were Gabby and Brianna gone?'

'Half an hour, maybe. I wasn't keeping an eye on the clock.'

'You weren't keeping an eye on the clock. But you know what time you left?'

'Approximately.'

'Right. Even though you'd be drinking. Had Gabby?'

'Yes.'

'Did she do drugs?'

Culloden averted his eyes. 'Yes.'

'A pregnant, high, drunk woman. She sounds like a wonderful mother-to-be.'

'Objection!'

'Withdrawn. Mr Culloden, isn't it true that you and Gabriella had a physical altercation?'

'Yes.'

'That she chased you out of the house in a rage?'

'Yes.'

'So she has a propensity for violence?'

'She didn't kill anyone!'

'But you don't know that, Mr Culloden. She was still there when you left, wasn't she?'

'Yes.'

'No further questions.'

Chapter 66: Gamble

After a brief break from lunch, the defence resumed their case. Kieran was still reeling from the unexpected loss of his star witness when Elliot Morgan-Bryant stood, shot him a nasty look and announced: 'The defence calls Brianna Jackson.'

'Objection!' Kieran leapt to his feet. Heenan looked over at him quizzically. Kieran didn't really have any grounds to object. *I'd better say something, quick.* 'The defence didn't notify us that they intended to call Miss Jackson as a witness.'

'Nor should they have. You know S21A doesn't apply to defendants. Sit down.'

Kieran sat, and watched as Morgan-Bryant began to paint Brianna as a victim.

'Miss Jackson. You admitted to killing Ellis DeLange, didn't you?'

The jury perked up. They sat forward and stared intently.

'I did.'

A gasp went around the courtroom, then Brianna held up a hand. 'But *she*,' Brianna pointed towards the dock, 'had a knife to my throat at the time.'

'A knife to your throat?'

'Yes, she took me hostage… At my sister's funeral.' The jury gasped again.

'How would you characterise Miss Curzon?'

'She's insane,' Brianna said simply. 'She's pregnant, hormonal and addicted to both drugs and alcohol. She held me hostage and forced me to confess to a crime I didn't commit.'

'You didn't kill Ellis?'

'No, I did not.'

'Then where were you that night?'

'I left early. I went back to apologise. I found an empty house with the lights off, so I turned around and left. Gabriella must have been waiting in the shadows.'

Kieran stood. 'Objection! Speculation.'

'Noted,' Heenan said. 'The jury will disregard Miss Jackson's last comment.'

Like hell they will. They can't unhear it. Kieran watched as Morgan-Bryant pressed on.

'You never saw the body?'

'No. Not until the police released it.'

'And there's no forensic evidence that incriminates you, is there?'

'Objection! Defence counsel is testifying.'

'Withdrawn. Miss Jackson, did you see anyone that night when you returned?'

'No.'

'So as far as you know, no one saw you either?'

'That's correct.'

'Almost as if you were never there at all.'

'Objection!'

'Withdrawn. Nothing further, My Lord.'

Morgan-Bryant sat back down, a smug look plastered across his face.

He thinks he's won. We'll see about that. Kieran stood. 'Miss Jackson, is it true you supplied Ellis with drugs?'

'No.'

'Then it's a coincidence we found them in your flat?'

'No. *She* must have planted them in my flat.' Brianna nodded to indicate Gabriella.

'She planted drugs from your workplace in your flat? Does she have a key to your flat?'

'No, but–'

'Or your workplace?'

'No–'

'They were your drugs, weren't they? You sold them to Ellis in return for the two thousand pounds a month she paid into your bank account.'

'I didn't!'

'Isn't it true you've lied to the police multiple times during this investigation? Didn't you tell Detective Chief Inspector Morton that you went home before midnight, and never came back?'

'I suppose I might have. I knew how it would look.'

'And you used a Pay As You Go Oyster card to hide your return journey.'

'That was an accident!'

'And then you walked around for a half hour, only arriving at the exact moment Miss Curzon happened to be in the bathroom?'

'I don't know when Miss Curzon was in the bathroom.'

'You're Ellis' heir, aren't you?'

'So they tell me. I didn't ask for that.'

'You didn't ask for three million pounds, but you'll take it all the same, won't you?'

'How dare you! I didn't kill my sister. *She* did. She did it, and she's setting me up! She held me hostage.'

'She admitted that.'

'Then why isn't she testifying?' Brianna asked.

This time, it was Hollis' time to leap to her feet. 'Objection. Witness is asking the prosecution a question. Shouldn't it be the other way around?'

Heenan's eyes twinkled. 'Ask another question, Mr O'Connor.'

'You testified you arrived back at Edgecombe Lodge at approximately half past twelve.'

'Correct.'

'And you're sure you didn't see Gabriella there?'

'Quite sure. She must have been hiding.'

'But you couldn't know that. Unless you planned the murder together. Did you?'

'Of course not. She did it!'

'You keep saying that, but the evidence points to you too. Nothing further.'

Heenan turned to Hollis. 'Do you wish to cross examine your client's co-defendant?'

'No, My Lord.'

'Then we are adjourned until nine thirty tomorrow morning.'

Chapter 67: Equal

At the start of the morning session, a juror passed a note along to the bailiff, who handed it up to Judge Heenan. It read *'Do we have to assume the evidence means the same for both defendants?'*

'Ladies and gentlemen of the jury, one of you passed up a note to ask me a question about how to interpret the evidence that has been put before you. You must consider the evidence as you see it. Evidence which is circumstantial in nature must be weighed and considered on its merits. If you find evidence of this kind to be true, then you may draw inferences as to the existence of the facts implied by that circumstantial evidence. If, on the basis of that evidence, you are sure that the defendant, or defendants, are guilty then you must convict. If you are unsure then you must acquit. Where there is circumstantial evidence, you must consider it against each defendant, and consider it in the round. If you believe that such circumstances can only be rationally explained by the guilt of the defence then you may rely upon that evidence to find a guilty verdict.'

The jurors seemed to nod off during Heenan's speech. Kieran shook his head almost imperceptibly. It was a rare judge who could explain things in terms that juries would understand.

Chapter 68: Damned Silence

Before Morton knew it, the trial had reached its end. The defence case took no time at all to present, for there was scant evidence to support their theory.

The jury had listened in horror when Elliot Morgan-Bryant had introduced the tape recording of Morton's surreptitious call to Ayala at the crematorium. Morton had felt a burning sensation when that evidence was presented. He was sure that the entire jury was fixated upon him, that they knew of his involvement, how he had stepped in to disarm Brianna and cuff Gabriella. It was silly of course. He was just another face in the public gallery, and no one was paying any attention to him.

He looked around the courtroom. All twelve jurors were captivated by Kieran as he stood before them with his chest puffed out and his back straight, ready to deliver his closing speech.

'Ladies and gentlemen of the jury. You've heard a great deal of testimony. You know that at the time Ellis was murdered, there were two women in the house. These two women conspired to enrage Kallum Fielder by making him think Ellis had emptied his wallet. They made sure no one else was at home. Gabriella went home with a man that night, a man she freely admits is unattractive. She made sure the police knew about it. She's since married a different, though equally unattractive, man.'

Kieran paused as the jury tittered. Heenan glared as if to warn him to stay on topic.

Kieran let the awkward laughter fade to silence. The next part of his speech would be crucial. He had to balance pre-empting the defence speech against the chance that he would lend their arguments credence.

'We know these women are not innocents. Brianna has been supplying her sister with pentobarbital, and was paid handsomely for it. The timing is no coincidence. Ellis was about to go into rehab – which would have cut off Brianna's income. She was also going to marry Kallum Fielder, which would have prevented either sister from ever inheriting a penny.

'It's all very neat. Two women who have everything to gain just happen to be alone in the house together, one of whom had already staged her exit and then doubled back using every method available to her to conceal that she done so. Brianna used a second Oyster card to hide her return, a trick which would have been utterly futile had she been coming back to apologise as she claimed. She's since lost that Oyster card.

'The same two women who were then involved in a hostage situation. A hostage situation in which they scream blue murder at each other, but miracle of all miracles, they both walked away without a scratch – and Brianna, the alleged victim, has since spoken out in support of her sister.

'It's a charade, a means to profit from the death of Ellis DeLange. They plotted to kill her, set up Kal as a suspect by inducing an argument, pretended not to be alone, and then made sure they were...

'The pool brick used to bash Ellis' head in, along with all the other pool bricks she owned, are long gone. A set of three, and none of them can be found. Every last piece of evidence has been lost or destroyed. And now the women are running a cut-throat defence. It's the oldest trick in the defence lawyer's playbook. The lie is simple – "she did it, not me".

'Every time the police questioned either of them about the murder, they refused to answer pertinent questions. No comment, they said. You heard from Judge Heenan that you can infer guilt from silence. I'm asking you to do so. There is no good reason to decline to answer a question about your sister's murder – unless you were involved in that murder.

'In a moment, you'll hear from the defence. In their closing speeches, they're going to try and argue that there is no definitive proof, no smoking gun. That's because the defendants have hidden it. There's no way for Ellis to have been murdered, other than by one of these women. And neither could have committed the murder without the other knowing. They were both there. They both had means, motive and opportunity.

'If you believe as I do that they killed Ellis DeLange then you must give Ellis the justice she deserves. Find Brianna Jackson and Gabriella Curzon guilty of her murder.'

Chapter 69: Ten Guilty Men

All eyes were fixed on Genevieve Hollis as she prepared to give her closing speech. It was to be the second of two by the defence lawyers, for Morgan-Bryant had given his speech before Morton arrived.

'Miss Hollis, we have perhaps half an hour remaining on the docket today before we recess for the weekend. Do you wish to proceed today, or would you prefer to finish the defence case this afternoon?' Judge Heenan had asked.

'Today, My Lord. Thirty minutes will be ample.'

'Then proceed when you are ready.'

Hollis produced a bottle of water from a bag underneath the table, took a big gulp and began.

'My client, Gabriella Curzon, is far from perfect. She was brought up in the system with no real family to speak of, and no idea that she was a part of the DeLange dynasty. A chance meeting brought Ellis into her life, and gave her the sisterly connection that she had always craved but never known. Ellis helped her find work as a model. She gave her houseroom, and nurtured her modelling career. Ellis was the consummate big sister.'

Morton watched the jury's gaze flitter from the lawyer to her client. Gabriella was biting her lip, trying to hold back the tears.

'Gabriella and Ellis became close. When Ellis' parents died, Gabriella was there. When Ellis fell from grace after her own dalliance with drugs, Gabriella was there. When Ellis was on the cusp of getting engaged to

Kallum Fielder, Gabriella was there. Gabriella did what she thought any good sister should do. She tested. She poked and she prodded. With hindsight, she relied on Brianna too heavily when they plotted to test Kallum's trust in Ellis.

'Should she have? No. She regrets it deeply. Just as she regrets her actions at the crematorium. She owned up to those actions, fully and immediately. She apologised. She wants to serve her time for that wrongdoing. But she did not murder Ellis DeLange.'

Hollis paused, and look hard at the jury as if to gauge their mood.

'The prosecution would have you believe that my client colluded with Brianna Jackson. That the two decided to commit murder together. Or that my client is setting herself up to inherit Ellis' estate. There is absolutely no proof. Yes, she was in the house. But so was the true culprit, Brianna Jackson. Miss Jackson orchestrated the trick played on Kallum Fielder. She came back in the early hours of the morning and let herself into the house. She sold Ellis drugs, despite Ellis' attempts to get clean. She is the sole beneficiary of Ellis estate. My client should never been charged with this crime.'

The jury stared at her, unemotional, almost listless. Hollis was barely halfway through her time but the jury looked like they were already beginning to tire of her monotone. It was no surprise. They'd been in court for weeks. Morton knew from experience that the last few minutes would make or break her case.

'Ladies and gentlemen, the standard in a criminal prosecution is beyond reasonable doubt. If you have any doubts as to the guilt of my client, and you should have, then you must acquit. It is a fundamental principle of British justice that innocence is a shield against persecution, for if one cannot rely on a lack of criminality as a bulwark against the tyranny of injustice then the entire system of criminal justice shall fall.'

Hollis paused to survey the jury. She needed to get their attention, and fast. As though reading Morton's mind, Hollis smiled and changed tack.

'Think of it like a spam filter. We have to accept that occasionally spam emails end up in our inbox. It is better that we sometimes get spam emails in our inbox, than our real emails end up in spam where we never read them. It is the same principle that guides us when discerning guilt and innocence.'

The jury perked up. This wasn't what they were expecting to hear.

'It is better,' she continued, 'that ten guilty men go free than one innocent woman be sent to jail. My client is that innocent woman. Vote to acquit – because she didn't do it.'

Chapter 70: Recess

Court recessed at five for the weekend, and Morton loitered for a moment to say hello to the prosecutor. Kieran appeared a few minutes later, his wig and gown safely tucked inside a blue damask cotton bag.

'Evening, David. Got time for a swift pint?'

'We'll never find a table, nor somewhere quiet. But yeah, I'm not seeing Sarah 'til eight.'

'I know a place,' Kieran said.

'Lead on then.'

They walked towards the Holborn Viaduct. The streets were awash with sunshine, and it seemed all the various lawyers and publishers who worked in Holborn were either dashing home or dashing to the nearest bar. They passed by a couple of Morton's usual haunts, Ye Old Mitre and The Melton Mowbray, which were packed to the rafters with young professionals, and carried on until they reached High Holborn.

'What've you got planned for date night, then?'

'We're going to an outdoor cinema in Hackney. Some art film that Sarah picked.'

'Very hipster. Turn right,' Kieran said.

They ducked under an archway before The Cittie of York and trudged along a hidden path. The sounds of legal London fell away as they passed by a guard hut. Kieran nodded at the guard, who gave a cheerful wave and said, 'Evening, Kieran. You in for a beer?'

'That I am, Kev. You stuck working?'

'Only 'til six,' said the guard.

'Well, come find us then if you fancy a half.'

They walked past the guard, and into a tree-lined courtyard in the middle of an office block. Kieran led Morton into a building on the left.

'Didn't expect this, did you?' Kieran grinned.

'If you're taking me off to be murdered, can we have that beer first?'

'Hah. Up these stairs.'

They walked upstairs, and through a couple of doors – and emerged into a private bar.

'Two pints of Pride, please,' Kieran said to the barman, and moved to sit down at a table.

It was a small bar, almost empty, with views over the courtyard they'd walked through to the south and another to the north. The barman brought over their beers.

'Cheers,' Kieran said, raising his glass to Morton's with a chink. 'You happy with how the trial is going?'

'Happy… no. But I don't think Hollis' wordy speech did her many favours. The jury has had a long week. Nobody wants to listen to a mini-lecture on a Friday afternoon, especially when it's this nice out.'

Morton put his drink down. 'Do you think that could influence how they decide a case?'

'Absolutely. It shouldn't but jurors are human, and they've got lives to get back to. The big guy on today's jury–'

'In the suit? Pinstripe shirt?'

'That's him. He's been checking his phone every time court recesses. I'd bet ten to one that he's trying to seal a business deal. On the other hand, the skinny kid with freckles looks like he's delighted to be out of work for this. Jurors bring their own problems into a jury room. If they want to go home, they'll reach a verdict more quickly, even if that verdict isn't necessarily right.'

'Then why did Hollis take the afternoon session?' Morton asked. 'If a tired jury is a bad jury to pitch to, then surely she should have waited until Monday.'

Kieran shook his head. 'That would have been suicide. If she'd let them leave, they would have had the entire weekend to mull over my closing speech without the context of her defence. It would have won me the case. It's one of the many reasons we shouldn't use juries.'

'What's the alternative to using a jury?'

'Trial by judge alone. Let qualified judges adjudicate on the law and the facts instead of just the law. Then again, even the Judiciary are human. They have other places to be, other things to think about. I've seen drunk judges. I've seen judges who've become jaded after presiding over trial after trial until they think every defendant is guilty. I guess we just live in an imperfect world.'

'Speaking of imperfect, who leaked the missing witness to the press? Paddy Malone's refusal to testify has been splashed all over the headlines.'

Kieran held up his hands. 'Damned if I know. Paddy could be the leak, or that sneak Morgan-Bryant might have talked to them.'

'But wouldn't that hurt the defence case?'

'Sort of. Having two defendants complicates things. Paddy was going to put Gabriella alone in the house, which shows that she had the opportunity to kill. Without Paddy, my case against Gabby is significantly weakened.'

'Which makes it more likely Brianna did it.'

'Exactly. They're running a cut-throat defence,' Kieran said. 'If Gabriella didn't do it, Brianna looks guilty. It's in Morgan-Bryant's interest for the reason that Paddy didn't testify to become public. It makes it look like Gabby is hiding something, and supports Morgan-Bryant's finger-pointing.'

Morton drained his pint. 'I'm so glad I only have to catch 'em. You might have the nicer office, but I don't envy you the job. I'd best get going. I'll see you Monday.'

Chapter 71: Unanimity

The jury was recalled at 9:55 on Monday morning, and immediately sent out to deliberate.

They stayed out through lunch, a good sign according to Kieran, and returned to Court One at 13:45.

They shuffled back in.

'Madame Forewoman, have you reached a unanimous verdict?'

Beebie stood, clasped her hands together and said: 'We have not, My Lord.'

'I need not remind you that each of you have taken an oath to return a verdict which is true to the evidence. You have been out for four hours. Each of you takes into the jury room your own experience with which to discuss the case and reach a verdict. Do you feel that further discussion might enable you to reach a unanimous verdict?'

The forewoman shook her head. 'No, My Lord.'

Brianna grinned. She thought she was off the hook.

Judge Heenan looked at his watch. They were well over the cut-off period to put the case to a majority verdict.

'Then I shall ask you to return to the jury room only a little longer, and deliberate further. I am willing to accept a majority verdict. If ten or more of you concur then I shall accept the verdict of the ten.'

The forewoman looked much happier. 'Thank you, your honour.'

The jury trooped out single file to deliberate further.

Chapter 72: Deliberations

Mitch twiddled his thumbs as he sat in his usual chair at the end of the table. For three weeks it had been his, the closest door to the exit. *Not that we'll be getting out of here any time soon.*

'We just don't have enough evidence,' Beebie declared again. No one in the jury room was in any doubt as to her position. The woman next to her, whose real name Mitch could never remember, nodded sagely in agreement.

'There's loads of evidence,' the youngest juror, a student called Amelia Glenn, said. 'They were both in the house when she died – and no one else was.'

'But how do we know that? We know Brianna was there. She admitted it. But Gabriella didn't testify.'

Mitch raised a hand. 'She didn't testify for a reason. If she was innocent, she'd say so. Aleksander Barchester puts her in the house when he left. So did Kallum Fielder. If she had left, then she'd have said so, right?'

'Not if she didn't want to be cross-examined,' Amelia said.

'Why would an innocent woman fear cross-examination?' Mitch asked. 'Life in prison must be much scarier.'

'No,' Beebie said firmly. 'She did not have to testify. I don't blame her. Those lawyers would have twisted anything that she said. There is reasonable doubt. She should go free.'

'She's hiding something, Beebie, and you know it. Why didn't that Patrick testify? The prosecution clearly expected him to.'

'I don't know. You tell me.'

'Didn't you spot the ring on her finger? I know it wasn't much of a diamond, but one of you must have noticed it.'

'She's married. So?'

'So she's married to him. It's the only reason that he wouldn't be able to testify. You must have seen cop shows on the television.'

'No.' Beebie folded her arms across her chest. 'She'd never marry him.'

'Not even to get away with murder?'

A small hand went up at the back of the room. 'Excuse me?'

Beebie turned. 'What is it?'

'She did marry him. I saw it on the front page of a newspaper.'

'You looked up the news? Judge Heenan told us not to.'

'No… Someone left a copy in the jury room. I found it on the table this morning. I put it in the bin. Over there, look.'

Beebie stood, and walked across the room. Sure enough, a copy of the newspaper was in the bin. 'We should tell the judge.' She walked towards the door, as if to call back the bailiff.

'Wait!' Mitch said.

'What?'

'She didn't read it. Did anyone?'

Each of the twelve shook their head.

'Then let's get on with deliberations. If we didn't read it, we didn't do anything wrong. We've been here for weeks. It must be costing the taxpayer millions of pounds. You don't want all that to go to waste, do you? Can't we just ignore it?' Mitch implored.

Beebie sat back down. 'They don't look like newlyweds,' she grumbled.

'I think we've deliberated enough. We all want to go home,' Mitch said. 'Unless someone wants to discuss something specific again, I propose a vote. With your permission, of course, Madame Forewoman.'

Beebie nodded. She picked up a notepad from the centre of the room, and tore the first sheet into twelve. On each piece of paper she wrote the names of Brianna and Ellis. 'Tick for guilty. Cross for not guilty. One next to each name. Everyone understand?'

The papers were passed around, and each wrote down their verdict in secret. The papers were folded, and passed up to Mitch, as he had proposed the vote. He counted them all, then nodded.

'Miss Beebie, would you like to confirm the count?'

Beebie took the papers, and double-checked the tally.

'Do we have a verdict?' Mitch asked.

Beebie nodded.

'Bailiff!'

Chapter 73: The Jury Returns

They marched back in, chatting freely among themselves with a jovial, almost party-like atmosphere. They were finally going home. The bailiff summoned the judge from his chambers, and paged counsel to return.

When everyone was back in the courtroom, the judge asked the jury again: 'Madame Forewoman, have you been able to reach a majority verdict?'

'We have, Your Honour.'

'On the charges against Miss Brianna Jackson, how do you find?'

'Guilty.'

Brianna collapsed in her seat, the grin wiped from her grace. She glared stonily at Gabriella.

'And on the charges against Miss Gabriella Curzon, how do you find?'

'Guilty.'

Gabriella wailed, and collapsed against her lawyer.

'How many of you are in favour?'

'Ten.'

'And against?'

'Two.'

Judge Heenan nodded appreciatively. 'I would like to thank you for your service. You are dismissed.'

Morton looked over to Kieran, who gave him a thumbs up. But Morton didn't share the prosecutor's glee. Gabriella's tears seemed to be real. Morton exhaled deeply. To him it seemed that two women had been convicted for a murder that only one of them had committed.

A killer had been caught. But had justice been done?

A Note from the Authors

Thank you for reading Ten Guilty Men. We appreciate how valuable your time is, and we're delighted you chose to spend it finishing our novel. If you have a spare moment, we'd really appreciate it if you could leave a review on the site where you purchased this book. Honest reviews help other readers find books they will enjoy, and let authors know what their readers want.

If you'd like to find out when we release new eBooks, please join our mailing list.

You can also join us:

on twitter @90daysnovel

email us on authors@90daysnovel.com

or like us on Facebook at www.facebook.com/90daysnovel

Also by Daniel Campbell & Sean Campbell

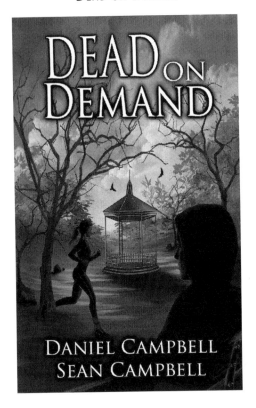

A career man, Edwin Murphy has always put more effort into his work than his family. Everything changes for Edwin when his wife files for divorce. On the brink of losing his home, his job and his little girl, Edwin orchestrates an intricate plan to eliminate his wife and regain his former lifestyle.

The police are baffled when bodies begin to appear all over London with no apparent connection between them. Inspector David Morton must think outside the box as he investigates the deadly web of deceit behind the murders.

Also by Daniel Campbell & Sean Campbell

CLEAVER SQUARE

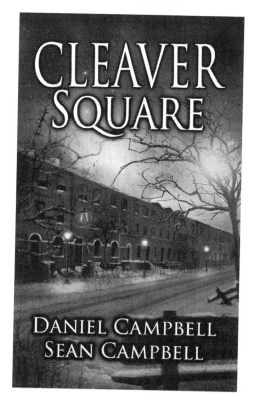

The bleakest winter on record and a gruesome discovery bring DCI David Morton to the Hackney Marshes in search of a clue, any clue, as to the identity of a dead child found near the Old River Lea.

Meanwhile, closer to home, Morton's long suffering wife Sarah comes to the conclusion that her man has been doing more than work during his late nights at the office. As he closes in on the mystery of the boy's identity his life begins to crumble and a terrible wrong is done to someone he loves.

Printed in Great Britain
by Amazon